Clayton found it unnerving—a whole world filled with Brothers and Sisters who looked exactly like each other. Dr. Rollan had cloned them all from the cells of a great genius of the last century.

"A simple formula, really," Dr. Rollan said. "But fashioning the right personality mix and making it breed true in the conception tubes—that was no trifling matter."

"I see," Clayton said. "To get the right sort of worker for—"

"No no!" Dr. Rollan was agitated. "The point is that Earth societies contain a contradiction, a dialectical one, if you will. Earth, with its billions of citizens, preaches the virtue of tolerance, of passivity, of conformity. But who does it reward? The heads that poke up above the crowd! It is impossible to free them of their adulation of the special unless it becomes impossible to *be* special! So I constructed Brotherworld to prove that Uniformism will work. Here we can illustrate the central tenets of progressive thinking, begin the true evolution of socialist man."

—From "As Big As the Ritz," Gregory Benford

GREGORY BENFORD ★ JOHN M. FORD
NANCY SPRINGER

UNDER THE WHEEL

BAEN BOOKS

UNDER THE WHEEL

Copyright © 1987 by Baen Publishing Enterprises

A Baen Books Original

Baen Publishing Enterprises
260 Fifth Avenue
New York, N.Y. 10001

First printing, January 1987

ISBN: 0-671-65611-2

Cover art by Bob Eggleton

Printed in the United States of America

Distributed by
SIMON & SCHUSTER
TRADE PUBLISHING GROUP
1230 Avenue of the Americas
New York, N.Y. 10020

CONTENTS

AS BIG
AS THE RITZ

Gregory Benford

Recently The Village Voice *ran an exposé on a New York City "utopian" colony not all of whose members found it to be the perfect circle they had hoped for.*

The "Sullivanians," *devotees of the Sullivan Institute for Research in Psychoanalysis, evolved from a therapy institute experimenting with alternative lifestyles into a coercive, repressive "cult," according to members who have left the group. Its leaders are strongly against the concept of the nuclear family, and have decreed that husbands and wives shall not live together within the group's communal houses. Parents have been coerced into surrendering their babies to other group members, and members are encouraged to sleep (though not necessarily have sex) with a different person every night. Some members have not spoken to their parents in fifteen years.*

A number of Sullivanians have fled, taking their children with them. Still, the group has about 250 members. To some, apparently, it is Utopia—merely a recent version of humanity's grand experiment.

In his story about the asteroid colony Brotherworld, Gregory Benford creates a utopia made possible by future technology. On Brotherworld, the men are all strong and the women good-looking—not surprisingly, as they're cloned from a single genotype. Their world is the birthplace of Uniformism, a society in which being "special" or "different" is unheard of. . . .

3

It is youth's felicity as well as its insufficiency that it can never live in the present, but must always be measuring up the day against its own radiantly imagined future—flowers and gold, girls and stars, they are only prefigurations and prophecies of that incomparable, unattainable young dream.

—F. Scott Fitzgerald
"The Diamond as Big as the Ritz," 1922

Kings and fools
Make their own rules.
             —*Joan Abbe*

1.

A lingering respect for the niceties of an Earthside education was the bane of the asteroid communities. Yearly it drained them of their brightest young men and women.

Thus the parents of Clayton Donner persistently pressured him to attend Harvard or Cambridge or Tokyo General, picking these names from a list as unfathomable as a menu in Swahili. Each locale was pictured in verdant 3D as a cultured pinnacle, a doorway to a different life.

The asteroids had been colonized by those who respected no conventional wisdoms but instead made their own. Those ancestors, now in their vacuum-dried graves, would have wrinkled their noses at the odor of flatlander-envy that pervaded the discussions of Clayton's destiny. The boy was quick, studious, clever. He would have made a fine metal-ceramics man, bio-integrater or syntho-miner. Instead, his parents relentlessly pressured him into an Earthside education extracted from books rather than from the gray tumbling worlds.

After his first year flatside Clayton was a convert to their cause. For a young man a career is a distant, fuzzy goal. Earth was concrete and *fun*. Gaudy. Effervescent. Deliciously lurid. He made friends, saw the sights, learned about sophisticated women and the chemical consolations of civilization. He even visited what was left of Africa, sampled the original abode where men had evolved, and came away with both a skin rash and a faint incredulity that anything worthwhile could have started there.

The east coast of the Americas was rather better, though clearly past its great days. The focus of Earthside economic life had shifted to the pan-Pacific nations over a century before. The snug, smug eastern streets were steeped in murky history and claustrophobic assumptions. Clayton stayed in the Ritz-Carlton hotel in Boston, spending a week's worth of his father's profits in two days. The building was well preserved, eccentric by modern standards, and impressed him deeply with its timeless gilded swank. He tasted the now-rare lobster and savored the heady fragrances of orderly decline. A woman he met in the bar seemed to find his asteroid origins interesting, exotic, and within a few hours she was in his bed. It was a perfect setting to lose his virginity. He was only mildly disturbed when, the next morning, she firmly requested payment and even, when pressed, showed him the Greater Boston price sheet and luxury tax scale. He irritably paid up, resolving that the experience would not blemish his memory of the Ritz and its majesty.

He had ended up at UCLA, his ability and personality profile matched with the school's needs and strengths by an elaborate trait-sifting program; the education of the young was too important to be left to their vagrant tastes.

Like virtually everyone's, his life appeared dull from the outside, or at best made of elements from a soap opera, while from inside it had all the sweep and grandeur of *War and Peace*. Clayton went through the usual undergraduate crises. He learned to conceal his naive assumptions and be shocked at nothing. Fashion allowed one to be occasionally stunned, but only within severe limits. Dismay, however, was his for the asking; it implied a certain haughty despair. He tried the various exploits—sexual, social, hallucinogenic—appropriate to his age. Struggling, he ingested ideas from survey courses, earnest late-night bull sessions, Op-Ed pages and other fast-thought franchises. He imagined that he was crossing new frontiers, when in fact he was only crossing into Iowa; billions had been there before. He did not suspect that a decade later he would find these reaches a bit commonplace and not a little boring.

In his second year he met Sylvia. She was different from the other students—more intent, dedicated, severe. Her devotion to the cause of selfless politics was already well known at UCLA. He was mildly attracted to her, despite her habit of wearing loose-fitting, dowdy attire in dull browns and grays.

She was known as Sylvia Hammersmith at UCLA, but that meant little—at that time students often adopted the names of famous people as a gesture. As the young grew more and more alike, devices to distinguish themselves became ever more enticing. Sylvia's taking the name of an explorer, fatally crushed on Venus the year before, seemed only a mild affectation.

When he discovered her true last name, however, his interest deepened. Clayton was still immature and, compared to any savvy Earthy, downright naive. Still, he sized up Sylvia quickly and judged his best approach. She wore a perpetual frown, assaying even casual remarks for their moral gold, so—intuiting rapidly—he decided to not mention his major subject of study. Instead, he talked endlessly of his minor area, Analytic Economic Morality.

He was, without thinking about it very much, solidly for Earthside's social shibboleths of the era— strict equality of pay for all, abolishment of all inherited wealth right down to items of clothing and furniture, and numerous measures to alleviate any trace of economic envy. The university incorporated these ideas as best it could, but found difficulty staffing the scientific fields, since technical talent could easily find work elsewhere. Support for progressive ideas centered, naturally enough, among the professoriat devoted to such subjects as Greek pottery and interpersonal dynamics.

These notions met with Sylvia's approval, and she opened up a bit. He learned of her laughing, pouting mouth, her glinting sea-blue eyes, her natural and unstudied grace.

He knew he was making progress with her, but he was amazed when she invited him to spend December at her father's. Though this might be customary if she lived on Earth, or even in one of the crystalline orbital cities, she was Sylvia Townsworth Rollan, and her father was founder of the most bizarre enterprise in the solar system: Brotherworld. It orbited at a steep tilt to the ecliptic, about two astronomical units away from the sun. Getting there would have taken weeks by conventional transport.

Until this moment his interest in Sylvia had been entirely the pure, pointed lust of a young man. Mores of the era had swung back to a constraining reticence in matters sexual. Clayton was well socialized, and believed various unsupported assertions which had the effect of delaying marriage, postponing children and generally defusing the explosive power of adolescent sexuality. Sublimation is a subtle game, one the twenty-second century played well. His warmly remembered night in the Ritz now seemed to be a gauzy treat, unrelated to realities, like cotton candy eaten at a circus.

Ambition he had a-plenty. After Sylvia's invitation he went immediately to his Major Tutor and asked advice. The gray-haired woman listened attentively, then said flatly that he must go, of course. There was no question. It could make his career.

Clayton was slightly shocked to find his own secret thoughts so freely voiced. He observed a quickening in the Major Tutor's manner, a fine-drawn anticipation of possible benefits to herself. Clayton studied the dart of three-level traffic outside her window and remarked that he was reluctant to mix his regard for Sylvia and his other interests, especially since she had such fixed views.

The Major Tutor pursed her lips, tapping a yellow fingernail on her amber desktop. She began a set-piece mini-lecture on devotion to the profession, on taking every opportunity in a field where such things came seldom these days, on understanding that in certain unique circumstances he could not allow niceties to dictate.

Clayton had heard it all before but believed it anyway. He could see the elements of personal advancement in this, but something deeper drove him and the Major Tutor as well: curiosity. Among those with the souls of true scientists, this was the ultimate addiction which could not be deflected. Both of them wanted to *know*. If minor deception was the price, so be it.

The Major Tutor observed that he would, of course, need special equipment. She could arrange that. But even more important was care, a sense of timing, even downright guile. Clayton understood.

His Major Tutor gave him confidential summaries of Brotherland's construction, or rather, what little was known about it. The utopian colony was the outstanding enigma of the day. What's more, Dr. Rollan had been acquiring advanced technology of an unsettling kind: plasma containment vessels, superstrong magnets, high-quality ceramics and alloys. Could he be building something even stranger than Brotherworld?

These questions the Major Tutor implied with raised eyebrows, and gave him an inventory of recent purchases by the colony. Clayton tucked the inventory away for study at the site.

The task was not without risk. Clayton was an adventurous type, though, determined to get his kicks in life, even if some of them were in the face. He left his Major Tutor firmly resolved.

He accepted Sylvia's invitation, and changed his major subject to Undeclared, in case she should be of suspicious mind. Indeed, some of his friends did mention to him, as he was packing, that Sylvia had casually inquired into Clayton's doings. They took it as a sign of female caution; courtship was a rite given much thought in this era, and the preliminaries were often the most rewarding aspect. They slapped him on the back, made a few obvious jokes, and gave unsolicited and rather explicit advice.

Clayton took the precaution of leaving behind any reading cylinder which could give away his interests. Instead, he took texts on social responsibility, even one which denounced the anarchist-cum-free capitalist asteroid communities from which he came. He halfway agreed with the book, anyway. The 'roid clans were rude, unsubtle, even loutish, compared with the fine manners and delicate social distinctions commonly found in California. The books had a point.

2.

They took a standard commercial fusion liner from Earth to Ceres, the conjunction being good. It made the trip under boost, at full grav, and arrived in five days. There they changed to a slingship. Its electromagnetic accelerating rings squashed them at three gravs for aching, tendon-stretching moments, then abruptly set them free. They took a long arc across the solar system, out to the motes of asteroids. The ship moved like a darting wisp among the stately slow sway of worlds.

Their target was a lonely, rolling hunk of iron called Hellbent. The other people on the slingship were rough, silent types, ill-kempt and grimy, with no hope of ever getting far enough ahead to afford a true, full-water bath, or food not force-grown, or clothes of something finer than the fibrous weaves they wore.

At Hellbent men and women sucked a lean milk from bare, spongy rock. Economics had decreed Hellbent's smelted products valuable for one booming generation, and had then snatched away its blessings, leaving only a shadowy clan who had too much invested to leave the place. The large docking cylinders and electromagnetic accelerators were leftovers of the glory days, kept up now as the staple of the economy. Clayton and Sylvia found the maze of sheet-metal corridors forbidding and chilly. The sheen of bare phosphors made them squint.

As they waited near the air lock for her father's shuttle, Sylvia asked, "Did you see that skinny man on the slingship?"

"Uh, yes."

"He was an astrophysicist, I'm sure of it."

"Why?"

"The way he looked at us. He knows who I am."

"Maybe he just thought you were good-looking."

She shrugged this off, impervious to compliments. "*And* his fingernails were clean."

Clayton hid a grin. "A sure sign."

He sighed, and felt an itchy sensation as he breathed in. Hellbent was so poor they ran their public rooms at zero humidity. In their hour-long wait the system could extract a gram or two of vapor from their breath and sweat, an involuntary tax of fluids.

Clayton's home was never *this* badly off. He felt a twinge of guilt at thinking of his parents, laboring in the chilly grit of a rockworld not greatly different from this. He should visit them, but the cost was prohibitive. Sylvia had paid all the expenses this trip; he could never have afforded it. One of Clayton's classmates had even suggested that as long as he was out this far, he might as well nip over and look in at home, too—all this said with an oblivious groundhog smile, never thinking that Clayton's parents were on the other side of the solar system from here. To Earthsiders, like New Yorkers of the centuries before, everything beyond their neighborhood was a single, amorphous Elsewhere.

The shuttle arrived with a clanging thump. When the thrumming pumps had stilled, the two of them entered the bare, gloomy loading bay. A silvery body nestled there, sleek and chromed. From its nose a powerful beam of ruddy light turned and regarded them like a malignant eye out of the coagulated night. As they approached, Clayton saw it was a shapely fusion flitter, gleaming with polish. The slim craft was studded with portals that winked and sparkled as he passed, looking exactly like enormous green and yellow jewels. Its nose was asymmetric and spindly guidance rods studded its sides, deftly functional. It was a work of art.

Two men, dressed in Spartan simplicity, stood inside the welcoming ramp. Clayton saw instantly that they were Brothers, the famous product of Dr. Leon Rollan's cloning experiment. And indeed, he could not tell one Brother from the other.

"Welcome to the Gates of Paradise," one said, giving Clayton a warm handshake.

"I'm, uh, pleased to enter," Clayton replied.

The Brothers greeted Sylvia even more warmly, as was fitting. Clayton glanced back and saw a small clutch of Hellbent's miners, muttering to each other and staring with frank, wide-eyed awe at the magnificence of the shuttle. The well-lit interior had upholstery of woven silk and linen. Here and there were plump pillows of softness and subtly stated opulence. The bulkheads were a deep ebony, adorned with crescents of glittering ruby-like stones and iridescent splashes of some blue-white jewels. It all represented the firmament itself, artfully arranged to lead the eye from one glowing high point to another.

"Incredible!" Clayton cried out.

"Oh, this is the old one," Sylvia said nonchalantly.

"There are others?" Clayton could not take his eyes off the rich fabrics. An alabaster dome topped the passenger lounge, a miniature copy of the famous mosque in Cairo he had seen the year before—except even more glorious, here, in a sun-defying white.

"Of course." Sylvia gestured lazily at the Hellbent miners, who now crowded around the foot of the ramp. "It's for them, really. They like to see how well a truly different system works."

Soon they were boosting at a steady 1.5 gravs, the ship humming with solid assurance through slick blackness. Clayton could tell immediately from several constellations, and the orange disk of Jupiter aft, that they were arcing above the ecliptic. Hellbent was merely the nearest 'roid to Dr. Rollan's famous experiment. Hellbent chanced at this moment to be close to the point where Brotherland intersected the ecliptic plane every eighteen months in its oblique path.

The hectic, brawling life of the asteroid belt lay like a plate below Dr. Rollan's empire, and lonely miners perceived it as a glittering, sparkling speck high up in the darkness, orbiting serenely above the affairs of ordinary men.

Clayton saw it within a few hours. The Brothers kept to their business, scarcely sparing more than a few phrases after their warm greeting. They spoke to each other in a strange argot, which Clayton could not penetrate, so he turned to staring dreamily out the faceted portals. These were unusual in design, not giving a clear vision at all, but rather a series of refracted images, as though peering through a jewel. Certainly the sculpt-engineer had gone to a great deal of trouble to create the effect. The multiple perspectives complimented the design of the walls, but Clayton found it hard on the eyes.

Through this layered set of images Clayton first saw the glowing eye of the Vortex. It was burnt-gold near the center, brimming with crisp light. Around it was a halo of red, and then an encircling, smolderingly blue haze, like a bruise. He strained to see the very center and was rewarded with a tiny, virulent twinkling. At first he could not be sure it was not an optical trick of the odd portal. The dot flickered like a will 'o the wisp in a distant, churning fog. Clayton felt his breath quicken, a tingle of excitement. The dab of light hardened. He was sure now. The dazzling white speck was the roiling glow emitted by matter as it cried out in its incandescent agony, flaring brightly for one long groaning instant before it plunged forever down the yawning Schwarzschild throat of a black hole.

3.

A massive star at the endpoint of burning has a central temperature of ten billion degrees and is nearly a billion times more dense than iron. Unable to burn any longer, its core collapses, the nuclei there break apart, and implosion begins. There is a "bounce" and the implosion turns into the classic supernova explosion. Vast amounts of matter initially near the stellar core rapidly expands and cools. Often the core left behind forms a neutron star or a black hole. These bizarre end products of stellar death throes were the principal focus of much twentieth-century astronomy.

—*Supernova Debris* (2nd edition)
Valerie Thompson, 2078

The glory of Dr. Rollan's virtuous empire unfolded in concentric rings. The fuzzy, glowering blue rim was a disk of dust that slowly worked its way inward, toward its death. As dust swarmed ever nearer the hole, friction among the particles heated them. Stirred by magnetic fields to a turbulent frenzy, they radiated. Farthest out, a blue oxygen line dominated the emission, giving an outer rim the color of a week-old bruise. Farther in, the faster-circling gas sputtered with an angry red. Radiation stole angular momentum from the dust. This minutely affected the orbiting particles, lowering them slowly inward.

Clayton quickly calculated in his head. It would take years for a dollop of dust to bleed inward, into the next band, a brimming mustard circle. Then the compressed dust flowed into the sunlike, white-hot hub where a fraction of its rest mass energy was released, fully thirty percent. There lived the black hole, the dynamo that made this work.

"You can't see it," Sylvia said helpfully. "It's only a speck, anyway, no bigger than your fingernail."

"Uh, amazing." He must not appear to know very much.

"See the collectors?"

A wide array of solar collectors orbited above and below the luminous disk. Sylvia said, "They provide the solar energy we sell to the inter-planet runs."

Clayton watched the filmy sheets turn in their own elliptical orbits, feasting on the light that burst from the rim of the black hole. They were hundreds of kilometers away, but the scene was lit with dazzling intensity. The collectors beamed microwaves across the solar system, he knew, providing in-flight power to ships. That cut the transport costs enormously. Rollan had been the first to provide the service.

"I don't follow the details, but it *is* lovely, isn't it?" Sylvia said with little-girl wonder.

Clayton agreed, but yawned and languidly said "Uh huh." He shouldn't seem too interested. He was, however, memorizing everything, and would make some sketches as soon as he was alone.

He allowed himself one more moment of rapt appreciation. The Vortex glowed with the mere waste energy of vast forces at work. The disks turned, a huge economic engine steadily rendering ordinary asteroid debris into limitless wealth.

"There's home!" Sylvia cried.

Until now the banks of dust above and below them had hidden the jewel of the system.

Further out, beyond the blue band, all was a mottled darkness, blotting out the stars behind. Further still, the infalling dust thinned. Beyond this shroud, Clayton could see the true marvel, the Hoop.

It was a thin glowing strip, as ripely blue-green as Earth on a summer's day. The inner rim of the Hoop was lit by the glow of the Vortex, the light funneled out and focused on the Hoop by the scalloped plates of the dust. This conserved most of the radiance and delivered it to the Hoop, bringing warm temperatures to its delicately contrived biosphere.

Clayton squinted. They were coming in at about thirty degrees from the plane of the Hoop. He knew from the sketchy information available through the UCLA library that a monolayer shield floated on top of the Hoop's atmosphere. He could see the sheen of Vortex-light scattered by that thin air-trapping film, high above a cottonball cluster of cirrus. Below, basking in radiance, were shimmering lakes and softly undulating hills. At the "equator," the inward curve of the Hoop, a long lake stretched, dividing the span.

Sylvia said excitedly, "Have you ever seen anything so beautiful?"

"Never," he said with complete conviction.

"The forests, the green hills . . ." Sylvia peered dreamily at the swelling Hoop. "Like Eden . . ."

Clayton realized she meant the "natural" beauty of the Hoop; he had thought she meant the marvelous engineering that made the thin slice of biosphere possible. He suppressed a disbelieving smile.

They slid outward toward the Hoop. He guessed the entire Hoop was a few kilometers across, and they were only perhaps twenty kilometers from the black hole itself. Yet the tiny sucking mote provided brimming light for an entire ecology.

The hills swept by, revolving cool and serene, as he watched. The Hoop circled the Vortex every seven minutes, a giant bicycle tire without spokes. But perspectives were awry here, the irreality of a glowering, gnawing mass-eater so near to placid forests was too jarring. He shook his head, dazed.

A faint pattering came through the alabaster dome of the improbable ship.

"Ah!" one of the Brothers said. He hastily dipped the nose down toward the Hoop.

"What was that?" Clayton said, alarmed. Any accident so near the virulent maw—

"A small error," Sylvia said calmly. "We probably hit a cloud of dust that strayed from its course, is all." She smiled with the confidence of a person for whom the technical problems were always someone else's. Clayton had noted that she was becoming more easy-going, less severe, as they voyaged out from Earth's bright confusions.

Once told, he understood. The infalling dust was supposed to be channeled down in a parabola,

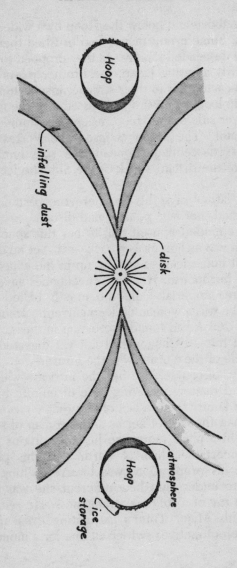

flowing above and below the Hoop by a wide, safe margin. Some errant matter had brushed them.

They descended rapidly. As they dropped toward the slowly gyrating Hoop, the Brother pilots warbled to each other in their strange, insular tongue. The ship looped outward and passed over the night-like outer side of the Hoop, where ice rimmed the terminator. The Hoop eclipsed the Vortex and darkness descended. Beneath the sole luminescence of the distant speck of the Sun the ice was blue.

"My father says this is where the past ends," Sylvia said, her face pensive and distant.

He reminded himself that to her this spectacular vista was as homey as a back yard. Yet he could see that homesickness welling up in the expectant pout of her mouth. Her high cheekbones gave her a severe, imperial look; the mouth belied that now. She was a woman of deep currents, emotions that at UCLA had found expression in ideas.

"And this—" Clayton had not yet digested the spectacle of the Vortex—"is the future?"

"Why, of course." To her the intricate waltz of light and matter, wheeling here in infinite black, was the family farm, a fact of nature.

He had thought of her as a kinswoman of sorts, reared in a place more like his 'roid origins than the comfortable plush of Earth. But this place, despite his preparation, was bizarre to him. He began to understand how different she was, and felt the tug of a sublime strangeness. He remembered his Major Tutor's calculating eyes and a confusion of motives swirled in him for a moment.

Only the grandeur of the spectacle outside made
him put all thoughts aside.

They came over the rim of the Hoop, clouds
allowing brief glimpses through to the verdant
fields. From the Vortex a wedge of light poured
outward, trapped between the blanket of infalling
matter. The twin sheets of dust resembled plates
that necked in to intersect at the hot central spark.
As they converged the plates glowed, giving the
bands of blue and yellow and brilliant white that
he had seen earlier.

They arced around the face of the Hoop, toward
the permanent high noon of the equator. The
monolayer sheen was turquoise here, with dis-
torted cumulus clouds wedged against its restraining boundary by the rising heat from below.

There—a lessening of the smear of turquoise.
That was the entrance hole, a swiftly-forming leak
in the system which allowed ships in and out. It
would be open for mere moments.

They turned and glided through it, thrusters
focused down now. Here the jockeying was difficult. The ship dropped through the hole, through
thick cloud layers, and emerged suddenly above a
careening landscape. The Brothers worked furiously now, vectoring sidewise and up, and now
down and aft, as they matched velocities and ac-
celerations in an intricate gavotte, descending
toward their landing field.

The ship, so graceful in vacuum, now seemed to
have the aerodynamic properties of a brick. Clayton shrank into his couch, dizzy.

What was a simple problem in vector mechanics

back at UCLA became a sickening whirl. He felt the eternal power of matter over abstractions. This was nothing like piloting among serenely orbiting asteroids.

Thumps, rattles, a hollow *whoosh*.

Landfall. The side of the ship furled up. Clayton followed Sylvia down the ramp into a lush valley. A golden haze hung idly over the vast sweep of lawns, azure lakes and artfully arranged forests. The Hoop curved away in both directions, arching up into a blue fog. In the middle distance groves of oak studded the tawny hills, reminding him of California. Farther away, rough masses of pine swathed the rumpled land in a grip of dark blue-green.

"It's . . . lovely," he said.

Three deer emerged from a grove of elms nearby, never giving them or the ship a glance, and meandered into a wooded gully. A falcon wobbled on changing air currents high overhead, then began a descending gyre. Above all this hung the incessant technicolor blaze of the Vortex.

"Hail!" came a voice nearby.

Clayton turned to see a ruddy-faced man of about fifty walking stiffly toward them. The famous Dr. Leon Rollan showed his years, yet his eyes vibrated with resolve beneath the golden glow of the haze.

The next moments' customary greetings went by Clayton without leaving any lasting impression, for he was fascinated by Rollan's presence. It is common to be so overwhelmed by the celebrity of the great that at first the actual person seems

unreal, too small and compact and mortal to have
been the source of such renown. Clayton had never
met anyone of remotely the stature or mystery of
this tanned, fuzzy-bearded being who shook his
hand slowly, blue eyes self-assured and calm and
questioning. He could think of absolutely nothing
worth saying. His mind hung in a vacuum, spinning fruitlessly as Sylvia hugged and kissed her
father and peppered the grizzled, indulgent man
with questions. They exchanged affectionate jokes.

Then Dr. Rollan said, as if prompting Clayton,
"I gather you are a young man deeply committed
to our ideas here."

"Sure am," Clayton said, without specifying which
ideas he meant. This place was certainly ripe enough
with demonstrated ideas, with practical applica-
tions of huge forces.

"Fine!" Dr. Rollan slapped Clayton on the back
with gusto. "Out here we used to get lots of the
other kind, you know, good Clayton."

Clayton nodded, supposing that Rollan meant
the grimy, no-nonsense inhabitants of the asteroids. They were interrupted by Rollan's dog, a
mongrel who seemed to become immediately fond
of Clayton's leg. On Earth dogs were rare, other
than as a delicacy, and Clayton did not know how
to respond. The dog was trying to embrace his
knee. Rollan was distracted, pointing out the sights,
so Clayton gave the dog a quick, experimental
kick. It backed away.

Dr. Rollan took them to a handsome dinner in a
vast, green stone country house, termed the Hostel. "Just something the Brothers made up as a

greeting," he said, ushering them into a vast communal dining hall. "Do you know what this is?" he asked Clayton.

"Well, uh, a cafeteria," Clayton said uncertainly.

"No!" Dr. Rollan cried good-naturedly. "It is our equivalent of church."

They stood watching the throng for a moment, and soon Clayton saw what he meant. The Brothers dined with a ritual seriousness, passing food and observing social graces with a deadpan earnestness. Evidently the sharing of food was a crucial observance to them.

Clayton found it unnerving—a huge long room, filled with Brothers and Sisters who looked exactly like each other. Dr. Rollan had cloned them all from the cells of a great genius of the last century, a social philosopher who had updated Marx and mixmastered in a blend of oriental religion, self-help, and moral philosophy. The high steepled wall above bore the statement.

A WEED IS MERELY A PLANT SOMEONE
DOESN'T LIKE.

Clayton frowned, trying to figure out the implications. Rollan's dog reappeared, this time eyeing Clayton's leg avidly but keeping a respectful distance. Fascism evidently worked with dogs, Clayton deduced.

"The Brothers and Sisters, they're really all alike?" he asked, to be saying something.

"Exactly," Dr. Rollan said.

"Nothing's *perfectly* copied every time," Clayton said.

Dr. Rollan answered crisply, "Circus knife-throwers know it is possible to be perfect, and one had better be."

"In some areas," Clayton said, seeking a way to deflect the conversation to the dynamics of the Hoop.

"In *anything* truly earnest," Dr. Rollan said flatly.

"Yes sir?" a Brother answered at the doctor's elbow.

"Oh, I didn't mean you, Ernest. Meet Clayton."

Ernest was a burly version of the others, obviously the product of an extensive exercise program. He wore his shirt open to the navel, where a mat of brown hair exuded a husky scent. Clear blue eyes regarded Clayton closely. There were three women behind him, blank-faced, obviously waiting until his attention returned to them.

"Glad to shake the hand of anybody can give the Missy a good time," Ernest said, pinching Clayton's hand in a viselike handshake.

"The . . . the Miss?"

"Miss Sylvia," Ernest explained. "She's the untouchable around here."

"Ernest means I don't take part in their sexual calisthenics," Sylvia explained lightly.

"Not genetically allowed, you see, good Clayton," the doctor said. "Would pollute the strain."

"Ah." Clayton liked something in Ernest's direct, gruff manner and was pleased when they sat at a table together. The people all called Dr. Rollan the Handyman, as though he were some mere technical assistant. Clayton thought this odd, and even stranger that Dr. Rollan beamed at the nickname. There were greetings all around, but then the Brothers and Sisters fell into rapt conversation with each other, leaving the three genetically different people to themselves.

Food arrived, succulent and steaming. All vegetarian, of course. It was passed on plates of a hard, black, heavy substance which Clayton guessed must be a product of the Vortex itself, matter transmuted by the intense heat of the inner accretion disk.

Ernest quickly downed several glasses of sweet wine, smacking his lips and pronouncing in detail on its qualities. "Try more, good Clayton," Ernest said, slopping some on the table as he refilled Clayton's glass.

"Uh, thanks." He wished everyone wouldn't use the "good" preface, though he noted others routinely using it. It reminded him of old ideas about conditional training. Ernest began telling stories about the farming and labor of the Hoop, dominating the table talk for a while. Clayton grinned at the expected moments, though it seemed humorless. Ernest's most witty sayings could provoke a smile, but they were seldom quick and light, and more often had the leaden quality of pig irony.

Clayton got on well enough with Dr. Rollan, discussing his parents' asteroid community and the everchanging economics of the Belt. The Doctor had once been a rockhound himself and still remembered much of what a catch-as-catch-can existence it was. At first the venerable man merely nodded and grunted assent, but as Clayton described his father's company and their hardships,

Rollan began to break in with stories of his own, snippets of information, good-old-days counter-examples. Slowly, listening respectfully, Clayton knitted together a picture of the man, filling in the spaces that had remained obscure in the biographies he had read.

4.

Rollan had found the Vortex entirely by accident.

He was born Leon Vladimir Rollan, son of good socialist parents in middle Europe. At that time the planners were attempting to arrest the long economic slide of his native land, and so sent teams into the newly opened asteroids. Their National Mission was to return raw materials for smelting in high orbit.

Rollan was fully committed to the ideals of his government, and volunteered for prospecting duty. This was a chancy affair, involving long low-energy orbits between likely asteroids. Exploring robots, however intelligent, had failed; they had no intuitive feel for the crannies which concealed lucrative metal deposits.

The North Americans had gotten to the obvious candidate 'roids long before, so the European prospectors were forced to explore the lesser targets—those with odd spectra, or hard-to-reach orbits out of the ecliptic plane.

Rollan was not a lucky prospector. He turned up countless examples of the most common 'roid—a spongy assemblage of boring elements, with no seams of rare metals. He failed to find even one carbon-rich rock, which would at least have paid his expenses.

He was on his final run, having boosted up to three km/sec at an angle of thirty-seven degrees out of the ecliptic plane. He was fatalistically pursuing a lumbering mountain of unpromising rock. He never reached it. Fifteen hours after his pulse launch in a cramped, one-man slingship, Rollan registered a flash of x-rays that looked like the preliminary burst from a solar flare. Normally the warning system would give him an hour to find a 'roid and hide behind it, out of the sleet of protons spewing from the sun.

But when Rollan swiveled his 'scope around to confirm, the sun was an ordinary disk, undisturbed by the huge, magnetic-dominated plasma arches which, collapsing, generate flares. He checked his x-ray diodes and found a steady level of emission. Turning the slingship, he found that the radiation came from a spot high up above the ecliptic. Unless he had ventured off on this oblique orbit, he would not have been within range to pick it up.

He tracked the spiky, slow-simmering x-rays for hours. They came from a pinprick of UV emission which was swooping down toward the asteroid belt.

Rollan expended his remaining reserve fuel and rendezvoused with the firefly dab of yellow. As he approached he expected it to swell into a 'roid profile. Instead, he nearly collided with it, believing it must be still a long distance away. Only his acceleration meters warned him, seconds before it was too late, of a sudden steepening of the local gravitational potential.

It was a black hole, the first ever found in the solar system—still grinding up and devouring the small rock it had intersected, yielding the burst of x-rays.

Rollan was a competent astrophysicist and he knew a fortune when he saw one. Observation of distant quasars had shown that their dazzling energies came from matters processed by vast black holes at a galactic center. Matter cast into a disk around a black hole could yield an entire menu of radiation, exotic materials and useful high-energy particles.

He also knew the hole was dangerous. His Earthside training had included elementary magnetic fusion methods; this qualified him to fly a solo slingship craft and make his own repairs. That came in handy. He fashioned a magnetic trap for the hole, keeping a respectful distance. The hole, despite containing the mass of a medium-sized asteroid, was only a millionth of a centimeter wide. Rollan's magnetic bottle could be strong but crude. Slowly, gingerly, he towed it back to a grubby 'roid station, where he kept silent about the contents.

Only when he reached the tinny magnificence of Ceres Station did he begin to use the hole, injecting ordinary dust and extracting energy from the hole by driving magnetohydrodynamic generators. Electrical power was still at a premium and he—or rather, his National Mission—prospered.

The hole was kept a secret, but even its profitability did not stave off the effects of a general economic recession. Rollan's National Mission folded up. Most of his countrymen went home, but Rollan managed to keep the hole—he had never revealed, even to his superiors, what fed the generators.

These hard times were the crucible in which Rollan was hardened and formed. The decline of the socialist nations—democratic or totalitarian, second world or third world, strict or reformist—led him to believe that only a new kind of society could bring about the aims of the old utopian thinkers. He took the hole and began a series of brilliant economic coups, manufacturing exotic materials and plasmas for anyone who could pay. He bought his own asteroid and moved it to a concealing orbit at a steep tilt to the ecliptic. This isolated him from the Belt society, allowing time to refine ore as he refined his own ideas.

He hired trusted assistants, all idealogically pure. He went on frequent, high-boost journeys to Earth, carrying his wares, and returned with huge credit balances payable in the banks of the Belt. He was an early investor in the self-replicating robot companies, and bought over a third of them in the first decade of the industry.

Then came the long plateau of his life, during which he traveled little and worked even harder. Inevitably, news of the hole escaped. Eager, ferret-eyed scientists came to inspect. The nations of Earth attempted to confiscate it. The Belt laid claim to "mineral rights." The system-wide economic community demanded that it be classified as a natural resource, the "proper heritage of all mankind."

In a sense, it was. Astronomers had long believed that the solar system began with a nearby supernova explosion. The supernova occurred in a star of about ten times our sun's mass, blowing outward a huge expanding shell of debris. A sector of this outrushing, highly radioactive junk collided with a neighboring dust cloud, compressing it.

Once begun, gravitational contraction proceeds apace. Within a thousand years the jolt applied by the supernova made the dust cloud shrink into a sputtering, newborn star, with an attendant disk which would eventually form planets.

All this could be deduced from the unusual concentrations of rare elements in present-day meteorites. The radioactive elements of the original supernova had long since decayed into daughter and granddaughter elements, a telltale signature of a violent birth for the solar system.

What had *not* been anticipated, though, was the fate of the original supernova remnant. A black hole formed, from matter crushed inward while most of the dying star rushed outward. The hole was of relatively unimportant mass, scarcely more than a mountain's. It was swept along in the chaos and currents of the explosion, and eventually formed part of the collapsing cloud that made the solar system. It apparently reached the imploding dust cloud late in the formation, and took up an orbit not fully aligned with the ecliptic. This gave astronomers a fix on the original rotation axis of the supernova star, and helped formulate detailed nu-

merical studies of the event which gave birth,
eventually, to all humanity.

Rollan didn't give a damn. He regarded astrophysics as a mildly interesting but fundamentally
useless activity, unless it could be used to extract
further wealth from the hole. After giving the
scientists minimal time to study the hole—now
surrounded by a complex system of infalling asteroid dust, transmutation cylinders and furiously working robots—he closed the entire community to
outside visitors.

Earth had long maneuvered to gain control of
the hole. Rollan favored neither Earth nor the
asteroids, on grounds that it was silly to select one
bull over another on the basis of the beauty of its
horns, when what mattered was that you lived in a
china shop. He maneuvered the 'roidbelt interests
into successfully countering Earth. In return they
asked for preference in patents derived from the
hole. Rollan freely gave that, demonstrating again
his balancing act between the two economic giants.
However, patent rights were all he would grant.
All else was cloaked in isolation.

Scientists came to inspect and were turned away.
Observations from afar were neatly blocked by the
huge clouds of asteroid matter that were sent orbiting in toward the hole, masking whatever enormous engineering feats were going on below.
Specialists hired for the tasks were sworn to secrecy. Their memories were wiped clean when
they left Rollan's employ.

As the years stretched on, no scientists ever
managed to wangle an invitation to see Rollan. He

evaded government surveys of his holdings, keeping all but a few workers at a great remove from the actual hole site. Rumors circulated that his self-replicating machines were roving the high-azimuth orbits above and below the belt, searching for raw materials not claimed, or even other black holes.

The happy years of progress and expansion were punctuated by Rollan's marriage to a woman of the Lunar Nirvana Colony. The Nirvanites intended to bravely carry out the final stage in the anti-specie-ist revolution. Their short-lived experiments in "human-animal genetically altered communality" led to public outrage. There were some interesting, unanticipated side effects, however. The breakup of Luna Nirvana greatly enhanced the market in collies and cougars who could take care of the children and run the house, too. It created a whole new industry in big game hunting, promising more nearly even odds. But the experience left Rollan's wife a shattered vessel, a docile receptacle for his idealistic impulses. Sylvia was their only child. Inspired by his vision, Rollan thereafter devoted himself to the cloning program necessary for the new society he envisioned.

5.

Generally ignored in twentieth century astrophysics was a hard problem—what happens to the bulk of the mass ejected from a supernova? Does it all turn to mere drifting interstellar dust, as many supposed?

The explosion occurs in the "carbon flash," when the carbon nuclei begin to collide and fuse. The energy released by carbon-burning heats the core without letting it expand, vastly increasing pressure. This means carbon-level nuclei can remain bonded into a solid form even as they are ejected in the explosion.

—*Supernova Debris*

Morning. As Clayton awoke he saw drowsily that multicolored streamers of light lanced across his room, rippling the far wall with elegant traceries of shifting blues, greens and oranges. This resonated with his technicolor headache, a memento of the sweet wine from the night before. He groped from the bed.

Through curiously thick windows he saw the great plane of the accretion disk, a broad stripe that ran straight across the sky. The sky was a pale blue that stretched away into oblivion, merging with the fuzzy vision of the Hoop itself, arcing up and away to left and right. Clayton saw that the streamers of richly varying colors came from different portions of the inner accretion disk, where matter boiled and frothed under a perpetual stirring of magnetically controlled turbulence. Seed magnetic fields, injected into the infalling dust out at the rim of the disk, grew by compression and shear, until the heating and convection of the disk was dominated and controlled by the rippling, knotting fields.

This much he already knew; observing the effects, though, turned dry equations into exotic flourishes of almost kinesthetic delight. He longed to see better, to be able to pick out the robot shepherds who tended the accretion disk. They would be mere dots against this magnificence, lost in the glare, but they could tell him much from their location and movements. His heart pounded.

He tapped the window. It gave back a solid *thunk*. He felt its slick surface, marveling at the density and thickness of the glass. Each pane was faceted at its edges, refracting splashes of light. Even for a man of Rollan's expansive style, it seemed an incredible indulgence.

"Good morning, sir," a voice said behind him. He turned. It was Ernest, the man from dinner yesterday.

"Are you ready for your bath, sir?" Ernest asked, holding out a towel.

"Well, sure." He hadn't expected such service. And Ernest's respectful "sir" he liked better than "good Clayton." Ernest was so devoted to Sylvia that Clayton automatically took him for a rival. It was reassuring that the man apparently knew his place.

Clayton began to shed his pajamas, but Ernest knelt before him and undid the buttons, saying "Allow me." As the man slid the pajama bottoms off, he observed Clayton's state of tumescence (caused by the vision of the accretion disk, plus a full bladder) and offered to provide any sexual service required.

"Uh, well, no, ah—no, not my kind of thing," Clayton gasped.

"You're sure?"

"No!"

"Perhaps one of the Sisters, then? I can summon Angela or Hadley quickly, they are nearby."

"No, no, nothing thanks."

Ernest nodded gravely and then smiled. "Anything you want, that's what you'll get. Our ideal is selfless service here, sir."

"So I see," Clayton muttered.

"Hot rosewater and vanilla soap?"

"What?"

"Followed by a plasma ionizer rinse," Ernest suggested. "Stimulates the body, while quieting the mind." He nodded significantly at the still-horizontal member.

"Yes," agreed Clayton, smiling inanely, "as you please."

The bath was reached by a slick slide down from his room. The swift journey surprised him, even with Ernest's warning. He plunged into a communal bath, an opulent bowl which was unpopulated save for himself.

Ernest stood at the edge and asked solicitously, "Music? 3D?"

He selected a melody that featured flutes, their notes dripping like a waterfall. Through the translucent walls he saw a moving shadow and abruptly realized that he was surrounded by an immense aquarium. Huge fish, clearly the offshoots of the old Lunar Nirvana experiments, swam in amber light, gliding without curiosity up to the walls and peering at him. They mouthed something but he could not make it out. A poem, perhaps. The fish had been good at that, were frequently published. He wondered what they ate.

He had only a few minutes before breakfast to draw sketches of the Vortex and Hoop, from memory. At the ample meal Dr. Rollan held forth about the new agricultural production goals his world had set. "We hope to reach them ahead of schedule."

"Your aim is to run the 'roid farmers out of business?" Clayton asked.

Dr. Rollan bridled. "Nothing of the sort! I wish to demonstrate that our system here, Uniformism, is a superior model for society."

"What will you take as proof?"

"When we are the leading producer of food in the outer system."

"But that will run the 'roid farmers—"

"If they persist in their outmoded market theories, yes, perhaps."

"But there's limited market for food. People—"

"There will always be more people, too! Don't forget that," Sylvia put in.

"But not enough to eat up megatons of excess wheat or—"

"We are an example here," Dr. Rollan said forcefully, "an example of what human destiny must be."

"A shining destiny," Sylvia said warmly, patting her father's hand.

They were surrounded by the hubbub of the communal dining room. Brothers and Sisters everywhere brought forth and devoured huge glittering plates of eggs, toast, cereal, ham. The ham was a vegetarian substitute, of course, but Dr. Rollan assured them that it tasted remarkably like true pig flesh. They swilled it down with flasks of hearty coffee. The constant humid motion and talk in the overcrowded hall seemed systematic to Clayton, but he could not understand the streams of bodies or follow their odd accents.

"They all seem to be about, uh . . ." Clayton began.

"Twenty-five, on the nose," Dr. Rollan said. "They all came out of the cooker at exactly sixteen when I started the experiment, nine years ago."

"They're all sort of older brothers and sisters to me," Sylvia said. Clayton noticed she had forsaken her constant Earthside garb of severe pants and blue cotton work shirt. Now she wore a little white gown which came to just below her knees. He liked especially the wreath of marigolds clasped with slender blue slices of stone in her hair.

"All the same genotype," Clayton said. "And you hold the patent?"

"I have published the 'specs," Dr. Rollan said. "Anyone can clone more Brothers and Sisters if he or she likes."

"They *are* handsome," Clayton said politely. Actually, he was already tiring of them.

"A simple formula, really," Dr. Rollan said. "I hired the best DNA artists in the system to make me a chain with no inherited diseases, yes, that much is commonplace. But fashioning the right personality mix and making it breed true in the conception tubes—that was no trifling matter."

"I see," Clayton said. "To get the right sort of worker for—"

"No no!" Dr. Rollan was agitated. He stopped slicing the blue-brown fake ham and frowned furiously. "The exact personality type does not matter. I know my ideas are not widely known in the reactionary citadels of Earth—and of course they are roundly despised among the 'roid rabble—but you must have gotten some misinformation somewhere."

"I just—"

"The point is that those societies contain a contradiction, a dialectical one, if you will. Earth, with its billions of citizens, preaches the virtue of tolerance, of passivity, of conformity. But who does it reward? The heads that poke up above the crowd! It is impossible to free them of their adulation of the special unless it becomes impossible to *be* special!"

"That's a scientific fact," Sylvia put in. "Father gave Brotherland its own dialect, too—it's the easiest way to program their worldview."

"Ah."

"You are training to be a social scientist, Mr. Donner," Dr. Rollan went on, cutting his cube of ham precisely into smaller brown cubes, all alike. "You must realize the central problem! One cannot carry out reproducible experiments on human societies. They are not a controlled environment."

"Well, yes."

"So I constructed this world, to prove that Uniformism will work. Here we can illustrate the central tenets of progressive thinking, begin the true evolution of socialist man."

"Through controlled experiments."

"Yes. We will demonstrate that Uniformism produces more material goods, higher pleasures, healthier bodies."

"And you'll drive the 'roids into a depression."

Dr. Rollan chuckled. "It is *they* who preach the virtue of their vaunted free markets."

"But my father's operation—"

Dr. Rollan smiled shrewdly, his eyes rolling upward in amusement. "Free markets . . . can be costly."

When he returned to his room, Clayton quickly finished unpacking. He assembled the telescope which he had dismantled and hidden among his belongings. It was stubby and could not give fine resolution, but it did not need to. Its heart was the spectrum analyzer which attached like a lamprey to the base.

Clayton pointed the telescope at the huge strip of light that hung like a ribbon wrapping the sky. He would have liked to do this outdoors, but there he would have been quickly spotted. He sighted the telescope through the thick windows and thumbed the instrument into action.

Rollan's ingenious design of the inflowing matter made astrophysical observation of the black hole impossible from a great distance. The infalling matter masked the hole except for the thin wedge in the equatorial plane—which was blocked by the Hoop itself.

Clayton focused the telescope on each of the technicolored bands of the accretion disk in turn. The spectrum analyzer recorded emission lines, buzzing and humming to itself. It estimated concentrations, measured infalling rates from the Doppler shifts. There was a wealth of information here and Clayton began to perspire slightly, his heart thumping.

Odd lines poked up above the expected hash of spectra. Clayton could not recognize them. He turned the telescope directly at the blue-white blaze which masked the black hole itself, thinking the strong lines would go away, but they did not. Very well, an interesting problem for later. He punched in commands for a finer scan and then heard the door behind him opening.

"Clayton!"

He jumped. It was Sylvia.

"I, uh, I'm—"

"You *must* come to see the harvesting. The entire quadrant is there!"

He stood speechless for a moment before realizing that Sylvia could not see the telescope behind him. "Well, sure, just give me a minute, huh?"

"Just one!" she cried happily, and left.

He quickly stripped the telescope into its components and hid them.

As a festival of commonality it left Clayton feeling curiously left out. The Brothers and Sisters harvested the wheat, all right, using lightweight machinery and considerable skill. But they chattered together in the indistinguishable patois that was beginning to irritate Clayton.

They all referred to Clayton as "sir" on the few occasions when they addressed him. Clayton felt rather swell about this until Sylvia mentioned that to be exalted above the commonality was in fact a denigration, so "sir" was a term of polite contempt. Clayton thought of Ernest's seemingly generous offer that morning, and the fact that the man had used "sir" in very nearly every sentence since then. Had the man become surly over Clayton's romance with Sylvia? Clayton studied Ernest's brooding face, but could read nothing. He decided the man was either very deep or very shallow, and as with many people, it was difficult to tell which.

Dr. Rollan tried to labor with them, sweating profusely, stripped to the waist. The man was old, of course, even neglecting the times he had spent in the coldsleep vaults while his self-reproducing machines had built the Hoop. He so earnestly wanted to be included among the Brothers and Sisters that he ran the risk of overtiring himself. Indeed, he quickly became ashen-faced and had to sit down. Clayton had to admire the chaste and consistent selflessness in the man.

"See how . . . well they . . . work together," Dr. Rollan observed while he shakily took a drink at the water trough.

Clayton agreed. He and Sylvia watched from the side of the fields, since he, as an outsider, was not allowed to take any part in the joy of production. Sylvia was in rapture. She confided to Clayton that she loved everything in nature, except perhaps anchovies.

Dr. Rollan said meditatively, gesturing at the laboring lines, "They are the future, young man. Superior to the mess humanity has made of itself."

Like most idealists, Dr. Rollan loved mankind in principle and disliked it in very nearly every particular.

"Do you plan to spread the Brotherhood and Sisterhood?" Clayton asked mildly.

"Where?" Dr. Rollan seemed genuinely puzzled.

"Perhaps to those new worlds discovered around Tau Ceti?"

"Good lord," the old man said crankily, "I wouldn't *run away* from the problems of the human race. We have to face them here."

Clayton nodded, but frowned.

That night Clayton could not sleep. The vegetarian diet had proved an ineffective cushion for the weight of wine that had landed on it. Still, he was too cautious to go wandering about on his own. Best not to arouse suspicions.

He sat up reading, and quickly grew tired of reviewing the old text, *Supernova Debris*. It was the last major work on the subject. Dr. Rollan had denied scientists access to the black hole and to Brotherland, so astrophysics had gained little from his discovery. *Supernova Debris* contained many speculations which could not be verified.

He put it aside and turned to an old text on social theory, tracking down details of the half-remembered Model of Utopias created by the nearly unreadable but famous social theorist and nudist, Darko Drovneb. Brotherland seemed to have all the characteristics. The textbook discussion rang uncannily true.

The Brothers and Sisters made a point of communal values, keeping their culture pure and without diversity. Rollan's program of genetic uniformity helped that, and also aimed at the second Drovneb characteristic: no change with time. Experiments required unchanging conditions, after all. Even more important, change implied that something had been wrong before.

Drovneb's third signature—a nostalgic and technophobic atmosphere—fit, too. The Hoop was a giant farm, recalling Earth of centuries ago. And the Brothers and Sisters knew little or nothing of machines beyond their farming equipment. Robots and Dr. Rollan made the Hoop work, with nearly everything technical kept above the bottled atmosphere.

And Rollan himself provided the fourth characteristic—an authority figure. He insisted on being called the Handyman, but it was clear that his word was law. He had built the very ground they stood on, after all.

Only in the final Drovneb characteristic was there some doubt. *Social regulation through guilt,* the book said. *Responsibility is exhalted as the standard of behavior.*

Clayton frowned. The Brothers and Sisters seemed remarkably guilt-free, compared with the constricted folk of Earth. Maybe the rural surroundings simply made them seem more easy-going.

Certainly their absurdly low-tech agricultural methods was politically imposed, hopelessly inefficient. Yet apparently it worked well enough to make a profit for Brotherland. Of that the Handyman was proud. He kept the fields of the Hoop a nostalgic echo of the farms of centuries ago, and it seemed to work. The ghost of Rousseau walked here.

He wearily thumbed off the book, shaking his head. The Drovneb parameters fit nearly every utopian society of the last five centuries. The theory predicted a common end—as soon as the authority figure died, things began to slowly unwind. Diversity, curiosity, simple human orneryness—all conspired to bring down the golden dreams.

He wondered what would happen when Dr. Rollan was gone. Could this pinwheel in the sky roll on?

He sighed and fell into an uneasy sleep.

6.

Someone was following them.

At first Clayton thought he was projecting his own free-floating anxiety about being discovered, but after a while the signs became unmistakable.

Dr. Rollan had proposed that Clayton and Sylvia hike around the Hoop. There were striking vistas and pleasant forests in a world which was only five kilometers wide but over a hundred kilometers long.

While they were crossing a monotonous checkerboard of cultivated fields Clayton first caught

sight of a distant figure far behind. There were so
few Brothers and Sisters working alone, a single
person was noticeable. The Hoop rose up into the
sky, distorting perspective. The distant person
seemed above them, looking down from a blue-
green carpet that curved away into misty cloud. As
Clayton watched, the figure disappeared behind a
tree. Later, he glimpsed a flicker of movement as
they mounted a hill.

Always at the same distance. Always the quick
ducking out of sight.

A polite way for Rollan to be sure his daughter
didn't get into trouble? Or to keep tabs on Clayton?

Clayton dismissed this last possibility, and strolled
with Sylvia through lush fields of grain, bordered
by groves of fruit-bearing trees. He put the matter
from his mind and enjoyed the warm breeze, driven
by the compact weather patterns of the Hoop.
Birds fluttered among high limbs, incredible to
Clayton in their variety. His childhood in the asteroid belt had confirmed him in the faith that the
best biosphere was simple, direct. Rollan's sculpted
kingdom echoed Earth's mad profusion. Nature
seemed unnecessarily messy and indecisive. Why
both the crow and the blackbird, for example?

Moist and fragrant air billowed Sylvia's hair into
a flowing flag, distracting him from theoretical
points.

"Why are you so fancifully dressed?" he asked.

"Instead of the usual utilitarian shirt and pants?
You truly understand *nothing* of my father's work,
do you?"

He had to allow that he didn't.

"On Earth I had to show my support for austerity, my devotion to equality. Here, the final state of society has been reached. Real *experiments* are going on here, Clayton. So I am free to express my individuality. As long as I am the only one, naturally."

Clayton could not follow this logic at all, until he saw the reverence given Sylvia by the Brothers and Sisters. Clearly her father had raised her as the darling of them all, and then constructed some idealogical maxim to cover her own indulgences. He could scarcely quarrel with the idea, since Sylvia was, for him, the only intriguing female within several Astronomical Units. He found the Sisters' uniformity boring.

They explored the long equatorial chain of lakes which divided the Hoop into two shores. It was several days before he could adjust to the sensation of journeying only a few kilometers and finding a wholly new environment. Tropical pineapple fields gave away to Alpine forests, which yielded to fertile river-valley vegetable farms, all managed by dutiful Brothers and Sisters. Overhead, occasional flying robots adjusted the humidity, shifted the clouds, tinted the air with mixers and catalysts.

A leisurely walk around the Hoop took about a week in the half-g centrifugal gravity. They hiked through crisp rolling hills, wholesome flatland wheat and cloying dense jungle. Sylvia seemed to bloom with every kilometer of progress. One day they avoided the 'roidrock communal home of the Brothers and Sisters, and instead camped in a dense

knot of oak trees. Their canopy blotted out the
Vortex, bringing a false night.

Sylvia luxuriated on a bed of moss, which Clayton had gathered at her request from the moist
upper limbs of the trees. "Moss is a parasite, after
all," she had said. "It uses trees; *we'll* use *it*."

Clayton toasted compressed tofu bars over yellow flames. "*This* is home," Sylvia said langorously.
She sat on a large stump (careful thinning was
necessary for a balanced biosphere) and said, "*Real*
nature."

"Um," he agreed.

"Where people can be people again." Her dress
fluttered like a white sail in a breeze, a craft
promising far destinations. Oak leaves stirred above
in the firelight, making moving shadows as does
the wind on the sea.

"Right."

He took her some tofu, hot and jacketed in a
crisp black crust from being held too long in the
flames. He collapsed to his knees before her as she
bit into the creamy warm taste inside. She smiled
in lazy acceptance and he kissed her. He drew in
his breath deeply, feeling himself on the verge of a
great abyss. She parted the dress and shrugged
free of it. The cloth fell like a table cloth on the
broad stump, herself as the meal. He was tired of
trying to be underspoken and witty. He inhaled
and a musky scent of her swarmed into him. Insects chirruped in the twilight. "Ah," she said.
The filmy dress, the thick air—if he had been
sensible, he would have worried about his heart.

She smiled, silkily stroked his neck, and slid the backs of her knees over his shoulders.

As they hiked the next day, the technicolor ribbon overhead rippled and flexed, like a living flag. Clayton watched it as closely as he could, a hand lifted against the glare. He could see now and then a chunk of asteroid debris escorted in by robots. The tidbit then slowly wound its way through the outer edge of the accretion disk. From this equatorial angle he could see much that was unknown about the disk—the coal-dark lanes of thickening dust, the sudden yellow flares of magnetic reconnection further in. When alone, he took notes and used the finger-sized camera tucked snugly into his belt.

He was pleased at the greeting they received toward the end of each nominal "day," at one of the living halls which regularly dotted the hoop. There they were received with full hospitality, given large rooms and ample food. Clayton had expected close questioning by the Brothers and Sisters about the 'roids, or at least Earthside. He was surprised to find that each evening he and Sylvia wound up talking to each other. The others politely answered questions, but asked none of their own. Clayton ascribed it to the fact that these people were, after all, mentally only nine years old.

Rollan had used Earthside techniques for constructing their basic platforms of emotion, integration, and left-right balances. Anthology personalities, the press called them. The techniques were derived from the new methods of compressed indoctrination developed in some of the more deplorable nations. Rollan still imported earth technology, and used mindtech when it seemed in accord with the aims of Brotherland.

Clayton had respectfully brought up the subject of contact with Earth. Rollan had visited there several times, making mysterious business arrangements, and brushing aside questions from scientists. "Why go to Earth at all?" Clayton had asked. Rollan had rolled his eyes and replied, "Why do people go to zoos?" and would say no more.

They had nearly circumnavigated the Hoop when Clayton saw a craft many kilometers up in the air. That seemed impossible, and indeed it was—there were no clouds at that moment, and he was staring straight through the cap on the atmosphere, into space. As he peered upward the silvery craft glided across the eggshell-blue bowl and dropped below the hills to his right.

Sylvia was becoming tired, so he left her to swim in one of the shallow, sparkling lakes. They were partway through a jungle zone and he found the going rough as he hiked the kilometer upward, into the hills.

He had never thought about precisely how the Hoop atmosphere was held in, so the shortening of the jungle trees came as a surprise. Here and there, dotting the thick tangle of vines, were great mango trees, their fruit purplish red or vivid yellow among the massive leaves. Among them loomed rubber trees, each with a tap to catch its milky sap, cool columns stretching up into air thick with moisture.

They were all cut at the top. And as he struggled upward amid green, cloying vegetation, he saw why. The monolayer which capped the atmosphere curved down to the ground nearby.

Their trunks sheathed in vines, the trees were stately among screaming cockatoos and pigeons which boomed through the leaves on whirring wings. He saw that the Brothers and Sisters must have kept the trees trimmed at the top to avoid their puncturing the thin, shimmering layer of blue that arced down out of a clear sky and came to earth not much further up in the hills. Clayton struggled on.

Abruptly he came to a steep drop—or so it felt. The trees stopped and he was looking straight down to ice. In a dwindling perspective he saw the silvery craft slow and fire mooring lines into a great cliff of sea-blue ice, scarcely more than a hundred meters away.

He nodded to himself. The Hoop's rotation gave a centrifugal gravity pressing outward, which was "down" on the Vortex-facing face. On the night side the effect was reversed, making it useless. Why would a ship land there, among the ice which Rollan used as backup fluid storage?

A cargo bay irised open in the ship's side. Robots edged something bulky from the bay. They towed it across to the ridged ice, which to Clayton's perspective curved down and away. He squinted as the robots and their cargo drifted into shadow.

Their chunky load looked like ice, too.

But why bring ice here, where there was plenty already?

And where did they get it?

He leaned forward to see better. His foot twisted on a last root that clung to the edge of the soil. He pitched forward, arms windmilling.

A large hand grabbed his shoulder, hauled him back.

Panting, he turned to see who it was. Ernest said, "Dangerous up here, sir."

"Uh, yes."

"Sightseeing is fine but you have to watch yourself."

"Yes, I didn't expect—"

"Not good to leave the Miss alone like that, either."

"Well, no, but—"

"You're supposed to enjoy yourself, sir."

"Well, I was merely looking—"

"Don't concern yourself with those machines," Ernest said solemnly. "They're different from us."

Flustered, Clayton wondered what the man could possibly mean. "Yes," he said, "they have more arms."

"Huh?" Ernest's heavy brow wrinkled in puzzlement.

"Forget it."

"Thing is, like the Handyman says, you got to stick to the good and true."

"What?"

"The fine way the light from the Vortex plays on the pebbles in a brook. Hard and true."

"Oh." The man seemed a cretin.

"Bright and clear."

Clayton nodded, though Ernest seemed neither of those things.

"You shouldn't be up here," Ernest said stolidly. Then, as an afterthought, he added, "Sir."

7.

It had been Ernest following them all the time, of course. Once revealed, he stuck like glue, taking none of Clayton's broader and broader hints.

They stopped for the "night"—really just a scheduled time when the windows were firmly covered against the steady Vortex glow—at a Hostel. As usual, the Brothers and Sisters were polite, generous, and totally uninterested in their visitors. Clayton got a haircut from them, at Sylvia's request. Ernest, whose muscles rippled beneath a tight T-shirt, attracted his usual covey of Sisters. Some were quite graphic in their intentions for recreation after the dinner hour, stroking him as they passed and cooing voluptuously. He grinned and accepted this as his due without making much of it. Clayton became uncomfortable at these continual erotic interruptions of their dinner conversation. There was also an embarrassing moment in the restroom. He had gotten used to the fact that there were no separate facilities for Brothers and Sisters, but was still surprised when Ernest offered to compare the lengths of their members while they stood near each other at the urinals. From Ernest's laconic remarks, Clayton gathered that Ernest felt the winner would have proved something.

Rummaging for something to say, Clayton bitingly remarked, "You can't compare flowers until they're fully grown."

Too late, he realized that Ernest might easily take this as a frank invitation, so he fled without even pausing to zip up.

Back at the long communal dinner tables, Clayton deliberately kept Ernest's glass filled with the sweet, red wine all the Brothers and Sisters drank. It was undistinguished, but it loosened Ernest's tongue.

"Sure, we ship the good grain to the 'roid people. Good trade," Ernest said.

"Profitable?"

"Pays expenses."

"Do you work on the engine repair for those tugs, the ones that haul the grain?"

Ernest nodded. "Don't like it much."

"Why?"

"Me, I like the simple work."

"Growing food?"

"Right. We've all got to rotate jobs, though."

"Why?"

"You know—prevent elites from forming." Ernest pronounced it "aye-letes," his brow furrowed at the thought.

"I've noticed you don't use much farm machinery."

"Work's not so good if you got to use machines all the time."

"You all agree on that? Even the ones who're doing the hoeing and plowing?"

Ernest looked irritated. "Why should any Brother or Sister think different?"

"Well, on Earth there's a different opinion every ten feet you go."

"That's Earth's problem."

Sylvia nodded. Clayton did not wish to get into an argument with her, so he probed in a different direction. "Do you work on other kinds of propulsion engines?"

Ernest sat very still. "Like what?"

"Well, fusion drives, that sort of thing."

Ernest looked confused. His small eyes darted around the room, but the long rows of Brothers and Sisters were babbling to each other with rapt attention. "Why would I do that?"

"Well, to carry cargoes further around the solar system."

Ernest became more agitated, simultaneously trying not to show it. The man obviously had no grace under pressure. "I don't think about those things," he said lamely.

Clayton didn't believe Ernest thought about much at all, but a few moments later in the conversation he let drop the term "ramscoop" and Ernest visibly started. *Ah*.

By this time a Sister was tugging Ernest away for what promised to be only the first bout of the night. Sylvia explained demurely that the Brothers and Sisters—who referred to themselves as the People—were agreed that the Hoop should be filled to the limit with more People. "The greatest good to the greatest number," she said. "That's the rule, isn't it?"

He could hardly disagree, especially since it promised to keep the already drink-sodden Ernest well occupied throughout the "night."

Two hours after Sylvia fell asleep in their small monk-like cubicle, Clayton rolled soundlessly from bed. He made his way through the cool ceramic hallways of the Hostel, easily dodging the small staff that went about necessary chores. The Hoop's advantage in having a constant source of Vortex-light, and thus a relentless growing cycle for crops, was somewhat offset by the inconvenience of tending to the fields even at "night." Still, Rollan's prescriptions for social unity decreed that a vestige of Earthside ritual be maintained, not least because it gave a rhythm and unity to the communal experience. So the Hoop ran on the standard 24-hour day, with few workers staying up through the nominal night.

Clayton slipped away from the Hostel on the side away from the central fields, since he was bound for the edge. No one followed.

He reached the Hoop's rim quickly. He had tucked into his rucksack for the circumnavigation a small infrared telescope. By standing on the very edge of the Hoop, he gained the greatest angle of observation, and thus could see furthest into the accretion disk near the black hole. Puffing from his run, he settled into the roots of a towering elm tree and steadied the telescope on his knee. He sat near the edge of a cliff. The monolayer buried itself into a rock ledge only meters away. Beyond that began the blue ice. He wondered momentarily about the curious incident of the day before,

and why robots would deliver ice to an already
ice-heavy outer face of the Hoop. It seemed innoc-
uous, but Rollan's obsessive secrecy throughout
the construction of his clockwork world naturally
made Clayton suspicious.

He shrugged and set to work.

More than ten kilometers away, straight up the
sky, blankets of dust curved in toward the glowing
disk. Clayton strained to pick up detail in the
murky cloak. It blotted out the stars, but against
the infalling, circling sweep there hung glittering
ivory motes. Robots, shepherding the ground-down
'roid dust. They looped gracefully among the
shrouded dark lanes, probing and pushing with
electromagnetic snowplow fields.

The telescope translated infrared into visible,
and gave a smoldering complexion to the slowly
churning dance above. High out on the Hoop's
axis, robot trawlers swarmed like fat beetles around
an asteroid. They picked it apart like insects dis-
mantling unlucky prey. They they crunched it into
the dust which spiraled inward, toward—

Something glimmered at the edge of percep-
tion. He had idly swept the 'scope by the accretion disk, knowing that the virulent glare there
would soon blind the instrument. But somehow
the glowing region near the black hole was lit by
mere twilight flares. He peered at it by looking
away, using the edge of his vision. Yes, the luminous core was dimming. But the brilliance of the
disk to both sides did not ebb. Then, just as he
was sure he was not making a mistake, the momentary darkening waned. He had the impression

that a mask was being drawn away, both physically and metaphorically. For only a few seconds, something had blocked the light from the innermost disk.

Something in orbit. Something big.

He calculated rapidly. If it was that close to the black hole, its orbital period—

He finished just as the dimming came again. A few seconds of twilight, then the returning brilliance.

Something about a kilometer in diameter was orbiting the black hole, about two kilometers from the hole itself.

Far enough outside the furnace heat of the infalling disk to keep it intact. But close enough in that no one would think to look for it. The glare of the inner disk blinded all but the most sophisticated instruments . . . and Rollan had made quite sure that no scientist with such equipment ever got near the Vortex.

Clayton nodded to himself. A perfect hiding place.

Or nearly perfect. After all, he had found it.

But what was it?

The ramscoop, certainly. His Major Tutor had supplied Clayton with enough information from around the solar system—invoices for machined parts, electromagnetic webs, pulsed power systems, superconducting magnets—to arouse ample suspicion. The authorities had let Rollan's pinwheeling utopia go spinning along its benign orbit for decades, as long as they were sure it was an essentially harmless experiment. Virtuous, even.

After all, Rollan did supply grain and other food to the 'roid communities. And his microwave net did transmit power at marketable rates to ships on fast boost between the planets.

But the accumulating evidence of the invoices suggested that Rollan was far more ambitious than he seemed. Rollan had built a ramscoop engine. With it he could launch cargoes into interstellar space, colonize other solar systems. This was illegal, indeed, immoral. Humanity had not yet agreed on a strategy for interstellar exploration. If Rollan sent a ship carrying the mere cellular ingredients for Brothers and Sisters, he would be able to colonize whole worlds with the seamless sameness of the People.

That could not be allowed. Obviously.

Clayton shook his head and muttered a string of unoriginal, but satisfying obscenities.

He had thought he would craftily reap a harvest of interesting astrophysics, and return to UCLA in triumph. Now his worse fears were confirmed. He would have to find out more about the ramscoop.

Crack.

He jerked to alertness. The snap of a breaking limb echoed through the stillness of the elm grove. Birds stirred and fluttered above. Clayton listened and thought he could hear the rustle of someone slowly prowling through a glade nearby.

He saw a flicker of movement. It was one person, following a remorseless rectangular pattern. Searching.

He crouched down and crawled away from the edge of the Hoop, careful not to disturb the rich piles of leaves slowly turning into loam. They would crackle and give him away, and anyway, the act would probably upset some ecological equation somewhere.

He wished that this "night" was real, could provide sheltering darkness. It occurred to him that the perpetual day banished the entire Earthly freight of associations planetary spin gave humans: darkness, gloom, evil, uncertainty, general bad news. Brotherland was a place where day reigned eternal, illuminating all with piercing light, permitting no obscuring dark. Even the shadows were technicolored mimics of the Vortex bands.

He wished fervently for a touch of darkness now.

Clayton moved cautiously, senses alert. Everything looked different from this angle. No wonder, he mused, that little children were hard to understand. Their world was dominated by anthills and tree roots, lakes of mud and mountains of garbage, chair legs and dog bellies, pant cuffs and big-toed feet, the musty mystery up mummy's dress. Who wouldn't be cranky?

A figure moved among distant trees. Clayton considered making a run for it and then realized that, after all, he hadn't really done anything. Just looked over the edge a bit, natural tourist curiosity.

Still, he didn't like being followed. He worked his way around an outcropping of rock, his soft-soled shoes making no sound. There was a rustling in the trees just below him. Clayton crouched. Only a meters away a man emerged, scanning the path with a careful eye. Ernest.

Without thinking, Clayton picked up a hefty rock and tapped the big man on the skull.

Ernest dropped like a felled ox. Clayton froze, horrified at his own act.

He had committed the first act of violence in a perfect world.

Ernest came to as Clayton staggered toward the Hostel. He had hauled the bulky man two kilometers in an over-the-shoulder carry and felt like a laboratory rat on an endless treadmill.

"Hey . . . whatcha . . . hey," Ernest muttered.

Clayton dumped him and told his rehearsed story, about finding Ernest where a small landslide had caught him.

"Yeah?" Ernest rolled up his eyes as if in thought.

"Uh, yeah."

"Well, man's got to get hit, head wound's the best."

"Oh?"

"Quick."

"Oh."

8.

The return of Clayton and Sylvia to the Central Hostel, where Dr. Rollan lived, was cause for festivity.

The Brothers and Sisters grouped in two long, straight ranks, a welcoming avenue. They cheered with sweaty enthusiasm, pounded Clayton on the back, made risqué remarks about the slowness of their journey. Sisters tossed flowers on them, Brothers called out hoarse jokes. Clayton found the entire ceremony enjoyable. Dr. Rolland was affable and cordial, though quite tired.

Clayton downed several glasses of the sweet wine. The crowd spontaneously broke into whirling knots. Some danced, others performed. Aerobatic drummers leaped and tumbled, all glistening torsos, touching their drums with the merest passing tap, yet the booms and rattles rolled through the humid, scented air. Fire jugglers spun orange nuggets through space, leaving in Clayton's eyes the after-image of traceries woven by centrifugal art. Potters and scroll painters crafted smoky visions, displayed them with broad grins, pressed them upon Clayton and Sylvia. Yet, curiously, Clayton had the uneasy impression that the Brothers and Sisters performed for each other, with the two visitors as mere conductors of private messages.

Even Dr. Rollan's dog was glad to see them, yelping and leaping at Sylvia. The dog eyed Clayton's leg adoringly but kept a respectful distance, eyes glinting with what Clayton took to be the *Fueherprinzip.*

The mad, heady celebration spurred Clayton to down more wine, unmindful of consequences. He was just warming to the experience and found it unnerving when, within an hour, the entire crowd had melted away, the spirit of the occasion evaporated into gauzy memory, transparent as the layered, moist air.

Dr. Rollan beamed, laughed, was the perfect host. He was no longer uncomfortable at signs of affection between Clayton and Sylvia; in fact, he beamed at their closeness. He even commented warmly on Clayton's hair, mentioning that it now resembled the Brother style, simple and utilitarian.

"Glad to see it, good Clayton," Rollan said.

Clayton chose not to remark that he had gone along with Sylvia's haircut proposal primarily because of the pleasant effect she had anticipated that the soft, short brush would have on her upper thighs. Instead, he had more of the aromatic wine.

That evening, as part of the sporadic celebration, Dr. Rollan instructed the worker robots who tended the Vortex to perform for Clayton and Sylvia. In they came, hundreds of the ivory motes streaming out from the glossy bands. Further legions descended from the banks of infalling dust, leaving only a skeleton crew of robots to keep the dark shroud on its slow sure gyre.

They flitted gnat-like through a momentarily opened hole in the monolayer. At Rollan's wrist control, the puncture spread. It was a suddenly swelling black circle, into which the robots swooped. Then it zipped shut, summoned together again by intricate molecular commands.

The robots extended silvery wings and swarmed through the Hoop's upper atmosphere. They formed letters, symbols, pictures. Against the sky the metal fleets swooped, performed adroit feats, defied gravity. In fact, Clayton realized, there was no gravity up there. Centripetal force held him pinned, but only the mild brush of the air acted on the flying robots. He craned his aching neck to follow their darting arabesques.

As they set to work on a large cloud, Clayton

stole away. The crowd went *ooh* and *aahhh* as the
cloud purpled, swirled, reformed. The robots were
crafting some momentary sculpture from it. An ear
poked out. An eye appeared, winked. Then a full,
round lip.

"Oh, it's Daddy!" he heard Sylvia cry as he
slipped inside the Hostel. The Handyman made
some self-deprecating reply.

Clayton quickly found what he was looking for.
Rollan's private quarters were encrusted with command and control modules, detailed sequencing
arrays, luminous graphics—the nerve center which
controlled Brotherland and the Vortex. He felt
like a spy, slipping through the doorway. He
strained to follow the complex interactions which
unfolded before him. Myriad columns and rows of
data rolled on opalescent screens. If he could enci-
pher even some of this, the right scrap of information—

"Why—*Clay*ton!"

He jerked his attention away from the hypnotic
welter. Sylvia stood in the doorway, eyes round
with shock.

"I, uh . . ."

"What are you *doing*?"

"Ah, I just wanted a look around the place."

"Daddy *never* lets anyone in here."

"I've seen Ernest—"

"Well, of course a few of the Brothers and Sisters. But no guests."

"Why not?"

"*You* know."

"The family secrets, right."

She said archly, "I'm sure you really do understand. You're just being difficult."

He put a hand gently on her arm. "Don't tell your father, okay? I don't want him getting mad."

"Well . . ."

"Come on, let's go see the rest of the show."

"It's nearly over. Robots bore me, really." She looked at him from the corner of her eyes, a lightly enticing smile curving her cool lips. "Besides . . . wouldn't you really rather go to our room?"

Her invitation was irresistible, her buoyancy contagious. Her dress fluttered in a vagrant breeze, as though she herself had just returned from a short, graceful, effortless flight in the uplifting air. Clayton sighed and gave himself over to her, though he knew he would have to try something daring if he was ever to make any real progress.

9.

. . . As the supernova expansion continues, the shell will fragment into clumps whose size is difficult to predict. Despite turbulence and magnetic disruption effects, some clumps should survive. They should have densities in the range of their initial formation. Rapid radioactive decay will leave many of them in states of virtually pure silicon, magnesium, or carbon. Indeed, carbon chunks will be most common, probably in the form of graphite. However, if at the onset of expansion the incipient lattice structure were face-centered

cubic, this form could persist. Numerical sim-
ulations of this stage are costly and unrelia-
ble, so it appears unlikely that theoretical
work on this topic can proceed further without some observational spur. Since such solid
supernova debris is not luminous, attempts to
observe it near supernova remnants in the
galaxy seem doomed. This area of research
thus appears to be at a dead end.

>   —*Supernova Debris*
>   Valerie Thompson, 2078

Later, he tugged her along the passageway, ner-
vously watching the doors ahead.

She whispered, "But honestly, I don't see why
we have to—"

"Shhhh!"

They walked softly through the rest of the Hostel, avoiding the distant sounds of movement as the
skeleton night shift went about domestic duties.
Sylvia led him through an obscure side exit and
they stepped into glaring daylight.

She began sleepily, "I still don't see—"

"I want a better look at the Vortex robots," he
said. "And I'm pretty sure your father wouldn't
let me."

"Did you *ask* him?"

"What you don't ask for, they can't deny you,"
he said nimbly.

"But he might get angry if—"

"Where did you say they usually landed?" If
they stood here and talked it all out, eventually
somebody would come by.

"Over there, beyond that hill. The maintenance station is buried under that grove of apple trees." She pointed reluctantly.

They skirted around the Hostel and made their way, keeping well back in the leafy shadows. A section of hillside slid aside at Sylvia's command; he was quite sure the voice-actuator would have rejected him, perhaps set off a jangling alarm. He had gently gotten information from her after a sweaty tussle in bed. She had drifted into sleep, but he had been unable to as a plan bloomed in his imagination.

After their graceful aero demonstration, some of the Vortex robots had stayed on the Hoop, for routine repairs. There were at least twenty of the things, each standing in its own auto-servo pod. Small robots worried across them, clacking. Bored, Sylvia began describing how the entire Vortex was virtually self-repairing, so that the Brothers and Sisters seldom bothered with the robots, or even noticed them. Clayton nodded respectfully. Sylvia walked through the quick-moving teams of shiny robots without giving them more than a glance, assured that they would get out of the way. They did, too. Awake now, she was quite willing to show off more of her father's vast empire, though it became obvious that she knew very little about how any of this worked.

In the back row he saw a huge bulging cylindrical thing, as big as his bedroom, perched on a launch platform. Atop it was a transparent bubble. A giveaway; automatic machines don't need observation walls.

"Can I take a look inside that one?" he asked with just the right touch of casualness.

"Well, sure, I suppose so."

She was alert, yet quite willing to go along with his curiosity. The point, she had reminded him regularly, was to free people from machines, so that they could think primarily of each other again. She repeated this as they climbed up the rungs of the large, pear-shaped vessel. A hatch hissed open. Inside, she tapped a command phosphor and a voice obediently asked, "Yes, Missy?"

"We'd like some drinks."

"Of course. I have fresh squeezings of fruit, pure water, sniffer ale—"

Clayton was no longer listening. His eyes swept the control panel, understanding its elegant simplicity immediately. His hands flitted over an actuation pad and the boards lit up. He tapped in a command. Standard stuff; his 'roid experience paid off.

The drinks were already splashing into opulent crystal glasses. The disembodied voice interrupted its offerings of food with, "Oh, sorry, I shall have to belay catering while we are under acceleration."

Sylvia blinked. "Acceleration?"

"Yes. Please be seated."

Clayton felt a gentle throbbing under his feet, then a tug. "What—ow!" Sylvia cried, as she tumbled onto a divan which had sprouted from a bulkhead.

"We're taking this personnel robot for a ride," Clayton said. "To see the sights."

Sylvia's eyes widened. "You, you . . ."

"Quite."

The craft rose with obedient, smooth competence. The hillside rolled away and they sprouted from it, a thin tongue of orange fire licking at the tail. Clouds wreathed them, visible through the transparent dome above. The ship asked, "Destination?"

"The Vortex," Clayton said.

Sylvia could have rescinded his order at any moment, he knew, but something strange had come into her eyes. She stared at him, a prettily puzzled frown marring her forehead. He had taken a move without consulting her; perhaps she was so surprised by this unique event that the possibility of a serious outcome to this adventure had not yet occurred to her? Somehow her crisp intelligence, so apparent at UCLA, was submerged. The true Sylvia seemed ever more unfathomable. She sat on the divan, stroking its gold lamé upholstery with a slow, distracted rhythm.

Clayton had worried about the monolayer, but he needn't have. It parted as they rose, unzipping a slice of raw black sky. The ship poked through it and free.

Sylvia said, "You don't mean to—"

"Oh, but I do." He smiled.

They sped swiftly toward the brimming disk of light. Dust thumped and rasped and sang against the hull.

"You'll tell me when the x-ray or UV count gets high?" Clayton asked the ship.

"Of course, sir. But I shall rotate my body away

from the disk itself, so as to absorb the radiations
before they reach you."

"Good idea."

"I was designed to think of such things."

"For what mission?"

"To take Dr. Rollan on his journeys to the
Vortex."

"To study what?"

"That I do not know."

"Does he go often?"

"Sadly, no. He has seldom made the trip this
last decade."

"Any idea why?"

"No sir," the ship said stiffly, and Clayton wondered if its programming used "sir" as Ernest did.

"Clayton, I want to go back," Sylvia said. He
recognized the petulant vixen approach—pouting
lip, whiny singsong. But somehow he knew she
did not mean it.

"No. I want a look at this."

"My father will be angry—*very* angry."

"Ah, threats. "I think he'll understand. He
was like me, once."

She said irritably, "I doubt that."

"Come on. Your father had curiosity."

"He was thrown into a place and a time, by
impersonal historical forces," she said, as if she
had memorized it from somewhere.

"Is that from one of your father's speeches to
the Brothers and Sisters?"

She looked surprised. "Well, yes."

"There's another similarity."

"What?"

"He was an astrophysicist, once."

She looked blank. "You're not, you're—" Then a furious look crept over her face.

"Right. I'm majoring in astrophysics."

Sylvia gritted her teeth and swore bitterly, her words like spat tacks. He said nothing.

She began to shout at the ship, commanding it to turn back. When there was no answer she pounded on the firm but padded walls.

"It's no use," he said mildly. "I've switched the ship to control panel operation only."

"How—why—"

"I'll explain later. Don't think badly of me simply because I did what I had to do. Just . . . give me time. And watch."

He knew there was little time before Dr. Rollan would be after them, and less still before the ship would reach the inner edge of the accretion disk. His heart thumped as he swung into the observation chair. It was mounted on gymbals and shafts, allowing easy movement about the transparent dome. Filtered telescopes and array sensors hung nearby, available at a gesture.

The central riddle of Brotherland came riding toward them, trailing clouds of glory.

They were coming down now, falling at an angle toward the accretion disk. It turned like an immense technicolor phonograph record. Luminous bands shaded from blue to orange to red and finally, at the furiously spinning inner edge, a startling glorious white. Clayton felt a giddy, seasick sway as the ship matched orbital velocities with the disk. Each striated section was at a different temperature and gave off its own speckled, roiling glow. He could see flecks of still-solid stone being swallowed at the outer rim, then ground into fuel by friction's raw rub.

But toward the center, where the burning fire was a searing point, he caught a flicker of movement. Something solid, something large . . .

Sylvia was talking to him, using reasonable tones of persuasion, softly undulant. To Clayton it was babble, lost in the background pops and rumbles that echoed through the ship. He could not follow her quixotic changes. He concentrated on the shadowy thing ahead.

He punched in directives and the ship smoothly shifted, pressing them into their couches as it set off in pursuit of the inky thing that—Clayton saw clearly now—was orbiting at the edge of the disk, but not *in* the disk.

Distances were deceptive. The plate of fuel for the hole revolved below, each arc gathering orbital speed as it worked closer to the fiery pinwheel death which awaited. The white-hot center cast stretched shadows across the disk, which Clayton estimated as several kilometers across.

Clayton was startled when abruptly the dark thing ahead expanded rapidly, filling half the dome with shadow.

"It's in orbit around the hole, but at right angles to the disk," he said wonderingly.

"*What* is?" Sylvia asked sharply, but even she was puzzled, frowning up at the strangely somber, gleaming thing.

The distorting sweep of light made it hard to be

sure. "It's no ramscoop vessel, at least," Clayton muttered to himself. So the suspicions had been wrong . . .

The surface of the thing caught the disklight and threw it back in a shower of minute glimmerings, a thousand thousand wavering ice-blue candles buried deep in the slumbering mass.

Extract sample, Clayton ordered the ship.

A small flitter launched itself across the foreground, braked, then buried itself deeply in the target.

The bulk's slow rotation brought into view a long, webbed tube, then another, mounted on the surface.

"Accelerators," Clayton said. "That's what your father bought the electromagnetic guns for."

"What?"

"To adjust the orbit of this big mass. To make up for the friction it encounters when it punches through the disk. And people Earthside thought he was building a starship . . ." He smiled mirthlessly. Sylvia peppered him with questions, but he brushed them aside. They watched silently as the small robot returned and thumped into the lock. In a moment the ship's flawless servants had conveyed the sample case up to the receiving bay. Clayton snapped it open.

Into his hand floated a brilliant, icy stone.

"What . . . I don't . . ." Sylvia touched the cold, hard thing.

"It's a diamond."

"Are you . . . sure?"

"It fits with some studying I've been doing.

Supernova debris is mostly rubble, junk, hydrogen gas. But the compressed star could form solid matter. At those temperatures . . ."

"Solid carbon? That's what diamond is, like graphite, isn't it? Only harder."

"Yes—far more compressed. The supernova star did that. The center imploded into a black hole, the outer layers blew away—and somewhere in the middle, *this*."

He looked wonderingly out at the slowly spinning mass. It had lumps and hummocks, like any other small asteroid. Yet each minute turn brought forth myriad fresh facets of hard, cool blue, of russet, or sulphurous yellow.

"But who would ever have thought : . . we always considered molecules, maybe a few pebbles at most. *This* . . . a chunk so big . . ."

He estimated distance, angle. He tried to think of something on a human scale to compare it to, something as worthy of this rich relic from a time beyond the first dim stirrings of earthly life, beyond the first raindrop, beyond the blind dumb buttings that formed the sun itself.

He whispered, "It's one whole stone, a diamond as big as the Ritz."

"The what?"

"A hotel in Boston. A fabulous hotel."

She said sardonically, yet distantly, "For the rich only, I'll bet."

"For the different."

"Sure they're different. They have more money."

Clayton could not argue of such infinitesimal

things, could not take his eyes from the blissfully turning body, host of a billion starlike blue-white promises.

10.

"Good Clayton!"

The rasp of Dr. Rollan's voice on the radio yanked him from his reverie.

"Daddy! Look what we've found," Sylvia cried gladly.

Clayton put out a hand to block the small TV camera she swiveled, to transmit the image before them. Sylvia veered it away from him, and focused on the vast stone.

"Think of it!" she said. "It must have drifted in here from those dust clouds the robots are always working on, bringing in from the Belt. Dummies! They didn't recognize what it was."

Clayton began carefully, "Sylvia, you should wait and—"

"No, don't you understand? If Clayton—I know he's impetuous, Daddy, and I have to admit it, a liar, too!— If Clayton hadn't stolen this ship and come out here on a jaunt, we would never have known this was here. It would fallen into the hole!"

Clayton said, "It's moving exactly perpendicular to the disk. That minimizes the friction it feels when it passes through the plane of the disk. Anyway, it's far out, at the edge of the disk. A small, steady push could keep it in this orbit for a long time."

"That's quite right," Dr. Rollan's voice came crisply through the panel speaker. "This object will no doubt prove very interesting to study. Meanwhile, I must insist that you return at once to the Hoop and leave—"

"No, Daddy! I want to *explore*. A diamond this big, it's—why, I wonder if when you stand on the surface, you can see yourself, little pictures of yourself, waving back? All the way down to the center!"

"Sylvia, there is all the time in the world to—"

"Never mind, the charade won't play," Clayton said.

Rollan asked menacingly, "What?"

"A diamond asteroid, orbiting just so it won't fall into the hole easily? But perfectly positioned so that when it is above or below the plane of the disk, it's screened by the infalling dust? So no one can see it from the Hoop? The only way I suspected it was the quick little flicker of its shadow passing between me and the disk."

Sylvia said, "The robots put it there. They probably were wondering what it was. But with all they had to do, preparing for their air show and all, there probably hasn't been time—"

Clayton laughed, though he sensed this was not wise. "And it just happens to arrive now?"

Sylvia said irritably, "You're making a lot out of—"

"No, he is right, Sylvie," the Handyman said. "The stone has been here from the beginning. I discovered it at the same time as the hole itself. They were in orbit about each other, even then."

Sylvia blinked. Her mouth opened—first in amazement, then in perplexity, then in a sad, wondrous expression of confused defeat. Finally she shut it, having said nothing.

"Then your biography is wrong?" Clayton asked.

"In part."

"You didn't make your first money out of the hole at all, did you?"

"No."

Sylvia asked wonderingly, "Then how . . ."

"He sold chunks of the diamond," Clayton said. "Right?"

"Yes. A little private courier run to Earth, some quiet deals. It was necessary."

Sylvia said distantly, "To finance Brotherland?"

"Yes. I could extract power from the hole, but not enough to buy all I needed. I left the diamond here in the original orbit, where no one would find it."

Clayton added, "We always wondered why you put Brotherland out here. That didn't make astrophysical sense."

Dr. Rollan's voice said wanly, distantly, "Yes . . . a clue, one I could not avoid."

"But Daddy, why *hide* it?" Sylvia's lips hovered between stunned surprise and quizzical alarm. Yet her eyes studied the huge stone outside with keen intelligence.

"I used chips from it to finance the Hoop."

"But I thought . . . the black hole . . ."

Rollan said sadly, "Yes, I could make some profit from energy extraction . . . but I could see it would not be enough to accomplish . . . my dreams.

Certainly it alone could not support . . . the economy of the Hoop as it now exists . . . all the
Brothers and Sisters."

Clayton understood everything now. He opened
his mouth to speak when suddenly he glimpsed a
rapidly growing red dot, high above the diamond
asteroid. "What—?"

Ernest's voice boomed through the cabin. "I've
come to kick your ass back where it belongs, *sir*.
The Handyman, he's taking this pretty hard. I
decided to come out here and drag you back, you
lying little—"

"Oh, forget that hairy-chested stuff," Sylvia said
sharply. "Can't you see you've been outfoxed?"

Clayton found her sudden tart anger endearing.
All along he had wondered if she found Ernest's
sweaty—well—earnestness somehow attractive. To
find that she could so quickly size up the situation,
and automatically side with him, gave Clayton an
unexpected jolt of pleasure. He smiled at her and
gestured toward the immense gleaming stone.

"I believe the lady would like to take a walk
upon the surface first, Ernest. We'll suit up momentarily. Then I'm sure I'm quite capable of
escorting her safely home, thank you."

The sputtering exasperation that came from the
speaker only deepened his joy.

11.

Clayton took a moment to himself on the veranda. It was pleasant to get outside, away from
the hothouse festivities of the Hostel.

Dr. Rollan had declared a holiday. The Brothers and Sisters had set to with an endless round of dances, feats, athletic competitions, songfests and general revelry. Apparently they required no explanation of the holiday, no pretext, but simply gave themselves over to a mad round of heartwarming ritual good spirits. Clayton had never seen people with such capacity, and wondered how such a remarkable ability fit into the dry, acerbic Drovneb parameters. Breathing in the succulent air of ripe fields and sweet promise, he decided that narrow Drovneb had missed something vital.

"Are you going to accept?"

Sylvia's sudden question, coming from behind, made him jump. He turned to find her glowing with energy, perspiring from a whirling folk dance that was just now ebbing away in the hall beyond.

"I . . . I came here to think it over."

"You *have* to."

"Well, I . . . it's a big decision, Sylvia."

Her mouth formed an incredulous O. "But you could live here for*ever*."

"But I couldn't return to Earth, or even to the asteroids."

"What does that matter? Earth can't compare to *this*, can it?"

He gazed out across the verdant fields, the gentle curve of the Hoop rising up into the sky with a seemingly infinite promise of bountiful natural wealth. There was astrophysics to be done here, utopian visions, a self-contained universe. Even if it was founded, finally, on a deception. But even

that false center was a giant jewel, a marvel un-
equalled anywhere.

"No, it can't."

"Father *needs* you."

"Yes, he told me when he made the offer."
Clayton patted her hand uncomfortably.

Actually, Dr. Rollan had revealed more than
Sylvia or anyone else in Brotherland knew. Dr.
Rollan's health was declining, an arteriosclerotic
gumming combined with gradual, accumulating or-
gan defects beyond the healing powers of man or
machine. Rollan was the scientific sorcerer behind
the Hoop, and was finding the task more difficult
as the great ring spun on. Even minor excite-
ments, such as Rollan's confession to his daughter
at the discovery of the diamond mountain, sapped
his strength. He needed help.

"You know," he said distantly, "if you hadn't
invited me, I wonder how he could have gotten
anyone reliable out here."

"You mean any volunteers would have been
Earth agents?"

"Well, yes," Clayton admitted uncomfortably.

"Just like you."

"But I'm different, you know that."

"Oh yes, as I know," she said, an enigmatic
smile playing on her lips.

Clayton's arrival had seemed an omen to Dr.
Rollan, a possible eleventh-hour salvation. Rollan
had never trusted outsiders enough to think of
bringing them into his gyrating experiment. But
now he had to. Sylvia's chance invitation had provided an unexpected opening.

"Is he resting?" he asked to deflect the conversation.

"I checked a short while ago. He's looking better."

"He knows I won't leak information about the diamond."

"Of course," she said mildly. "We trust you."

"Mere knowledge that so many potential diamonds could flood the market—that alone would drive the price to nearly zero."

Sylvia smiled. "Your sacred market system. Too much wealth and it becomes worthless."

Clayton shuffled uncomfortably, rubbed his hands together. There had been so many signs, clues, hints. The thick windows of his bedroom were diamond sheets. The robots he had seen at the edge of the Hoop were bringing a chunk of diamond to store among the ice fields of the Hoop's backside. Ernest's discomfort at discussing technical matters arose from the man's lack of experience at keeping secrets from strangers.

Rollan had not been deeply disturbed by Clayton's discovery. Perhaps the years of keeping the secret had built up a kind of pressure to share it with someone who could understand.

The old man did trust him. Earlier tonight the Handyman—face lined, hands visibly trembling, voice reedy and faltering—had offered to bring Clayton forward as his inheritor, the Fixit Man. To transfer the mantle of humble power.

Rollan's dog came cautiously onto the veranda and sat a respectful meter from Clayton's revered leg. Curiously, the dog acted this way only toward

the Handyman and himself, as if all along the
animal had sensed some similarity.

"I . . . I don't know," Clayton said. "I'd have to
learn so much astrophysics, handle Brotherland,
teach people like Ernest enough to help me out."

"Father can teach," she said laconically.

Clayton nodded. Dr. Rollan knew the quirky
ways of the Brothers and Sisters, was sure that he
could smooth the way for Clayton. They needed
leadership, though of a gentle, self-effacing kind.
For in their blissful, nostalgic world, the Brothers
and Sisters were unprepared for the inevitable
threats the Hoop faced.

One danger was obvious. The mass which was
heated and thus lit the Brotherland skies was in
turn swallowed by the hole. As the hole's mass
grew, its gravitational field clutched the Hoop
harder, made it spin faster, stressed the steel webs
that underlay the warm green fields. This would
worsen. Only an astrophysicist could solve such a
long-term problem.

The Handyman had peered at Clayton for a long
time this evening, beseeching him wordlessly to
shoulder the task. And now Sylvia did, too.

To maintain this idyllic simple communality demanded vast, intricate, gyrating technology, but
even that was not enough. At the secret center
was not a dark secret but instead a diamond, a
luminous cliché of capital. Something in these con-
tradictions appealed to Clayton's heart.

He took her hand and walked inside, to the
railing above the large dance floor. Below swirled
the uplifted, perspiring, happy faces.

For the first time tonight, Clayton had begun to sense the strange social cohesion these people felt. They were the Handyman's ever more demanding and uncontrollable hostages to fortune, joyful souls born into a serene world shaped by unseen hands. They spoke to each other constantly, comparing their minor mishaps, accidents, confusions, fretful collisions with reality's unrelenting rub. The tireless torrent of pure, unashamed gossip shared out all misfortunes, tempered egoistic dread, purged anger of its uniqueness. There was a solace in such a thick net of mutually invaded privacies, sexual preferences confessed and exercised under an unblinking sun, angst exposed to the social glare like a skin disease shriveling away beneath searing ultraviolet. Like a heightened form of clubbiness, these people felt no oppression in their uniformity. They gained instead a reassurance that villages and tribes had granted their members down through millennia, the casual knowledge that no scrape or tragedy or disfiguring blemish was in fact new, that everything had happened before, or very nearly so, and could be shared, soothed. They were like a roistering army marching toward some battle they could not anticipate and so shrugged off, given strength to tramp forward by their own massed smell, their swelling songs.

Something in their innocent spinning dance endeared the Brothers and Sisters to him. Even dumb but useful Ernest, waving up at them, seemed like an old schoolmate. The fevered music, humid thick air, heady sweet aroma of wine—all blended into an illusion of ample community and endless uncomplicated joy. It was a dream he knew he could share, as the Fixit Man.

"They never seem to stop," he said dreamily.

"Yes," Sylvia said precisely. "Like sex, only too much is enough."

The remark surprised him, like many of her sudden shifts, and he studied her for a long moment. She seemed coolly oblivious, and yet . . .

What an obliging accident it had been, that the fellow student she invited for a visit was an astrophysicist, even though he concealed it. Despite her thoroughness, her quiet investigation of him at UCLA had no revealed that deception. How providential, too, that Clayton had the right combination of curiosity and timing to discover the diamond, and force Dr. Rollan to think about a replacement. In the long run, if Clayton could not surmount the Hoop's gathering problems, he had contacts among the freebooters of the asteroids. Their craft and their silence could be bought, without alerting Earthside. Clayton's 'roid origins could be useful. And finally, how lucky for them both that romance had bloomed here, and that Clayton was a man she could share this marvelous mad pinwheeling world with.

His eyes narrowed at the thought, and she gave him a serene, full smile. He would always wonder exactly what it meant.

FUGUE STATE

John M. Ford

If you're fond of a concrete, unchanging reality, don't read this story. John M. Ford, who won the World Fantasy Award with his novel The Dragon Waiting, *here creates a global police state that rules by revisionism. The Vogel apparatus has made it possible to control a man's mind on the deepest level of all . . . and the world may never recover.*

The rattle of the Russian gun seemed to go on long after the magazine was empty, and Forester's arms ached from holding it against the recoil. He looked around the room; no one was moving.

Forester threw the AKD into the fireplace; logs shifted, sparks went up. He turned around, began walking away from the lodge, up the hill toward the treeline. Around him the snow went on smooth and white and forever.

Forester wondered if any of the people in the lodge had any notion of what he had done for them. He struggled himself to think of the word for it. An act. An act of . . .

An act of compassion.

That was it. It had been so difficult to remember. Forester stumbled in the snow, and fell forward. There was no more sensation than of falling into soft white light. Words tumbled through Forester's mind as he tumbled through the light: pain, cold, weariness, death. But he had forgotten their context, and without context they were meaningless. Vogel had told him that, told them all that. Had any of the others understood?

Isolation was the last word. There wasn't anything after that.

The Memory cops kicked in the door. Margrave was sitting in the middle of a book-lined room. The heat and sound sensors on the helicopter hidrone outside said he was alone; gun muzzles swept the room, but there was nothing in sight but bookshelves and the kitchen. Closet doors were pulled open; there were clothes, more books, a duplicating machine.

"The copier is licensed," Margrave said. "You'll find that the seals are intact."

The cops had on helmets and ribbed black armor jackets. Margrave wore a red-striped shirt and brown wool trousers. Forester carried a pistol, Danny Baker a riot gun. The two local-force backups had D-Three-issue Urban Short Carbines; the Division Four tech was too busy with her Vogel rig to use a gun. Margrave was making a cup of tea.

Margrave was long-bodied, conventionally handsome, with sandy hair and strikingly dark eyes behind small round eyeglasses. He jiggled the chain of the tea ball, making it jingle in the cup, and said mildly, "I suppose you have some sort of warrant?"

Forester pulled the laminated blue card out of his breast pocket, flipped it onto the table. "Glenn Margrave, National Identity Number 4036–8248–1390, your premises are being entered on suspicion that your actions pose a threat to the safety of the citizenry—"

"The public safety. Noble old phrase."

"—of the World Federation of States. The bearer of these orders and his deputies are empowered to search and to pursue search, to seize and to confiscate property, persons, and data— "

"There are sixteen hundred twenty-four books in this room, give or take a few on loan. I hope you gentlemen can read very, very fast . . . but then, I forget. You're not readers, are you."

"—and to execute such other orders as the Federal authorities may prescribe."

Margrave said, "Look, I've been through this four times, two of them in this very room. I'll finish my tea, and we can go."

"And to execute," Forester said flatly, "such other orders as the Federal authorities may prescribe." He reached into his pocket again, pulled out the red card and threw it down across the blue one. Margrave stared at the card. Forester said, "Okay, Rennert," and the tech came in from the hallway, the steel briefcase in one hand cabled to the probe in the other.

Margrave looked hard at the Vogel apparatus. He knew what it was.

Forester said, "I now advise you, Glenn Margrave, that as Case VT-185441, the Federal Special Court has determined that you are to be given Vogel Conversion by a qualified operator at the time of your apprehension on the current charges. Because of the threat to the public safety, you are not to be permitted messages or other outside contact prior to the conversion procedure."

Margrave's face was very pale, but his body and voice were steady. "I don't suppose you'll name the charges against me?"

"You don't know?" Danny Baker said.

Margrave looked at Baker. "You ask that as though you meant it, Officer. Yes, I know. But it once was usual for the prisoner to face the court, even if the court had already reached its verdict. . . . No messages, eh. If I wrote a letter, you'd just burn it, wouldn't you?" He started to lift the tea ball from the water.

Forester's hand closed on his wrist. "Leave it there or I'll break something."

"It's cold anyway." He let go of the chain. Forester holstered his pistol and pulled Margrave out of the chair: he locked his right arm around Margrave's throat, levered Margrave's left arm up against his spine.

Margrave turned his head slightly, toward Danny Baker. "You're black," he said. "Don't you find any outrage at this, at one person doing this to another?"

Baker said calmly, "Not when he's the one man and you're the other."

The tech came closer, raising the probe. Margrave said loudly, "Is any one of you a Jew? Hispanic? Amerind? Are any of you *anything* other than police, that what's happening here should mean something to you?"

"There was a woman named Lacy," Baker said. "Other than police, she was someone's wife, someone's daughter."

"Yes, yes," Margrave said, "It is that basic humanity that I'm trying to reach—"

"Lacy's job was registering duplicating and printing machinery."

"Oh," Margrave said quietly.

"*Oh*," Forester said, and compressed Margrave's chest. "Lacy never even carried a gun. Aren't you going to tell us that the pen is mightier?"

Margrave didn't say anything.

The tech put the probe on the table and pressed a retina reader's rubber cup to Margrave's eye; Margrave shut his lids tight, but the tech just punched the inductor button and sprung them open again. "Okay, that's a match," the tech said, and picked up the probe again.

"If you are silent when the darkness takes those who protest against it," Margrave said, "who will protest when the darkness comes for you?"

"The tapes of this will be wiped tomorrow morning," Forester said in a tired voice, and pulled back. The tech shoved the probe against Margrave's forehead. The secondary contacts reached out on jointed metal arms to embrace his skull. Margrave struggled then, finally, tried to bite Forester's wrist above the glove, but too late; the probe's inductor system had control of his head and neck muscles and Forester had control of the rest.

Forester said, "Ready?"

"Another couple seconds. Grid's bouncing like crazy. Okay, we're in. No skin touching?"

"No skin. Do it. Danny—watch the door."

"Never left it, partner."

The tech said "Voltage," flipped the safeties and triggered the Vogel circuits. The wired-glass contact tips glowed blue-white.

Margrave jumped, but not much.

"Five seconds to failsafe," the tech said. "Mind the tears, they conduct . . . three, two, one, okay, from here on it's permanent."

Forester relaxed his grip, just slightly. Baker covered the hallway; it was quiet. The backups watched, curious; this was the first Vogelization they had ever seen live and close up.

The tech said, "Grid's nearly flat. . . . Okay, that's it." She punched a switch and the equipment went dead, the probe arms recoiling.

Margrave's eyelids fluttered. His head rolled and his knees went slack. Forester kept holding him, on the off chance that the conversion hadn't taken: Margrave hadn't crapped his pants and most Vogels did that.

After a moment, Danny Baker said, "He's done, partner. Let him down easy."

Forester let go. Margrave swayed, but stayed on his feet. Vogel conversion didn't reach down to the motor centers, but sometimes there was a temporary paralysis or blindness.

Margrave took a hesitant step. He looked around at the cops; his face was blank, his eyes wide. He shuffled to one of the bookshelves, ran his hands over the spines, made a gabbling noise. Drool ran down his chin. He got to the door, fumbled it open. One of the backups stuck his foot out in Margrave's path.

"Don't do that," Baker said, not loud but sharp, and the cop pulled his foot back and stood up stick-straight.

Margrave paid no attention. He walked out into the hall, turned, and made his way toward the building exit, fingers scraping along the walls.

"They all got such a sense of purpose, you notice?" the tech said, folding up the Vogel rig. "Ever wonder where it is they think they're going?"

"Every time," Baker said, and looked around the room. One of the D-Ones was asking the tech how long it took to teach a Vogel bladder control, and giggling.

Baker said to Forester, "You notice something funny about the way this place is laid out?"

"What?"

"Where's the john?"

Forester looked around, then nodded slowly. "Yeah. Take a look at that." He pointed at one of the floor-to-ceiling bookcases; its right edge was out of line with the case next to it.

Baker reached for the edge of the case. It began to swing out easily, silently on hidden hinges.

Forester touched his shoulder, said "Remember Penny Lacy?" He turned to the tech. "Read the hi-drone again."

"Moment . . . no change. Can't get anything on heat or sound."

"Right. Okay, you clear out and call for a disposal team." Forester pointed at the backups. "You two, back into the hall and cover us from there. Danny—"

"I'm on it, partner," Baker said, and crouched oblique to the door, using the table for shielding, his gun leveled at thigh height.

"Right," Forester said. He took some books off the shelves. "There's a hole back here. I see a loop of wire on a hook. I'm going to unhook it."

"Could be open-circuit."

"He had to leave himself a way in and out. Hell, the toilet's back there." Forester flipped the loop. Nothing happened. "Opening the door."

"As you say."

Forester raised his pistol, eased the concealed door open with his left hand. It swung wide. Then he and Baker and the backups saw what was in the next room, suspended from the ceiling.

One of the D-One city cops took a step forward. "Sweet Jesus Christ!"

"He's nothing to do with this," Baker said. "You stay right where you are. You too, partner."

"You think she's wired?"

"Give me a minute to figure out what to think. . . .

Look. Middle of the room, right in line with the door where we'd be sure to see her. Oh yeah, it's a setup, all right. Is she dead? Or is it a dummy?"

"Those are real scars," Forester said. "Can't tell if she's alive."

Baker moved closer. "Looks like clay all over the walls. Insulation, that's why there wasn't a heat trace. And if *that's* what he's been doing in there, the room's *got* to be soundproof."

"Not clay," Forester said. "Plastic explosive. You hear Disposal coming?"

"They'll be here. Is that wire, or cord?"

"Can't tell. It's shiny, but it could be silk cord. Tight—can't be any circulation in her arms or legs." He walked through the open door.

"Where you think you're going, partner?"

"I wanted a look at her face. Come here, Danny. Look at this. Do people still *make* stuff like this?" He brushed her hair back to show black leather, tight across her cheekbone.

"Depends on what you mean by people. . . . Oh. Oh. These are her eyelashes, caught in this zipper. Is she breathing? She'd better be breathing."

"Yeah."

The Disposal team came in from the hallway, looking alien in their heavy armor and waldo claws. They stopped cold when they saw the figure suspended in the next room. Forester and Baker stepped back and let them go to work.

"I'll call Airmed," Baker said. "One of us ought to ride with her. The Commander will want her screened."

"I'll go," Forester said. "If I go out on the street just now I might see the Vogel. And if I do that—" He drew his pistol, took it off cock and put it back in its holster.

Baker nodded and herded the backups out, with a last glance at his partner; Forester stood in the open bookcase, quite still. On the street, one of them said, "We're local guys . . . what your partner said, you know, that can be fixed."

"My partner was blowing steam," Baker said, not looking at the two cops. He pulled off his helmet, the sweat beaded on his dark face. "When Division Five blows steam, D-One don't hear the whistle. You understand me?"

"Yeah." They were sullen and nervous at once.

"All right. You did all right. Explosives in there makes it combat pay, you know."

"Where *did* that guy go, anyway?" the other cop said, looking up and down the street. There was no sign of the Vogel.

"Forget him," Baker said. "He doesn't exist any more."

The Division Five Commander's office was more like a room in a comfortable old house than a place of business. There were rugs and wood furniture, soft lights, framed prints of hunting scenes. Behind the Commander's huge oak desk and leather chair was a curtained window, small panes of colored glass set in black leading. The window was a fake: the office was several levels underground, and even if it had not been, the Commander would hardly have sat with his back to a window.

The Commander was reading the action report by the light of a green-shaded brass lamp. He was old, and his face showed all of it. His hair had gone from red to white, and hung a bit unfashionably long over his ears, but his mustache was as precise as if filled in by a draftsman. He wore an ordinary dark suit and red ascot scarf, his badge pinned to his breast pocket.

He finished reading, tapped his large thick fingers on the report, and then looked up at Forester and Baker.

"You shouldn't have gone near the woman," he said. His voice was very pleasant, and his tone was moderate. Forester and Baker, like everyone in D-Five, had once been deceived by that voice, but no longer. "Forester had no business staying in the apartment after Disposal arrived." The Commander looked up. "Since you apparently did not believe there was any danger, your danger pay is disallowed. Yours too, Baker, since you let your partner stay there . . . the woman *was* wired?"

"Simple closed circuit, nothing complic—"

"If you want a transfer to D-Four, Forester, do it through channels. There wasn't anything special about the bomb that got Lacy, either." The Commander tapped the report again. "It pisses me off, you know that, Forester? You do a clean, sharp Vogelization, not a shot fired, and then decide to hang around and sightsee at a goddamn bomb disposal. Next time you want to be an idiot, Forester, do it off duty." After a moment, the Commander said, "The woman made it to the hospital all right?"

"Yes, sir."

The Commander nodded once. "That's all, Officers. The erasure orders on this case are through Judicial and active; if there's anything you want to look at, see Officer Caladon."

"Thank you, sir."

"Thank somebody you're here to say that. Dismissed."

Forester and Baker went through the paneled oak door into the hall, which was dull painted metal like any reasonable office corridor. Forester said, "I think he was actually angry this time."

"Losing Penny Lacy got him hard, I think. That has to be why the Vogel order went through so fast. . . . He wasn't even being screened until the last couple of days."

"Must be why we didn't know about Irene Kiel."

"Who?"

"The woman in the back room."

"How long have you been a cop, partner?"

"Long as you."

"Uh-huh. And you have been witness to, shall we say, a bad scene or two in that time?"

"I'm all right," Forester said. "It was just— watching her, while the Disposal crew worked around her . . ."

"Yeah," Baker said thoughtfully. "Yeah, I think I know what the Commander was so mad at you for. Let's go look at some tape."

Data Control had its own corridors, and its own air-cycling and sealed-nuclear power systems. There was a sign inside the outer Vaults Area door:

ALL STORAGE MEDIA PAST THIS POINT
WILL BE DESTROYED

Forester and Baker traded in their badges, which had buried microchips, for DCVA passes. They handed over their bank cards, watches, and Baker's pocket calculator. They kept their pistols. Then they went down a long hall with patterned metal walls, the Amnesia Tunnel.

"Ever feel the microwaves crawling around your shoe nails?" Baker said. They had both heard the joke about the guy with metal snaps in his shorts, and the one about the underwired bra, and most of the others. The jokes were considered sort of funny, at least enough so to take your mind off the buzzing in your head as you went through the Tunnel.

They went through a door into a small, velvet-walled cubicle, both a light trap and final checkpoint (a sign read HAVE YOU LEFT ALL DATA MEDIA BEHIND?) and then into Screening Room 8. The room was half-circular, about ten meters across; the curved wall tapered inward toward the ceiling, to tilt the double row of screens that covered it at a comfortable viewing angle. Facing the screens was a crescent of console, live with pilot lights, illuminated controls, digital counters; it was also covered with papers and loose data cassettes and empty cardboard coffee cups.

Jane Caladon made a note on a green-glowing digital clipboard, then looked up. "Hi, Danny, Forester. Clean off a chair and sit down. Want some coffee?" She took a swallow from one of the cups. "Rephrase that. Can you possibly live without some coffee?"

Caladon wore a light jacket over a high-necked sweater, dark slacks; proper enough for a cop on duty and comfortable enough for sitting all day alone in the dark. She had middling-dark hair, brown eyes, and her face was plain—no insult, just plain. Caladon was one of the top undercover people in D-Five, one of the reasons she kept hidden in Data Control when she wasn't on the street.

"Coffee'll wait," Forester said. "What we got to look at?"

"On your Vogel? We've got plenty." She waved an arm at a cluster of at least a dozen vault boxes, each the size of a two-drawer file cabinet. "He was a busy little bomber. Last one's coming up from the Vault now." On the room's straight wall, a chime sounded and a light came on above a small steel door. Caladon rolled her chair to the door, inserted a key; the door opened and another box rolled out on tracks.

Caladon read its label. "That's it. Fourteen cubes." She pushed the box with the others, flipped through a printout on the control desk. "Let's see. We've got books: your Vogel wrote eleven books. Lasting classics of the human spirit like *Evaluating the Latino Subfederation of States in Historical Perspective* and *A Statistical Survey of Torture in Police-Dominated Regions*. Nice. Any interest?"

"No," Forester said. "He said something about books loaned out. They get those?"

"They got 'em." Caladon made a note on her

clipboard. "Okay. They're already deaccessed at all libraries and terminals. Hard copies to the shredder. That takes care of half a cube. . . . Next, monographs: two hundred and, my god, forty-three. Care to take a look?"

"You run a title series?"

"Forester, I'm wounded. Was there any special word you wanted?"

"Bombs."

"Let's see. We have here 'Dynamite and Human Freedom.' But it's historical again, not practical. He seems to have gotten all his hardware from the usual cookbooks."

Danny Baker said, "There's must be some way of getting rid of those damned things."

Caladon said, "Hey, you want to see this month's memos on it? Trouble is, the data's all redundant in military and industrial publications, perfectly legal—not to mention chemistry textbooks, though Havlicek's got a team working on that one."

Forester was looking through the index print-out. "What's 'They Scream in the Fire'?"

"Oh, you noticed that. It's poetry."

"The 'they' are books, right?"

"That's the impression I got. Do you want to see a copy?"

"Burn 'em."

"On the list. Now we've got screening reports, arrest records, the usual stuff. Not as much of it as most Vogels."

"He went early."

"Lacy?"

"Lacy."

"Not early enough," Caladon said, and they were all quiet for a moment.

Baker said, "Do we have anything on just after the conversion? He disappeared off the street faster than I would have expected."

"Just a moment, Danny. You had a hi-drone, right? It should have gotten something." She went to the console. "Case VT-185441, Vogelized, that's flag 101. . . . Running now." Frame counters began rolling, and one of the wall screens lit up with an overhead street scene, in the harsh imaging of hi-drone cameras, the case number and time burned in along the top of the frame.

The street was empty except for three police units: Forester and Baker's car, the D-Four van, and the D-One local cruiser. Two pedestrians came into view, and crossed the street to avoid the parked vehicles.

The Vogel came stumbling out of the building. He sat down at the foot of the steps and began staring at his hands, as if puzzled by what they might be for—which of course he was. Then he stood up unsteadily, wandered back and forth. There was a small puddle where he had been sitting. Another pedestrian came by, and quickly scurried out of the frame.

A small van pulled up to the curb. A stylized image of joined hands was painted on the side. Two people in bright blue jackets got out.

"Council of Friends," Caladon said. "I always wonder how they got on the scene so quickly."

"Friends of friends," Danny Baker said.

The two took the Vogel gently by the arms and guided him toward the van, put him inside.

"Freeze it," Forester said. "Give me the cursor."

Caladon stopped the picture, Forester picked up a hand controller. He spun the frame wheel, running the recording back until the three figures stood just outside the van. He moved a hollow red square over one of the Friends' chests, zoomed in. The screen showed the Friend's jacket, his white shirt, an angular dark area against the shirt.

"Friend with a gun," Forester said. "That's a new one."

Caladon reached for a telephone. Baker already had one. "This is Baker, 50113, suspect priority. I want a vehicle trace, license number—" Forester worked the zoom controls—"NYF 234 GEA. . . . Yeah. Yeah, got it. Copy to my desk, will you? Thanks." He put down the phone. "Plate belongs to a car reported wrecked four months ago, fleet car for a delivery service. Not a van, and not the Friends."

Forester nodded. He said to Caladon, "Is Irene Kiel being screened?"

Caladon worked the keyboard. "Yeah. She's at Presby."

"Put it up."

Another screen lit, showing a woman, heavily bandaged, lying in a hospital bed. There were several pieces of machinery surrounding her. Her eyes were closed; she stirred slightly.

"We have access to the medical data?"

"Only what you see here. This is custodial screening. Want me to call Judicial for an order?"

"Quicker to go over and look. Call D-Four and have a medical tech meet us there." Forester was looking straight at the woman in the bed. "Let's go, Danny."

Caladon said, "What about this stuff?" She pointed at the data boxes.

Baker said "Whoever's got him, he's a Vogel now. Burn it."

In the car, Forester sat forward, leaning on the wheel, silent.

Baker said, "So do you want to use the lights and siren?"

"No."

"Guess you're right. Anyway, we'll just annoy the patients when we get there."

"Don't ride me, Danny."

"Partner, if someone's riding you, it is *not* me. Look, I saw the lady too. But we did for the guy, remember? Put the wire to his head and wiped him clean. He's gone as old Vogel himself."

"Books about torture. Christ."

"What books? I don't remember any books."

Then Forester laughed.

Irene Kiel looked worse in person than on screen. She was sweating, and kicked and clutched at the sheets.

"Is she sedated?" Forester said.

"Of course she's sedated," said the floor physician. "She's dreaming. It's better for the patient not to have REM sleep depressed—"

"This is healthy?"

"Her temperature and heart rate and blood pressure are all under control," the physician said, irritated. "If she seems likely to fall out of bed, we'll tie her down."

Forester looked sharply at the physician, but just said quietly, "Is that tech here yet?"

"Coming now," Baker said.

Forester said to the physician, "Is there a Vogel scanner you can get up here, right now?"

The doctor stared. Baker's eyebrows went up. Kiel twitched and moaned softly. The doctor said, "You can't just order that sort of thing."

"I didn't say a full Vogel rig, just the grid scanner. Your psych ward has one, doesn't it?"

"I'll see if it's available."

"Call from here," Forester said. "If it isn't, we'll get one of ours. It'll just take longer." He looked away from the doctor, at the woman.

"Used to getting what you want, aren't you?" the physician said.

Forester said, "Aren't you?"

The integrated sensory grid as displayed on a Vogel scanner was a complex network of colored lines, shown in isometric; it resembled a relief map of a mountain range that continuously pulsed and shifted. Number and letter codes flashed across the screen almost too fast to follow. Interpreting the grid in real time required a two-year graduate course.

Forester hadn't taken the course, but he'd Vogelized over two hundred people, seen a lot of grids, and there was something wrong with Irene Kiel's. The lines bounced too rapidly, too wildly.

The tech had taken the course, and he didn't understand it either. "What in hell happened to this woman?"

Forester just looked at Kiel. Danny Baker told the tech a little of it.

"No, no, this isn't a pain pattern, I've done interrogations. Look at this flip-sector . . . Is she a psycho?"

"All right, take it down," Forester said.

"Whatever you say—hey, look at this."

They looked. The jumps in the pattern were gone. The grid was normal. They looked at Kiel. She was sleeping quietly.

Forester said, "Is your rig working right?"

"My rig is working just fine. That lady's head, that's what's not working right. You still want me to pack up?"

"Yeah."

"I'm gonna have to put in a report on this."

"Yeah."

"I mean, I'd have to file on machine use even if nothing happened, but this pattern—"

"We understand," Danny Baker said. "You see it gets to my desk, and you're covered, okay?"

"Sure. Sure. Look . . . who is she?"

"I guess we're going to have to find out," Baker said.

When the tech had gone, Forester was still watching Kiel, who was very quiet and still now, breathing evenly.

Baker said, "You want to go get some dinner? Corrie's got the chicken pie today."

"No. You take the car in. I'll get a bus home."

"Sure. Look, partner . . . you want me, call. I'll be there."

"Yeah."

After a moment, Forester looked up from the bed; but Baker was gone.

Baker checked the car into the police garage, then went upstairs to his desk and unlocked it. The display screens lit up with waiting case memos. He sorted, read, shuffled, filed. The phone didn't ring. He started to punch Forester's number, then broke off. He went out of the building, took the subway home.

Baker unlocked his apartment door. He shoved it open. He felt the slight catch as it swung, just saw the loop of wire pull loose from the detonator clip; then he was enveloped in white light, white heat, white noise.

Danny Baker woke up. He hadn't expected that.

He was lying on his left side, on a hard surface, his arms out straight behind him. He couldn't see, couldn't see *anything*: there seemed to be bandages over his eyes. And something against his tongue, tight.

Suddenly quite awake, he could feel the cut of the wire into his wrists and elbows. Something cold was pressed against his temple, and there was a voice, tinny-sounding through a bone-conduction speaker.

"This is awkward, but I'm certain you're quite deaf otherwise. And there are a few things to say."

The voice was whispery—no, Baker thought, hoarse with excitement.

"Didn't I tell you, Officer Baker," said the voice, "that one day the darkness would reach out for you? And there would be no one to protest?"

The speaker fell away. And then the hands came down, with horrid expertise.

The D-One cops had a cordon around the block, there were four hi-drones up, cruisers and tac-vans lit up the night red and blue and white. Forester was there, the Commander was there. Danny Baker was there, but he had been closed up in a D-Four medical van and would not be coming out.

"Concussion bomb on the door," the woman from the Forensics team said to Forester and the Commander. "Not a big one. Just enough to bring one man down."

"And no one else heard it?" the Commander asked.

"They all heard it," Forester said. "They heard doors slam, tires blow out, noisy television shows, new dance steps. They all heard something they could turn around and forget about." Forester looked up at the apartment building. There were faces in many of the windows, faces backlit and featureless. "Ask most of them, they'll swear they didn't know Danny was a cop. Sure as hell not a Memory cop."

"Officer Forester's right, sir," one of the locals said. "We're not going to get anything useful here."

The Commander folded his gloved hands against

this chest, breathed out fog. "All right. Get the rest of the statements and—*what in hell?*"

A man was walking toward them, throwing a long shadow ahead of himself on the wet pavement; he wore a long leather coat that flapped as he walked. A D-One cop followed a little behind him, trotting to keep pace, riot shotgun in both hands.

"Good evening," the man in the long coat said. "Excuse my curiosity, it's a vice of mine—but of course you'll know that, won't you?"

"Sir," the pursuing cop said, "he wanted to see you—sir, we read his eye, and—*nothing,* sir—"

"I've also agitated this young man. But you know about that bad habit, too . . . good evening, Officer Forester. Good to see you again."

"It was you," Forester said, not stopping to think how it could possibly be. "The bomb, and the wire . . . you did it." And then Forester's pistol was out, and leveled.

"I? How could I have done . . . whatever it is? I don't even *exist,*" Glenn Margrave said.

The Commander said, rather slowly, "Make the arrest, Forester."

Margrave said, "Oh, you can't do that. But I'll willingly go with you to headquarters, if you'd like."

The Commander said, "What do you mean, *can't?*" His voice was calm; his tone was withering.

Forester lowered his pistol. "I know what he means."

"Well?"

"To confirm an arrest," Forester said, "we have

to get a voucher. To do that, we have to ID him. The locals already found out what happens if we try that."

"No records," the Commander said grimly.

"Not any more."

"Shall we go?" Margrave said.

Forester called out "Granger!" and a D-Four Med came over. "Yeah, Forester?"

"Trank this agitated and dangerous suspect."

"Agitated? I?" Margrave said coolly. "This is going to look very bad on tape, Officer Forester."

"This man's a danger to himself and others," Forester said, without raising his voice. "Trank him."

Granger drew his air pistol and put a dart into the side of Margrave's neck. Margrave's hand went toward it, like a man trying to brush away an insect; he never reached it. "O-oh," Margrave said, and his legs buckled and he went down. Forester caught him and put him on the pavement. "Call another med van," Forester said.

Granger said "There's room in—"

"He's not riding with Danny Baker," Forester said flatly.

"That's right enough," said the Commander. "Call another unit."

Margrave sat in a chair in a plastic-walled room, metal and plastic bands around his body and head. Forester and the Commander watched on a screen in the Commander's office; the screen was edged in oak and brass to match the room decoration.

"He's been talkative enough," the Commander

said, "naturally about everything but what we need to know." He pushed a button and the audio track cut in:

". . . had a test for female potential recruits," Margrave was saying. "I would take her home, position her on the bed, and put something by Harry Partch on the tape player. If she said 'What is that appalling noise?' we could proceed to the next stage. If, however, she continued in her doe-eyed infatuation with the bold revolutionary, I threw her out—and I mean on the moment.

"You see, you've destroyed the appreciation of the unusual: anyone who would pretend to it must be either a police spy or too stupid to be useful. . . . You're scowling. Have you perceived some profound linkage in that statement?"

A light on the band wrapping Margrave's temples lit red, and he twisted against the restraining straps. His mouth opened.

The Commander cut the sound off.

"We are faced with an impossibility," the Commander said, "and every attempt to reduce it to possibility has failed. The Vogel equipment used has been checked and works perfectly. The operator has been interrogated and did not falsify the readings."

"What about the Friends?"

"They deny ever having held him. Judicial still refuses to grant us a search warrant for their schools. They may have to change their minds after this one."

"Suppose it's not Margrave."

"Margrave has no twin brother, there is no question of makeup . . . and if this man isn't Glenn Margrave, then who is he? Either someone has learned how to restore a Vogel conversion's memory . . . or they have learned how to erase our records on a person. I find that an even more disturbing possibility. I don't pretend to understand the Vogel mechanism; but I *know* our files."

The Commander switched off the screen. "We have three options. We could interrogate him until he breaks. This might be useful, *if* Margrave knows how the restoration was performed—but we have no reason to believe that he does, and if he does not we would be left with nothing.

"We could re-Vogelize him, and wait to see if his memory is again restored. But if it is not, we again have nothing but a broken lump—and even if it is, we need to understand the process.

"What we are *going* to do is let him think he's won. Let him go, and see where he leads us." He looked at Forester. "It's your case, of course. You did the Vogel, you have the background, know his associations. Speaking of which, the woman in the apartment—what was her name?"

"Irene Kiel."

"What have you found out about her? Aside from the fact that she didn't like avant-garde composers."

"Not very much, sir."

"No? I'd understood that you were with her when Danny Baker was killed."

"I was at the hospital, sir. She was sedated."

"Yes."

"Commander—I was Danny's partner for five years, but I wasn't his shadow."

"Of course not, Forester. And if you had followed him home, I might have lost both of you. I'm not blaming you. I just wanted to make certain you didn't blame yourself."

"Yes, sir," Forester said, and then after an awkward pause, "He'll know he's being screened, and probably guess he's being followed. He's too smart to lead me to anything."

"That's just why he will," the Commander said. "Margrave's a grandstander; he needs an audience. If we keep him from his contacts long enough, he'll have to make a play: when that happens, I want you to be the audience."

"He knows me."

"Then you don't have to waste any time establishing your credentials, do you?"

Forester nodded.

"One more thing, Forester. I *am* giving you this one because of Danny Baker . . . but not for the reason you think.

"After what happened to Baker—and I have to remind you that we haven't got any evidence at all that will stick—Margrave's going to expect you to be out for blood. Fine that he thinks so; fine that he sweats. But that's not what you're after, Forester. We have to find out how he shook the Vogel; that's more important than anything else right now. You can scare him, you can make his life absolute eight-cylinder hell and I hope you do, but you don't touch him. Understood?"

"Understood, Commander."
The Commander nodded.

Margrave didn't seem surprised at his release.
He didn't even show his usual smug confidence,
except when he was issued a new NID number
and credit card. "Now I can be arrested without
causing everyone an inconvenience," he said
brightly. "How generous of you."
For the next several days Forester followed Margrave twelve hours a day. It didn't produce much.
Margrave visited museums, ate in restaurants, slept
at the Plaza Hotel. He made no contacts. Division
Four Cryptography did analysis runs on everything from his walking route to the pattern of
uneaten fries on his plate. Thermography established that he had poor circulation in his legs
during sleep.
On the fifth day, Irene Kiel was released from
the hospital. Now Forester had something else to
monitor, but she didn't do anything interesting
either.
On the night of the seventh day, Margrave went
to a jazz club on the Upper West Side near Co-
lumbia. Forester went too. He sat down in a dim
booth, with a good view of the musicians and of
Margrave, and ordered a beer.
Margrave showed no sign of noticing Forester
for the first hour and a half. The musicians took a
break. Margrave got up and came to Forester's
booth.
"Can I buy you a drink, Officer?"
"I have one, thanks."

"But the minimum here is two. Another of these for me," Margrave said to the waitress, "and bring the officer here another of whatever he's drinking." He leaned against the booth. "You don't mind having it pointed out that you're a policeman, surely? Not even a Division Five policeman?" He didn't speak loudly. Still, heads turned.

"It's no more than a statement of fact."

"Good. Very good. I like a devotion to the truth."

"So tell some. Who are you?"

"Surely you know that. You're a policeman, after all."

"Tell me anyway."

"All right. My name is Glenn Margrave. I was born on the fourth of April, thirty-four years ago. For fifteen of those years I've been publicly critical of the policies of the government, especially as they concern police powers. Now, I remember all of this very clearly, Officer Forester. But lately there's been a little trouble with the memories."

"And what's that?"

"I was a writer, Officer Forester. I wrote books and papers and poetry, and caused them to be published. I have a perfect memory of that fact. Yet in all of this city I cannot find a single copy of any of my works. I've tried the terminals, the hard libraries, the bookstores, the *used* bookstores—nothing. Isn't that curious?"

"Maybe you should talk to your publisher."

"Oh, I've spoken to all of them, Officer Forester. But that's curious too: they don't remember my work. They don't remember *me*. Now isn't

that strange, Officer, that men and women I knew
and worked with for years should suddenly have
no recollection of our meeting?

"It's as if I'd been *edited out*, Officer Forester.
As if some great blue pencil had stricken all reference to me and my work. Now tell me, Officer, if
such a pencil existed, who would have the right to
use it? Who would have the right to reach down
and censor a life out of existence? Drink your beer,
Officer Forester, and think a bit: even if the power
existed, how could the right?"

Margrave sat down across from Forester. A few
people were looking at them; a few people had
gone. The musicians were starting up again.

"This is a nice tune, isn't it?" Margrave said.

"I like it."

"This is by Miles Davis. Now, suppose you woke
up one morning and all of Miles's music was gone—
not just no longer played, but *forgotten,* so that
you had these tunes in your mind that no one else
had ever heard. In time you would get used to it.
Until the morning you awoke and found Charlie
Parker gone. And then Basie, and Bix. And you
would say, well, there's still Armstrong and Corea,
and keep your silence, for fear that if you spoke,
one morning you would wake to find no music at
all. You're nodding, Officer Forester. Does this
argument strike any chords, you should pardon
the phrase, in your memory?"

"I was just listening to the music."

"Yes. This is a brilliantly sad piece, isn't it? . . .
which reminds me, I did want to tell you how
sorry I was about your partner."

Forester said flatly, "What partner?"

Margrave lost a beat. "Officer Baker . . . your late associate."

"I don't know anyone in the division named Baker. The last partner I had was named O'Shaughnessy. That was three years ago. She works in Cheyenne now."

Margrave said carefully, "You don't recall a Danny Baker? A black man, tall, quite nicely spoken? I believe there was a bomb . . . yes, I distinctly remember it was a bomb that killed him." He watched Forester's face, Forester's eyes.

"I think I'd remember that. But I don't."

"Ah. I must be mistaken, then."

Forester drank his beer. After a moment he said, "I understand the University is having a Partch concert next week, with some of his original instruments. Will I see you there?"

"You listen," Margrave said unpleasantly, making heads turn away from the musicians, "you constantly listen, but you hear nothing." He emptied his glass and went out of the room.

Forester followed. Margrave was standing at the bar on the other side of the club, talking to a woman. She nodded, picked up her coat. As they started for the door together, Margrave glanced over his shoulder. He grinned at Forester.

Forester moved toward the door. Someone tried to trip him; he sidestepped and went on without looking at whoever it was. Someone else bumped into him, hard. He pushed on by, to the door, and he pushed it open hard.

The man who had been waiting outside the door

was knocked off balance. Steel glittered. Forester hit him twice very hard and the knife fell to the sidewalk. Forester kicked it away, pushed the man against the wall, drew his pistol and shoved it under the man's chin. "Who told you to stop me?" he said, not loudly at all.

"A guy—gave me twenty. I wasn't gonna hurt you, man. Just slow you down, he said."

"Sure. Just a guy?"

"He said he was a cop. Memory cop."

"Sure. He show you a badge?"

"Shit, man, everybody knows Memory cops don't have badges."

"You're too stupid to be lying," Forester said. "Guy gave you twenty?"

"Yeah."

"I'll give you ten." The man blinked. Forester took a step back, leveled the gun. "One," he said. "Two. Three."

The man got the idea. Before Four he started running. In another three seconds he was gone.

Forester put the gun away. He got on the subway downtown. The idea now wasn't to follow Margrave, but to let him run. And then find where he'd run to.

The screening record inside the club was useless, as Forester had expected; music and bar noise covered everything Margrave and the woman he'd met had said. Between crowd and bad viewing angle, it wasn't possible to get an identifying look at the woman.

On another screen, Irene Kiel was reading, something by Sartre. Forester had been watching her for about half an hour; he'd checked the earlier records and Margrave hadn't made any contact. Kiel was nervous; she kept looking up from her book, glancing around.

Forester picked up a phone from the screening console, punched a number. After a moment, Kiel's phone began to ring. She nearly dropped the book, then set it down carefully and picked up the phone.

"Hello?"

"This is Glenn Margrave," Forester said.

On the screen, Kiel relaxed, closed her eyes. "Then it did work," she said.

"Yes. It worked. I'd like to see you."

"I want to see you," she said. "But—I'm sure I'm being watched." She rubbed at the skin behind her ear. Forester dialed up the magnification, but she stopped scratching, apparently without noticing anything.

"Naturally," Forester said. "So you know where to meet me."

"Yes. . . . When?"

"When better than now?" Forester said, and broke the connection. He dialed another number.

Kiel looked at her phone for a moment, chewing her lip, then put it down. She went to her closet.

Forester said, "This is Forester, 50135, case priority. I want an immediate hi-drone surveillance, and a vehicle link."

As soon as it was confirmed, Forester went down to the garage. His patrol car was parked with a half-dozen other identical ones, and he scanned the row of rear plates for his number.

A civilian plate among all the blue police tags caught his eye. It was on the back of a small, unmarked carryall van. NYF 234 GEA. The number was familiar for some reason. Forester got into his car, started it and brought up the onboard screens. The visual display lit with a bright, grainy picture from the hi-drone. The map screen located Irene Kiel coming out of her apartment on 97th Street, and the text display annotated everything for the case record.

Forester punched the LIC INQ button and entered the license number.

```
VEHICULAR LICENSE INQUIRY
NYF 234 GEA
= = = =
NO WANT
NO WARRANT
DO NOT STOP OR APPREHEND THIS VEHICLE
ACCESS RESTRICTED
ENTER AUTHORIZATION
```

Forester stared at the screen. The car terminal should have automatic authorization. He entered his personal passcode.

```
VEHICULAR LICENSE INQUIRY
NYF 234 GEA
= = = =
REGISTERED TO: NORTH AMERICAN POLICE
                DIVISIONS CENTRAL VEHICLE POOL
ASSIGNED TO: DIVISION 5
                SPECIAL CASE SERVICE
```

= = = =

DO NOT STOP OR APPREHEND
THIS VEHICLE

Forester still couldn't remember why the number was familiar. But there wasn't any more time
to think about it. Kiel was getting on the subway.
Forester picked up the phone. "This is Forester,
50135, case pursuit priority. I need a subway track
on a tagged suspect, entering at 97th and Broadway.
The tracer is Alpha Tango four eight four, and I
have a hi-drone operating. Suspect is not aware of
the tag and not to be apprehended. Keep me ad-
vised." He drove out of the garage.

The New York subway had always been one of
the best places in the world to lose a tail, right up
there with the sewers of Paris and the Casbah. It
still was. Unless you had a double-diode passive
tracer circuit implanted under the skin behind
your ear, in which case you weren't safe down
there at all. Tracers in the cars and stations followed Kiel to the Port Authority station, and when
she came out the hi-drone took over again and led
Forester to the West Side docks, Pier 92. She
went into a warehouse that was supposed to be
empty.

Forester parked the car and followed her. The
building did look empty, and it was dark, except
for a few drips of luminous paint on the floor.
Those led right to an office door, still slightly ajar,
with light coming through. Forester moved silently up to the door and looked through the crack.

Kiel stood in a sort of office. There were books and tapes in crates, and a desk with a lamp and a small audio player. No one else was there, but on the far side of the room were double doors, and beyond the doors the sound of footsteps; the doors opened just slightly, and Glenn Margrave came through them and closed them again.

"Well," he said, "good evening."

"We did it," Kiel said.

"We did indeed," Margrave said, in a pleasant but tense voice. "Who told you to come here? Who was stupid enough? Connelly? Dwyer?"

"You said—"

"You *knew*. Someone's going to have to be removed from the organization, my dear. You'll have to give me the name." He looked her up and down. "You should be required to perform the removal . . . but you won't be."

"You called me," Kiel said.

"I did what?" Margrave closed his eyes, shook his head. "Ah. Ah, Irene. You dear sweet trusting acquiescent idiot. Did you password the call? Did you arrange a meeting? Did you do anything but run here to see me?" He put his hand on Kiel's shoulder and pushed her into the desk chair. "Now I must be moving on again. And you . . ." He pulled open a desk drawer, reached inside.

Forester drew his pistol and kicked open the door. Margrave looked up. Kiel turned her head.

"Hello, Officer Forester," Margrave said. "We must stop meeting like this. . . . But you're alone this time? No dragons at your back, no Vogel wizard bringing up the rear?"

"They'll be along soon enough."

"No. Not soon enough. After all, how are you going to persuade me to wait for them?" He looked at Kiel. "The officer won't kill me, Irene. He can't. Not after his people have spent so much effort in following me. And they won't kill you, either, because you're part of this as well." He looked up at Forester again. "Oh, do drop that gun, Officer Forester."

"I'll keep it."

Margrave's hand came out of the desk drawer, holding a short black metal tube with a rubber grip. "Do you know what this is?"

"Prowler tube." It was a one-shot, short-range weapon firing a sort of heavy beanbag, designed to knock the target down and out without doing much real damage. Forester said, "I can shoot you without killing you, no problem at this range."

"I'm certain you can," Margrave said. "But I'm aiming at Irene's head. And at *this* range, the shot will crush her skull. Put your gun on the floor, Officer Forester, and kick it toward me. Gently, of course."

Kiel sat quite rigid in the chair, not looking at Forester or Margrave. Forester did as he had been told. Margrave turned the prowler tube on Forester and held it steady as he picked up and pocketed Forester's gun. He stepped away from the desk, from Kiel.

"You're thinking that I've chosen the wrong weapon, that I still have just one shot. That you might rush me, and I might miss. But you won't do it, will you, Forester? Because if I do hit you with my one shot, you'll be helpless. At my mercy. And you've seen my mercy, haven't you, Officer Forester?"

"I've seen what you did to her."

"Yes. But you can't figure out why, can you?"

"I've got a fair idea."

"No. You *did* have an idea. You were certain you knew my weakness. Until you tried to scare my dear Irene with my name, and she came running to me instead. So many of you have done that: thought my weakness was love, when it's your failing instead.

"Look at you, Officer Forester, hating me, despising me, yet fearing me desperately. Afraid of a little pain before the dark, but perfectly willing to take my memory, my work, my life, and flush them all down the toilet. Could you bring yourself back from that oblivion, Forester? Could you climb out of the shit-pot as I did?"

"You had some help," Forester said. "You pressed your memories on her."

"Gave them, rather. There was no force involved. . . . You don't believe that, do you? Because you don't understand communication. You see the whip and the chain, and you think they're only your tools for maintaining the status quo; you can't comprehend how they could be used against you. You can beat a man as you read him the law, but you cannot beat him and read to him of the revolution."

Forester said to Kiel, "You believe this crap?"

Kiel looked slightly dazed, distant. Finally she

said, "I held on to Glenn's memory. We brought him back from the Vogel conversion."

Forester said, "I suppose this was a scientific experiment."

"It was a test of a hypothesis. We needed a link. But true love would not do." Margrave smiled at Kiel. "It had to be completely objective. We couldn't risk losing any part of me to a lover's forgiveness. . . . Come here, Irene, and kiss me. There isn't anything we haven't shared, after all."

She stood up, walked over to him. He leaned slightly toward her. She closed her eyes and, hesitantly, kissed him on the cheek.

"Now, there," Margrave said. "I knew you would do that. Didn't I learn as much about you as you did about me? More?"

"All right," Forester said, "you've proved your superiority to the whole damn world. Now what?"

"Now Vogel," Margrave said.

"Vogel's long gone."

"So you've been saying for years. But he's gone *somewhere*. Maybe the state knows where, maybe it doesn't. But you *have* to find him now, because your system is in danger; the bad men have learned to beat the conversion, and you must stop that before we learn even more devastating tricks."

Margrave turned to Kiel. "I told you the officer couldn't kill me. I wouldn't be surprised at all to find out they were helping us along—all in secret, of course. I might lead them to Vogel, and that's more important than any mere crime I might commit."

"Don't be too sure of that," Forester said.

"Don't be too sure you know your masters," said Margrave.

He pulled at the double doors, and they slid apart. In the next room was a small metal table, and a chair, and a bright light shining down on the chair.

A woman sat in the chair, her arms dangling at her sides, her feet flat on the floor. She looked up—or rather, her head bobbed up; her face was blank and her eyes were glassy and unfocused, unseeing. Her head rolled a bit.

"This is Audrey," Margrave said. "Audrey can't hear you right now . . . she's in a very suggestible state, and so she's been instructed to hear no voice but my own." He turned toward her slightly, still holding the gun steady, and smiled. "I am the universe to Audrey just now. I am the voice of her God."

"Hypnosis or drugs?" Forester said. Margrave was the easiest man in the world to stall: just keep him talking.

"Both. It isn't very deep—one can't *communicate* with one in this state. A strong stimulant will bring her up. But it is helpful, especially at the beginning of a relationship. You're a policeman, Officer Forester; haven't you had trouble, sometimes, putting the cuffs on someone who didn't see that they were in her own best interest? Even my dear Irene, here, had to go through a phase of—"

"I never did any such thing," Kiel said, staring at the woman in the chair.

"Not at the very first, in that you were unusual.

But you were quite startled by the true art in the flesh."

"I accepted it, because I *believed*—"

"And believed, and believed! But the mask, ah, when I showed you the mask, you did not believe at all—"

"*You did not do that to me.*"

"What's this, forgetfulness?" As he spoke, Margrave's grin froze on his face. "What, are there gaps in that ideologically resilient mind of yours? That won't do, my dear, that simply won't do."

"I told you where the lines were drawn—"

"But I am a man unbounded by lines."

"You never drugged me—"

"With my own hands. Through your own lips, your sweet veins."

"What makes you think I would consent to such a thing?"

"Because, my dear, mind of my mind," Margrave said, warmly, sadly, "In the end, everyone consents. To everything."

Now, Forester thought, it depended on what Kiel did next. If she did love him, well, that was it.

She got up from the chair, moving awkwardly, disjointedly. She slapped Margrave, hard enough to knock him back a step. Forester moved.

Margrave moved faster. He brought up the prowler tube and hit Kiel with it, then shoved her into Forester's path. Forester caught her.

Margrave aimed the tube at the two of them, and said in an absolutely cold voice, "Pray I hit

her with this, Officer Forester, because I'll use
bullets on the other one of you."

The woman Margrave had called Audrey flopped
forward in her chair, her hands dangling near her
ankles. Margrave turned then, and the look on his
face was full of joy. He took a step toward her,
bending forward solicitously, lovingly. "Who knows,
this time . . . perhaps back from the larger
death . . ."

Forester took a step. Margrave said softly, "You
are not under the gun now, Officer Forester . . .
but sweet Audrey is. Stand quite still."

Suddenly the woman sat up again, quick as a
puppet on strings. Her hand held a little snub
9mm auto from an ankle holster, and aimed it
squarely between Margrave's eyes.

"Hugs and kisses, you son of a bitch," Jane
Caladon said crisply.

Margrave stood bolt upright; he shrieked and
fired the prowler tube, maybe on purpose, maybe
not. Caladon fired, once, wildly. The three sounds
and the bullet ricocheted off the concrete walls.
Margrave dropped the empty tube, turned and
ran through a door, his heels loud on the floor.

Caladon groaned and slid down in the chair, a
bright splash of blood on her left side.

Forester put Kiel on her feet and went to look
at Caladon. The shot-bag round had hit her hard,
but the bleeding was superficial; she probably had
broken ribs, maybe a torn lung. He supposed she
was full of drugs to block Margrave's control drugs;
he had no idea what that would do to her system
under this stress.

Her eyelids opened, and she seemed about to say something; then her eyes closed again and she breathed raggedly.

Forester picked up Caladon's hideaway pistol and went after Margrave. He went down half-lit corridors, moving quickly and quietly, looking for movements in the shadows, yanking and kicking open any door that showed a light.

The fourth door he opened had Margrave behind it, in the middle of a bare room, gasping like a drowning man. Margrave pointed Forester's gun and pulled the trigger; the round went into the ceiling.

Forester shot him in the left calf and he fell down. Forester walked over to Margrave, crouched, pulled his pistol from Margrave's loose fingers; he pressed its muzzle against Margrave's forehead and looked down into his wide, bright, eager eyes.

"Forester," Margrave said, out of breath, "do it, Forester. Make me immortal with a leaden kiss."

"What's the goddamn use," Forester said, put the pistol in his pocket and stood up.

"What's the matter, Forester? Just once, for a good reason, Officer Forester. Just once in passion. Just once, do it for love. *Do it*."

Forester said, "I forget how."

He turned to go, call cleanup, see about Caladon and Kiel.

"Forester!" Margrave howled, half-choked with rage, and Forester turned.

Margrave had pulled his jacket and shirt open. Taped to his chest were flat gray blocks of plastique. Wires led to Margrave's fist. The fist clenched.

There was brilliant white light—no sound at all. There wasn't anything after that.

"It is desperately important to me that my uncle be found," the woman said. "I am willing to pay you twenty thousand dollars."

Forester watched the woman. First on the phone, and again now, she'd said twenty thousand dollars . . . well, not as if it was nothing, Forester didn't know anyone who could do that; but certainly like it was streetcar fare.

Her name was Irene Kiel. She wanted a man named Vogel found. He was a scientist, and he'd been missing for a couple of weeks. That was about it.

"Do you have a photograph, Miss Kiel? Even a newspaper photograph would be very helpful."

"There are no photographs. My uncle detested publicity of any kind. I've given you as complete a description as I can."

Forester looked at his notes. "Heavyset, not tall, broad face, graying hair thin in front, brown eyes. . . . There are only about fifty thousand men in this city alone that answer this description."

"You're a *detective*," the woman said. "I'm offering you a great deal of money to . . . well, detect. If you aren't interested . . ."

Forester waited for her to say what she'd do if they weren't interested, but she didn't, so he said, "All right, Miss Kiel. We'll take the case. We do require expense money—"

She opened a thin crocodile wallet and put a thousand-dollar bill on the desk. Tom Edison's face smiled benignly up at Forester. "Will that be sufficient?"

"That will be fine, Miss Kiel." He opened the desk drawer and pulled out the waiver, and a pen. "Would you sign this, please?"

"What is it?"

"An agreement to have this investigation conducted according to the laws of the Republic of New York."

"I don't want anything illegal done, Mr. Forester."

"It means," Forester said calmly, "that you are retaining us, rather than the World Air League, for this investigation, with the knowledge that our authority is limited to New York Federal law. It also requires that you not request the intervention of the Air League without giving us formal notice of severance."

"I understand."

"Please read it anyway."

She looked once at the paper and signed it.

"Thank you, Miss Kiel. Where can you be reached?"

"I will be at the Plaza Hotel, room 821."

Forester wrote it down, so as to look serious. "Miss Kiel . . . Dr. Vogel is your mother's brother, correct?"

"He . . . well, of course. Our names are different."

"People do sometimes change their names, Miss Kiel. I'll be in touch as soon as we learn anything."

Kiel nodded and went out, taking one last look around the office. It was small, but well enough kept. Forester thought he could detect a little disgust in Kiel's look, but it was just a thought.

Forester watched from the blinded window until Kiel had reached the street. A black car—a Packard limo, not a taxi—took her off. It had an NY plate, but Forester missed the number.

He put on the gun that the Federal Republic of New York said he could carry, his coat and hat, and went downstairs, going two doors up the block to a diner.

Forester slid into a back booth, across from Danny Baker, who was pouring cream into his coffee. "If Corrie ever starts charging us for refills," Baker said, "we are broke tomorrow, partner."

"Maybe not." Forester shoved the thousand note across the table. "Twenty more Tommies on delivery, she says."

"O-o-okay. What's the catch?"

"What you'd think. No pictures, worthless description, no good contacts. The Junior Birdmen would have their hands full with this one."

"She signed the release?"

"Very quick she did. I'd like to know why she doesn't want the League looking for him, if he's worth twenty grand."

"Rules don't say we have to offer the alternatives."

Corrie, the diner owner, appeared with another cup of coffee and two slices of cheesecake. "Hi there, Forester. You going to smile for me today?"

"Do my best."

"Well, you keep workin' on it, honey. And this one's for you, Daniel." She handed Baker a slip of paper.

Forester said, "What's that?"

Corrie said, "That's what you detective boys call a clue."

Baker said, "NYF 234 GEA. Our client's license number. You *said* you didn't want her to spot me yet."

"Now there, honey," Corrie said, "I knew you could smile." She went back to the front of the diner.

Forester took a long swallow of coffee, straight and black.

"You're going to burn your gut right through, partner."

"We're going to do worse before we're through on this one."

"Okay. Where do we start?"

"Vogel's a scientist. He worked for something called American Dynamics Incorporated; they've got an office in Rockefeller City. I'll look at that; you keep an eye on our client. She's at the Plaza, 821."

"Comfortable place to watch, at least." He picked up the paper with the license number. "I'll call this in, too. When do you want to meet?"

"It's two o'clock. Meet me at Goldschmied's at five. If something happens before then, I'll have you paged in the Plaza lobby. Who do you want to be?"

"Have 'em call Benny O'Shaughnessy."

Forester grinned. "Yeah, they'll never peg you for an O'Shaughnessy." He stood up. Baker pointed at the thousand note. "You want to take that along?"

"You keep it. At the Plaza it might get you two cups of coffee."

Forester went out of the diner. Abruptly, the clear sky darkened; Forester and some others looked up. Overhead, a World Air League heavy cruiser blocked the sun, triple suspensorays brilliant blue against its broad black-winged shape. It was no more than a couple of thousand feet up, but made no sound audible from the street. Forester waited until the shadow had passed, then walked to Broadway and caught a streetcar downtown.

American Dynamics's office was on the twenty-fifth floor of the RCA building, a white limestone slab rising from the center of the Rockefeller City complex. Forester walked into the lobby, which was decorated in black marble and gleaming brass, paintings of the Power and Glory of Industry on the high walls. He got into an elevator decorated with brass geometrics, and stepped out into a quiet, cool corridor with travertine walls. There were a dozen frosted glass office doors with company names in block letters, faint sounds of typing and tele-phone bells.

Below AMERICAN DYNAMICS INCORPO-RATED was a small national flag, thirteen stripes and thirty stars. Forester opened the door and walked in.

Inside was an efficient-looking little office lined with green steel file cabinets, and an efficient-looking woman in a brown wool dress. "Good af-ternoon, sir." No offer of help.

"My name is Forester. I'm a detective." He showed the blue card. "I'm interested in one of your employees, a man named Vogel."

"May I ask the reason for your interest?"

"I'm simply trying to locate him on behalf of a client."

"And your client's interest?"

"I can't discuss that. Do you know Dr. Vogel?"

"No, Mr. Forester. But this is only a liaison office, employing only myself and a few clerical workers. Our principal operations are in the West. Dr. Vogel, you said? He is a scientist?"

"So my client says. Are you telling me you don't have any information available?"

"Not at all, Mr. Forester. Please sit down."

Forester sat. The woman opened a file drawer, riffled through folders, pulled one out. "Dr. Karl Lyman Vogel?"

"That's correct."

"Dr. Vogel is a staff researcher at our Wyoming Territory facility. If you contact our office in Cheyenne, they may be able to tell you more." She closed the folder.

"There's more than that in the file you're holding," Forester said.

The woman smiled. "Do you have a court order, Mr. Forester?"

"Do I need one?"

"Mr. Forester, American Dynamics does have competitors. I'd have to ask for an order even if you were from the Air League. I'm not trying to be difficult, I hope you understand; if you have a specific question, I'll do my best to answer it."

"Fair enough. Is Dr. Karl Vogel missing?"

"Missing, Mr. Forester?"

"Disappeared. Absent without leave. Gone, no forwarding."

"Not according to this file."

"Then would you mind asking your Cheyenne office? I'll pay for the call, Miss . . ."

"Jane Caladon. And I'll be happy to call them for you, Mr. Forester." She put the file on the desk, said "This will just take a few minutes," and went through a side door, closing it behind her.

Forester looked at the folder, sitting all naked and defenseless on the desk. It was a set-up; couldn't be anything else, not with efficient Miss Jane Caladon. The question was, what sort of set-up? She might just be doing the nice detective a favor. It didn't happen often, but it did happen.

The folder just sat there. It wasn't wired to explode. Not literally, at least. Forester picked it up.

Inside was a standard personnel file: same description Irene Kiel had given, no photograph. Vogel was Austrian by birth, naturalized. Never married. Nothing about other family. The IN EMERGENCY NOTIFY space gave the address of American Dynamics in Cheyenne.

Forester flipped the page. There were some sheets stamped CONFIDENTIAL. Obviously he was supposed to read them, so he did. They were cryptic reports on something called Tube Alloys Project: progress reports, completion dates. The last page had PROTOTYPE TEST DATE 4 APRIL circled.

Forester closed the file, put it back on the desk. Then he picked it up again, put it down a foot away from its original position.

Caladon came in, looking concerned. "I've just spoken with the Cheyenne office. Dr. Vogel is in fact missing, Mr. Forester. He hasn't appeared for work in almost ten days. May I ask now who your client is?"

"You may. But I won't tell you."

"Mr. Forester, this is important. Dr. Vogel is engaged in crucial research for us. Do you have reason to believe he might be here in New York?"

"I'm a New York detective. This is where I can look. You don't have someone looking in Wyoming?"

"Wyoming isn't a state, Mr. Forester. We're limited to our own hired security staff. And the head office has authorized me to retain your services—"

"I'm on retainer, Miss Caladon."

"We'll gladly speak to your current client about taking over the contract. We're after the same thing, after all."

"I'll ask my client."

"We'll double your fee."

"You haven't called the Air League?"

"It's under consideration," Caladon said.

"Good day, Miss Caladon. Thank you for your help. I'll speak to my client, and be in touch."

"I leave the office at five o'clock," Caladon said. "There won't be anyone at all here after that."

"I'll remember," Forester said.

At 5:15 Forester and Baker were sitting over pastrami sandwiches and coffee in a deli around the corner from the Plaza Hotel, trying to make some sense of the day.

Baker said, "The car belongs to Northeastern Courier and Forwarding. They're real enough to have a phone. But they don't hire cars."

Forester said "No?"

"I called twice, just to bracket 'em. They were sorry that they didn't have that service available for Mr. Ben O'Shaughnessy," he said in a light and entirely believable brogue. Then his voice became gravelly and slurred. "An' dey wann'ed to know jus' who Mist' Rastus Shine Jones thought he wuz, callin' dem 'bout hire cars." He laughed dryly. "Sometimes the rudest answer is the most honest one. What about your terribly efficient secretary?"

Forester said, "She hung the file out in the breeze for me to read, and then invited me to make a visit after closing time."

"Could be they want to catch you with your hand in the drawer," Baker said. "Or it could be that they want our client."

"I'd guess the second. Why would anybody want to embarrass a lousy New York cop?"

"The Junior Birdmen might."

"Yeah."

"Any hint of what this Tube Alloys thing is?"

"No. Even assuming there is such a thing, that the whole file isn't a phony. What did Kiel do?"

"She came downstairs for a newspaper and some candy, asked for mail and phone calls, but there weren't any. So what do we do next?"

Forester looked at his watch. "The RCA lobby's open till ten."

"We could call for a search warrant."

"That's three days and a statement of probable cause, and you know it. And I'll bet they know it too. No, we'll play by their rules for a while."

"You want company?"

"You'd better keep watching Kiel. Can you have the Plaza switchboard covered?"

"It'll be expensive. But I guess our client is paying for the best." He laughed.

Forester walked into the RCA Building lobby carrying a worn brown briefcase, and walking hunched down in his coat. He didn't pause for anything, or look around, just walked straight to an elevator and pushed the button for 25. No one paid any attention to him.

The floor was empty, all the glass doors dark. Forester paused before American Dynamics, thinking. Then he opened the briefcase and took out a piece of metal, something like a bent icepick. He raked the lock tumblers and was inside the office in fifteen seconds. No alarms went off, no lights came on.

He checked the side door, where Caladon had gone to place her call to the head office. There was a small switchboard in there, a desk with a typewriter, and a teletype machine. The paper in the teletype was blank, and the bin to catch print-outs was empty.

In fact, Forester noticed, all the wastebaskets were empty, except for one that had a white delicatessen bag and a sandwich wrapper in it. So they hadn't been emptied by maintenance; there was no trash, and *nobody* had no trash.

He went back out to the office with the file cabinets. He pulled at a drawer; the cabinet was locked. And it wobbled. Forester picked the lock. The cabinet was empty.

He opened the drawer Jane Caladon had opened. It was full of file folders. All of them were stuffed with blank paper.

Forester closed up carefully and went back downstairs. There was a man in a gray coat in the lobby, pretending to make a phone call and not doing a very good job of it. Forester went out of the lobby and the hood came after, hands in his pockets just like in the movies.

Forester knew he could lose the hood, but that wouldn't get him anything; besides, whoever sent him might send someone good the next time. Forester walked a couple of blocks west; sparkling Rockefeller City faded fast into dingy West Side warehouses.

Forester turned down an alley, went fifty feet and stepped behind a trash dumpster. The hood appeared, a black silhouette. He took a hesitant step.

Forester stepped out and said, "Like to talk to me?"

The man in the gray coat took out a gun and shot at Forester. It wasn't a very precise shot, but Forester didn't like being shot at. He took out his own gun and put one high over the hood's head. The hood ducked and flinched. Forester went back and grabbed him, made him drop his gun.

"Wait, wait," Gray Coat said.

"No." He was a kid, maybe twenty. Not too young to learn.

There was a movement up the alley, and a whining sound, and then blue lightning came at Forester and the hood. Forester stepped back. The light showed the hood's mouth open wide, his face pale as a dead man's in the instant before he was.

The bolt tore away half of the man's skull. Forester felt the blue fire tingling his skin. The body fell down, still wrapped in blue lightning, still twitching. After a few seconds the charge leaked away and all that was left was a mess on the ground.

A man stepped out of the shadows. He wore a gray leather jacket and whipcord trousers, high gray boots and a flying helmet. There was an enormous plumber's-nightmare pistol in his hand, still glowing blue. Forester got out his own gun, for what it was worth.

"Good evening," said the Air Leaguer. "Saw you were in difficulty, and couldn't just go by." He held the blaster loosely, but ready. "I trust you have a permit for that pistol of yours?"

"Forester. New York Federal Detective." He flashed the blue card.

"Well, that's all right then." The Junior Birdman holstered his blaster and held out his hand. "Glenn Margrave, Independent Flight Officer. Tell me, Mr. Forester, do you have one of your red cards for this . . . enterprise?"

"Not tonight."

"Ah. But you are on an investigation."

"The waiver's in my office."

"Of course. You wouldn't carry irrelevant items in the field. Any idea why this . . . gentleman was interested in you?"

"Not yet," Forester said, and reached inside the smoldering coat of the man at his feet. There was a wallet, burnt traceries across the leather. Inside was a driver's license in the name of Lacy, and an employee card for Northeastern Courier and Forwarding. Forester pocketed them without showing Margrave. There were also a dozen or so twenty-dollar bills. He held out the Wilbur Wrights to Margrave. "These are yours, I think."

"It was you he was shooting at."

"Fair enough." Forester took the money, dropped the wallet on the body. "Good night, Mr. Margrave."

"If you have time, Detective Forester, I'd like to ask you a few questions—I have an investigation of my own in progress, you see. There really isn't enough cooperation between our organizations, don't you agree?"

"I certainly do," Forester said, and walked away, leaving the Birdman standing by the smoldering body.

Forester took a streetcar a couple of stops, then swung off and went into a phone booth. He dialed a number from memory.

"New York United," said a pretty-girlish voice on the other end.

"My name is Forester. I'm a police detective. Tell the Commander I want to see him. Tonight."

"What might this be in reference to, Mr. Forester?"

"A death in the family."

"Will you hold, please?"

Forester held, watching the street for passing cars.

The voice said, "Mr. Forester, if you'll give me your location, a car will be sent for you."

"I know your location. I'll be there in half an hour." He hung up.

The building was between the financial district and Battery Park, with a beautiful view of the bay; a tall, modern building with automatic elevators and one of the most elaborate private telephone systems in the city. Forester went into the marble-and-gilt lobby and took the small express elevator to the top floor. Though it was quite late, no guards stopped him; the building had no guards, in the usual sense.

On the top floor there was an outer office with Persian carpets, old European paintings, museum-piece furniture, and a knee-weakening Eurasian secretary in a tight silk dress. There was also a big guy in a cheap suit that fit even worse because of the two big guns he wore under the jacket. He sat near a large wood-paneled door.

The receptionist said, "You are Mr. Forester?" The big guy didn't say anything, just got up and went over to stand a little behind Forester.

Forester said, "That's right."

"The Commander will be pleased to see you."

"I'm pleased to hear that." He turned around, drawing the gun from inside his coat, and handed it to the man in the cheap suit. The .45 looked small in the big man's hand. He looked at the gun, nodded, and stepped out of Forester's path. Forester went through the paneled door.

The room beyond the door was quite dark, heavy drapes blocking the beautiful view. Commander sat mostly in shadow, behind a massive wooden desk. One of his large, brown-spotted hands rested on the glossy desktop, near a row of intercom buttons. In a dark corner, a tall clock was ticking, its pendulum catching the light with each stroke.

"Good evening, Forester," the Commander said, in a voice that seemed very tired, or maybe just old.

"The lady said you were pleased to see me."

"My door is always open to New York's finest, Forester. You've known that since you joined the force. I'm pleased to see that you finally took advantage of the offer. . . . What is it you need?"

"I've got something for you." Forester tossed the ID cards onto the desk. "I took these off a dead kid a little while ago. He had a gun, and he wasn't a cop, so he was one of yours."

The Commander didn't touch the cards. "I'm not gunning for you, Forester."

"I know that. He had some fresh bills on him, too—enough so they had to be pay for a job and not enough for a hit. And he was just a goon, not a hitter."

"But you killed the boy?"

"A Birdman happened by. He killed him."

The long hand took the license, turned it over. "Very well. Keep talking."

"Do you own something called Northeastern Courier and Forwarding?"

"Not to my knowledge. That doesn't mean I don't, of course."

"Yes or no?"

"I'm not a charity, Forester. You want my help, it is for sale."

"I'll keep that in mind." He turned away.

"Forester. I remember the first time you visited this office. You swore you'd see me in jail. How long has that been? How long are you going to pretend you don't know how the world goes? You help me, I help you back. Except that you give me no help at all."

"You do okay without me."

"That's right," the Commander said seriously, "I do. So tell me the name of the Birdman who fried my boy."

"He was inside the law."

"Not *my* law!" The Commander's fist hit the desk.

Forester pulled the blue card out. "I'm the law in New York."

"Of course," the Commander said. "You work out of a hole in the wall, for anyone off the street with a few bucks. Most of your clients are crooks who don't dare ask the Birdmen for help. Why would anybody else come to you, when the Air League will solve their problems for free? But you *are* the law, Forester. I give you that." He jabbed a finger upward. "They keep you in the gutter. They keep this country on its knees. But *you are the law*."

"Were you this much of a patriot before they crossed the Atlantic?"

"Are you telling me you're siding with the bastards? Or do you think they'll give you a better deal than I will?"

"You know what side I'm on. And where I'm telling you to put your deals."

Forester walked out of the room. He took his gun back from the big goon, rode the elevator down and went out of the building. He spat into the gutter, as if to clear something out of his throat. Then he walked into Battery Park and found a telephone.

"Plaza Hotel, may I help you?"

"Would you page a Mr. O'Shaughnessy, please? I believe he'll be in the lobby."

"One moment, sir."

Forester looked across the park, at the water. A ship was passing, lighted bravely: it was a forty-meter torpedo boat, the *Yorktown*. It was one-seventh of the United States Navy as prescribed by the World Air League.

A couple of minutes later Danny Baker's voice said "Yes?"

"Dynamics is a front," Forester said, "but I wonder if our client knows it. I'm on my way over there to stir her up a little. Be ready to follow if she runs."

"You got it."

Forester took a cab to the Plaza. As he walked through the lobby, he scratched behind his ear, signal to Danny Baker, wherever he was. Forester couldn't see Baker, which meant nobody else could either. The man was the best.

Forester took the elevator up to 8, knocked on

the door of 821. Irene Kiel answered. She was wearing a high-collared dressing gown.

"May I come in?"

"Please do, Mr. Forester."

The room was ridiculously big, over-furnished, a typical Plaza room. Forester walked past Kiel to the bedroom door, opened it; there was a woman's suit laid out on the bed, but no one listening.

"Mr. Forester—"

"How long has your uncle worked for American Dynamics, Miss Kiel?"

"I—I'm not sure."

"Approximately."

"At least two years, I believe. Have you found anything?"

"American Dynamics would like to talk to you directly."

"You didn't tell them—"

"I didn't identify you, no. If you want to speak with them, that's your choice." He wrote the phone number on a piece of hotel stationery.

"Thank you, Mr. Forester."

"I haven't found your uncle yet, Miss Kiel. I have to get back to work now."

Forester went back through the lobby, nodding slightly to nobody, and caught a streetcar back to the office. Just as he opened the door the phone began ringing.

"Hello."

"Grand Central, partner. You flushed the bird all right. You want me to grab her or just watch her?"

"Just watch," Forester said. There was a thump

on the other end of the line, and no answer.
"Danny?"

Nothing.

Forester snapped off the lights and ran.

Grand Central was, as always, the greatest place
in the world not to find someone in. People flowed
and eddied, stood trying to decipher timetables or
cadge a dime, struggling with their suitcases and
the English language as spoken in New York. Forester checked under the clock, in the men's room,
by the lockers and the checkroom. Nothing.

There was a bank of telephone booths just off
the big vaulted hall. About half of them were
occupied, people huddled over phones, gesturing,
moving.

In the fifth booth were a hat and coat the color of
Danny Baker's, and no motion. Forester moved
closer. The phone was off the hook. A dark-skinned
hand rested against the glass of the door.

Forester opened the door, and caught Baker's
body as it slumped toward him. He was still warm,
but he was dead. Forester could see the splintered
hole in the wall: someone in the next booth had
pressed a gun against the wood and fired right
through it, into Baker's back.

There was no one in the next booth now. Forester looked at Baker's booth. Nothing was written
anywhere. Baker's hands were empty. Forester
took out Baker's wallet. There was nothing but
Corrie's ticket with the license number, a faded
photo of Corrie herself, and the $1000 bill.

A uniformed cop came over. "Something wrong here?"

Forester said aloud, "Oh, not much, my friend's just had a couple too many," and then he flashed the blue card and said quietly, "This man's been shot. Help me get him out of here."

The brassbutton cop nodded, and they got their arms around Baker and pretended to walk him to the station security office.

They were putting Baker on a bench as the shift captain came in. "Hello, Forester," he said, and then stopped short. "Is that Danny Baker?"

"It was."

"Goddamn it to hell! What happened?"

"Danny was tailing somebody. He must have been seen. Your man there knows as much as I do after that. Will you call a wagon, Havlicek? I've got to keep on this."

"Sure, Forester. We'll take care of him."

Forester went out of the office. He stopped at a phone booth, dialed a number. When the voice answered, Forester said, "You tell him I'm coming over, now. And he's going to talk to me." He slammed the receiver back on its hook and went out to catch a streetcar.

Forester walked straight past the receptionist, straight-armed the boy by the office door, and shoved the door open. The Commander was still sitting in the dark, sipping tea from a bone-china cup. "Good evening, Forester. Sorry to hear about your partner."

"You got that news damn fast."

"I do that." There was a noise behind Forester.

The Commander said past Forester's shoulder, "Go sit down, Dwyer. Shut the door."

"Yeah," said a disappointed voice, and the door closed.

"Northeastern Courier and Forwarding," Forester said.

"Are you working for the Securities people now?"

"Don't give me any shit. If they move stuff on the docks then you've got your finger on them."

"Forester. I want to help you. I like you, I liked your partner. But I've told you both, you want to play with me, play by my rules."

"Are you telling me this is because Danny didn't play?" Forester said harshly. "Do you know why he's dead?"

"No, Forester. I don't do things that way and you know it."

"I'd better know it for a gold-dollar fact. Because you're not gonna sleep nights until I do."

The Commander sighed. "I thought you were a smart man, Forester."

"I thought you were, too," Forester said. "But you aren't smart enough to know who some of your boys are taking jobs for. You want some information, Commander? Here's some: you're not going to like it when you find out what goes on at Northeastern Courier."

There was a silence. The Commander put his teacup down, picked up a telephone. "Get me Connelly, now," he said. "Good night, Forester. Pleasant dreams."

Forester went out. There was a taxi on the curb;

the driver took him back to his office without speaking or dropping the flag on the meter.

He went into Corrie's for coffee and pie. The waitress asked about Danny Baker; Forester just shook his head and was glad it wasn't Corrie asking. He'd have to tell her soon enough, but not just now.

When Forester got up the stairs, there was a light on inside the office door. He was certain he hadn't left any lights on. He took out his pistol and opened the door, went inside slowly, checking for wires, for god knew what.

The desk lamp was on. In the pool of light under it was a package in brown paper. It didn't tick, but it smelled faintly of grease and gunpowder. Forester slit the paper open.

Inside was a Colt .45, and a map of Wyoming Territory. On the bottom of the pile was a business card, torn in half. The pieces said NORTHEAST-ERN COURIER AND FORWARDING, PIER 92, NEW YORK CITY.

Forester hefted the pistol, checked its load: custom jacketed bullets, just the thing against Air League body armor. He knew the gun's serial number wouldn't trace anywhere. The Commander didn't leave loose ends.

He looked at the map. There was a circle drawn in red ink, around something called Bills Canyon, just west of Cheyenne. Folded inside the map was a Chicago & Pacific train ticket, leaving inside the hour. No loose ends at all.

Forester went to the closet and took out a brown canvas bag: inside were a couple of drip-dry shirts, underwear, a shaving kit, and a couple of hundred in old bills. He put the gun inside and zipped the case.

As the taxi took him down the West Side Highway toward Penn Station, they ran into some congestion: a warehouse was burning on the docks, just about where Pier 92 should have been.

Forester had to change trains in Chicago. As he stood on the platform, bag between his feet, chewing on a bad sandwich and drinking worse coffee, he saw a plywood construction barricade with a row of posters plastered across it. They showed a man in gray leathers, fists on hips, standing in the doorway of a sleek short-winged cruiser, his feet on the globe of the world. An endless stream of ships passed over his shoulder, a black and silver rainbow. PEACE, said white block letters, FREEDOM, STRENGTH. That was all. No more was necessary.

Before the century was twenty years old, the countries of Europe had managed to rip each other to bloody shreds. America had nearly impeached a President to stay out of the dogfight; a few adventurers, mostly war correspondents and fliers, went over to see the elephant anyway.

When they came back, they said that something was rising out of the ruins, a steel phoenix with blue fire in its belly and claws. A team of scientists had torn power loose from the raw stuff of matter: with the suspensoray they could cancel gravity, and with the atomic blaster they could cancel everything else.

The people who carried the fire called themselves the World Air League. They took their texts
from Wells and Plato, Kipling and Bellamy, King
Gillette and Thomas More. Some people, watching the phoenix rise, spoke of watchers in the sky
and law given like a dose of salts. But others spoke
of wings and peace and order.

What they all failed to say was that where the
phoenix flew, nothing else without feathers was
allowed to fly. Oh, here and there there were a
few who spoke, an American named Mitchell and
an Englishman named Dowding, but the American was too early and the Englishman was too late,
and neither of them was ever heard from again.

Forester looked toward Lake Michigan, where
black ships circled overhead, allowing only the
gulls to share their sky.

Thirty hours from New York, Forester stepped
off the C&P express on the west side of Cheyenne. The buildings were all low, and they sprawled;
Forester doubted there was a single elevator in
the city. There were mountains in the distance.
There was too much sky. A way off he could see
Air League ships, black against white clouds, visible for miles . . . the Birdmen able to see for
miles.

He found a telephone directory and looked for
American Dynamics. There was no listing. He
called the operator and asked for a number.

"One moment, sir . . . Sir, the only listing I
have would be radiotelephone, ten dollars for the

first three minutes. Shall I connect you to the Mobile Operator?"

"No, thanks." He hung up and began walking west.

About a mile out of town, when the buildings had gotten sparse to the vanishing point and the sky was even more supernaturally broad, there was a little cluster of wood-and-tin buildings, bright as a mirage in the sun. There were gas pumps and a few battered old high-slung Ford trucks. A sign said THOMAS JEFFERSON HONEST DOLLAR SERVICE AND GENERAL STORE.

Forester went inside. There was an old man behind the store counter, drinking a Coke. "You Thomas Jefferson?"

"I look like him?"

Forester took out a gold double-eagle, looked at it. The guy did look like Jefferson, gone to hell. He put down the $20 piece and the old man grinned.

Forester bought a leather jacket and a pair of hiking shoes, and fifty rounds of hardball and two spare clips for the Colt.

"I need a truck." He jerked his thumb at the clunkers outside. "Those for rent?"

"Five dollars a day, twenty-five a week. Sell you a spare tire for ten bucks."

"Am I going to need one?"

"Depends on where you're goin'."

Forester pointed at the hills.

"Might need two."

Forester put down some more bills and another

gold Jefferson. "Truck for a week, two spares.
How much gas does it hold?"

"Thirty gallons."

"Fill it and put another thirty in cans on the
back."

"Must be quite an expedition."

"Are you asking?"

"Nope." The old man slid the .45 rounds across
the counter. "Have fun, Mister."

Forester changed coats and shoes, loaded the
Colt magazines and started driving. The map
showed an Improved Road toward Bills Canyon.
Forester didn't want to know what it had been like
before the improvements. A few miles along, there
was a turnoff, and two signs: one said,

AMERICAN DYNAMICS INC
WYOMING TERRITORY RESEARCH FACILITY
NOT OPEN TO THE PUBLIC

The other said,

DANGER
TRESPASSERS WILL BE SHOT

There wasn't anyone visible to enforce either
sign. A bulldozed track led toward the canyon.
Forester drove on.

Bills Canyon was narrow, and maybe seven hundred feet deep. The road was dusty but otherwise
not too bad. About two-thirds of the way down,
Forester found a place large enough to park the
truck mostly out of sight. He walked to the inside

edge of the road and looked down, and saw the Facility.

There were half a dozen long steel huts, a radio shack with antenna wires running up the canyon sides, a big transformer station with two dynamos and lots of heavy conduits and insulators. Some heavy machinery stood around. Forester didn't see any people.

And then he did: three little figures moving from one of the Nissen huts to the radio shack.

Forester continued down. As soon as the ground allowed it, he left the road and picked his way down the canyonside.

He came out behind one of the huts, near a rack of steel drums. There was a gust of wind down the canyon, and the drums wobbled. Forester tapped a couple of them. Empty.

A shadow crossed the sun. Forester saw the blue streak of suspensoray overhead. A League airship was settling straight down the canyon. It was one of the powerful small cruisers, a Mark Seven or Eight.

Forester heard voices, and a hut door opening and closing. He put a clip of hardball rounds in the Colt and leaned against the corner of one of the buildings.

The airship landed and the suspensoray shut down. A man in grey leathers came out. In a moment there were five men around him, pointing rifles. The Leaguer indicated his empty blaster holster, put his hands up, and went with the others to the radio shack.

That seemed to be where all the excitement

was. Forester went too, circling around to listen at a dust-covered window.

There were a series of muffled thuds. Forester knew the sound well enough. Somebody was punching somebody else.

"Stop it," said a woman's voice, Irene Kiel's.

"Yes, stop," said another woman. It was Jane Caladon, the efficient New York secretary. "He isn't going to tell you anything."

"That's not why I'm doin' it."

"Is Dr. Vogel safely out?" Caladon said.

"Yes," said one of the male voices.

"All right. Pack up the notes and the proto-types. Burn anything you can't take. When our friend here doesn't report in, the rest of the Blackhawks will be right along; we don't want to leave anything for them."

There were sliding, scraping noises. The door opened, and people filed out. Kiel's voice said, "What about the Officer?"

Caladon's voice said, "His own people will find him."

"But—"

"You can stay here with him, if you like."

"No," Kiel said, and the door closed and the building was quiet.

Forester looked through the clouded window. He pushed it open and climbed through.

There was an elaborate radio setup against one wall, dials and breakers, large glowing tubes and heat sinks. A speaker crackled faintly with static.

In the middle of the room was Flight Officer Glenn Margrave, hanging by his wrists from a rope over a ceiling beam. He looked badly used. He raised his head slightly, looked at Forester. "Ah," he said. "Didn't expect to see you here."

The speaker squealed. "50135 Independent, this is Thunderbird," a voice said. "We are on approach. You must contact now to cancel. . . . 50135 Independent, do you read?"

"It's me they're calling," Margrave said.

"I don't know much about radio," Forester said. "Is this the microphone?"

"Yes."

Forester jerked its wires out of the console. For good measure he opened a couple of likely-looking switches. Some of the tubes stopped glowing. "Okay, now I'm going to get you down. If you do anything I don't like, I'll shoot you. Got that?"

"I believe so."

Forester cut the ropes. Margrave landed on the floor, sat there rubbing his wrists. "You're a bold man, Detective Forester. Have you ever thought about joining the League?"

"Ever since I was a kid," Forester said. "I was a Young Air Scout, had Rickenbacker's picture over my bed. Saw all the movies with Jimmy Stewart and Montgomery Clift."

"What happened?"

"Quebec. Manila. The Sinai business."

"Haven't you ever shot a fleeing criminal, Detective? Speaking of which, you do realize what you've done just now."

"I got you out of a spot. Now we're even."

"Because I didn't answer that radio call, this place is going to be attacked any second now."

"Yeah, I thought so." He looked out the window.

"You want that to happen?"

Forester gestured at the people outside. "I think *they* want it to happen. Didn't want to disappoint them."

Above the end of the canyon, a half-dozen black V and W shapes appeared from the clouds, blue fire along their bellies. More fire spat from their wingtips; the bolts hit the ground and tore out craters. "You'd better run for your ship if you want to take it out of here."

"I'll fly you out."

"I've got other things to do. See you in the movies." Forester went out of the radio shack. At the far end of the complex, a hut blew up. The transformer station was arcing brilliantly. The smell of ozone was overpowering.

He sprinted to the first Nissen hut, threw the door open. Inside, Jane Caladon was throwing matches onto piles of papers. Irene Kiel turned, gasped. Forester came up behind Caladon and took the matchbox from her hand. "The flyboys are going to save you the trouble," he said, pocketing the matches.

"What are you doing here?" Caladon said.

"Looking for Karl Vogel, like I was hired to do. But you said he's gone." There was an eruption from the power station, and all the lights in the hut went out. The fire from the papers suddenly seemed very bright. "I think it's time we went too."

Forester, Caladon, and Kiel went out of the hut. An Air League carrier swung by overhead, less than fifty feet from the ground; as it flashed by, a door in its belly dropped something big. Forester pushed Kiel down and covered her.

The dropped thing hit the ground, and bounced: it was some sort of off-road car, with a load of armed flyboys in gray. It ran on for a hundred yards or so, killing its speed, then turned around and drove for the compound again.

Caladon said "This way," and pointed toward a parked truck. Then a heavy blaster bolt mashed into the truck like a thumb into clay. There were signs a man had been inside. Margrave's cruiser lit its suspensoray and lifted off.

"—know what you've *done*?" Caladon said, and pointed a revolver at Forester.

"I'm starting to sort it out," he said, and calmly turned and started for the rocks at the canyon side. "I've got a truck up there, if you're interested."

Caladon put her gun away and followed Forester, grabbing Kiel's wrist to drag her along. They started up the slope. Behind them, the whole valley was erupting.

They reached the parked truck just as a cloud of dust from the Air League car approached down the track. The two women got into the truck cab, Caladon behind the wheel.

"Drive," Forester said, closed the door and vaulted into the back of the pickup. Caladon drove.

The Air League car gained steadily on them, weaving over the rough road and through the dust Forester's truck kicked up. The two Leaguers in the back stood up, bracing on the roll bar, and fired their blasters. Rocks exploded. Forester shot back twice with his armor-piercing bullets. One of the Birdmen fell down and out. There were two spare tires and three ten-gallon gas cans in the back of the truck with Forester. Another blaster bolt went by, acutely close to the gasoline.

Forester opened the jerrycans. He shoved two of them out, then tipped over the third can, trailing a stream of gas. He rolled out a tire into the road, and struck a match, held it cupped against the wind. He pushed the can out, and dropped the match.

Fire flashed back down the road, and erupted around the piled cans. The League car plowed into a sheet of flame, hit the tire and stopped. It caught fire. It blew up.

Forester banged on the glass and Caladon stopped. He got into the driver's seat. "Now I'm just like the rest of you," he said, and nobody answered him.

Forester drove back toward the city. When they reached the general store, he pulled the truck under an awning. The old man was standing in the doorway.

Forester took out his wallet, pulled out the thousand-dollar bill Kiel had given him a few dead people ago. "I want you to drive us to the railroad station, and then keep driving east, at least until nightfall."

"I like to drive," the old man said, pocketing the Edison note. "Let's go."

"Somebody may take a shot at you," Forester said.

"Hell, at the pay I figured that. You a lawman, mister, or the other sort?"

"Good question," Forester said.

There was a twenty-minute wait for the next train East. Forester and Caladon sat on either side of Kiel; she asked to use the powder room, and Caladon said, "You do and I go with you. Everywhere." Kiel sat.

"I could start screaming," she said.

"Get it through your head," Caladon said, "you're in this too, and you can't get out. The Air League will hardly trust you to keep quiet about your part in this. And quite frankly, we won't trust you either."

"So why don't you kill me now?" Kiel said, trying to keep her voice low.

"I'm not part of any of the 'we's," Forester said.

"That's right," Caladon said. "We're going East in Detective Forester's protective custody. When we get to Chicago, he can apply to the Illinois Federal Police for official assistance."

"Will I get it?" Forester said dryly.

"You will," Caladon said. "Then, Miss Kiel, we'll keep you away from the League. And safe."

"And alive?" Kiel said.

"And alive."

A couple of kids in the waiting room were playing cops and robbers. The one in the Young Air Scout uniform won.

The streamliner for Chicago pulled in. The two women checked into a Pullman parlor-bedroom, Forester into the adjacent bedroom. They opened the connecting doors and bolted the corridor doors.

"Now that we're all friends," Forester said, "where *is* Karl Lyman Vogel?"

"There is no Karl Vogel."

Kiel said, "But you said he had—"

Caladon said, "That was for the Birdman's benefit. Vogel and his project are phantoms, invented for the World Air League to waste its time chasing."

"I'm not certain of that," Forester said. "But how about you, Miss Caladon? Do you exist?"

"I beg your pardon, Mr. Forester?"

"How long have you worked for American Dynamics?"

"Since its founding."

"Which was how long ago?"

Caladon smiled. "Five months."

"And who founded it?"

"Certain people very close to the American government."

"But they didn't set it up in a state—out in one of the Territories, instead, so the American government was nicely out of it."

"The Territorial authority agreed to the building of the Canyon compound."

"Here's what I think. There is a Karl Lyman Vogel. He used to work for the Air League, probably in Europe—but he ran away from them, taking something along. What he took, maybe some parts, or some plans, or just what was in his head, couldn't be allowed to get away. He came to America—and then he disappeared. Now, you want the whatsit, but you don't know how to find Vogel either. So you pretended you had him. Set up a dummy company to work on his project, knowing the Junior Birdmen would notice. Is that something like the truth?"

"Very nearly," Caladon said.

Kiel said, "But American Dynamics wasn't a real company. What if the Air League had noticed that?"

"They knew very well," Caladon said. "Mr. Forester knew. But he didn't tell you, did he?"

Kiel looked hard at Forester. Forester said, "It was a nice piece of double-guessing. They wanted the League to think that, since this company didn't do any real business, it must exist only for Vogel's project—which is presumably important enough to build a whole company around it."

"It's that important," Caladon said.

"And since you controlled all the information about American Dynamics, the League had to play by your rules to investigate it. Of course, the League can double-guess too. They set a hood up to snipe at me, so I'd think the Birdmen were just bystanders. 'Course, they had to kill the hood to make the stunt work. . . . Why did you kill Danny Baker, Miss Caladon?"

She said, "You knew it was me?"

"I thought it was one of you ladies. Probably you. It was very efficiently done."

"It was a mistake," Caladon said. "Your partner was spotted trailing Miss Kiel, taking down her train number. I heard him say something on the phone about stopping her—"

"You made *Danny* tailing her."

"Yes. I didn't have a lot of time for a decision."

"Someone else fingered him. You didn't."

She ignored the statement. "We couldn't have her stopped, and we didn't want her followed by anyone but the League. I didn't know he was your partner, of course; I didn't know who he was. It was a terrible mistake."

"People do make mistakes," Forester said. "Is embarrassing the Air League over this man Vogel worth all the little mistakes?"

"It's considerably more than that," Caladon said. "If the League gets Vogel back, it tightens its grip, quite possibly unbreakably. If we get him—get the *real* Tube Alloys Project—it's the end of League domination."

"The end of the League, that's what you want," Kiel said bitterly. "You want weapons to destroy the League, destroy each other. What little peace there is in the world is the Air League's doing, and you'd bring it all down for the sake of your pride—"

"Shut up, stupid," Caladon said evenly. "Didn't you get enough of a taste of Air League peacekeeping at the canyon?"

"What did they tell you Vogel was?" Forester said to Kiel.

"That he was a scientist, kidnapped and forced to work on weapons for terror—"

"All right," Forester said. "What is Tube Alloys?"

Caladon said, "From what we can tell from Vogel's notes, it—"

There was a flicker of blue light past the train window, and a sizzling noise.

"Suspensorays," Caladon said, and then the windows were shadowed, and the car shook with an echoing clang. "He's grappled to the roof."

"Officer Margrave?" Kiel said.

Forester said, "Who the hell else?"

The train wobbled a bit, and then picked up speed. The blue arclight still shone through the window.

"But what can he do up there?"

"If that's a Mark Eight cruiser," Caladon said, "he can pull this train right off the tracks if he wants."

"What if we go into a tunnel? Or under a bridge?"

Forester looked out the window. "Do you want to tell her what happens then, or should I?"

Caladon said, "That blue light means he hasn't turned off the suspensoray projector. If we crash with that still on . . . it'll explode."

Kiel said, "Margrave will be killed?"

"Him and a few other people," Forester said.

"Why is he up there? What does he want?"

The train hit a curve. Steel wheels screamed.

"He wants us to jump," Forester said. "Or else everybody dies."

"He's an *Air League Officer*," Kiel said desperately. "Even if you're right—wouldn't murdering hundreds of people only be worse for them than anything we might say or do?"

Forester said, "Remember that movie serial, with Harrison Whats-his-name—*Deadline in the Sky*? Where the Birdman stops the runaway train with his cruiser, and saves everybody?" He pointed at the roof. "I'll bet Margrave's seen that one ten times. 'Course this time the trick won't work, but he was a brave officer to try it."

"All right, all right!" Kiel said. "I'll do it. I'll jump."

Caladon said, "Take your coat off."

Kiel said, "What?"

"Take. Your. Coat. Off."

Kiel stood up. As she took her left arm out of the sleeve, Caladon grasped Kiel's wrist, pulled her down. There were a couple of clicks, and Kiel was handcuffed to the arm of the seat.

Caladon put on Kiel's coat and hat. She took a heavy revolver out of her own purse, put it in a coat pocket. "Let's go," she said.

They went to the end of the car. Forester braced himself, then pulled the handle on the side door; wind sucked it open. He leaned out of the car, over the ballast ripping past at ninety miles an hour, tie ends fast as the teeth of a buzzsaw. There was a narrow metal ladder just around the corner, on the end of the car. Forester leaned back in.

"After you," he said.

"Forester . . . I'm sorry about your partner."

"Too damn late for that. Go on."

She went to the door, reached around to grasp the end ladder. Forester braced her left arm, and she swung a foot around, scraping about, getting a foothold. "Okay," she said, and Forester let go as she put both hands on the ladder, then both feet. She started to climb.

Forester followed her. The space between the cars was tight, and the wind was intense. He got a hand to the top of the car, and Caladon grasped his wrist, helped him up. The roof was smooth metal, sloped toward the edge. A couple of feet above was the lower hull of the Air League cruiser. The blue glow from the suspensoray was almost painful, and its crackle was louder than the wind.

Caladon pointed at the magnetic clamps holding the airship down, at a small hatch just forward of the ray chamber. Forester nodded. They crawled to the hatch.

Caladon pushed the handle, lifted the door, twisted through it. Forester gripped the edge of the hatchway and looked inside, from just below and behind Caladon's feet.

He was looking down a narrow corridor, lined with wires and plumbing for the airship's engines. The metal door at the end of the corridor swung open, and Forester saw a pair of gray boots step through.

"You actually made it," Glenn Margrave said, and then hesitated. "Ah, no, I see—"

Caladon fired at him. The boots disappeared through the doorway and the door swung shut. Forester pulled himself through the hatch.

"I didn't miss him," Caladon said, "but I don't think I hurt him very badly."

Forester squeezed past Caladon to examine the door. It was all metal, not to be forced without tools.

"All right, we do it the hard way," he said, and pointed to the hatch. They climbed back down to the roof. Forester drew the armor-piercing Colt, and traced along the edge of the air cruiser to one of the magnetic grapples. There was a thick con-

duit leading from the clamp. Forester shot it. Metal
burned, throwing sparks, and the grapple let go.
The cruiser lurched upward a few inches. The
suspensoray showed itself, and Forester and Caladon
shielded their eyes from the light. The airship
trembled, then settled unevenly back down to the
roof of the train.

Forester killed another grapple. This time the
cruiser settled at a skew angle, and the wind around
it turned turbulent. On the hull above their heads,
there was the clanging of boots from inside. Forester handed the Colt to Caladon. He pointed at
the magazine, held up three fingers. She nodded
and took the gun.

Forester went to the hatch. The boots were
very close. Forester moved to one side of the
hatch, reached out and flipped it open.

A blaster bolt tore into the edge of the hatch,
ripping the hinge apart. Forester moved, pushing
himself inside. Margrave was waiting for his gun
to recharge. Forester knocked it aside and chopped
the side of his hand into Margrave's throat. Margrave dropped to one knee; his blaster hit the floor,
and Forester stomped on it, hearing glass break, a
vacuum tube implode.

Margrave grabbed Forester's belt. Forester back-
handed him across the face. They both fell down.
Another grapple let go, and the airship bucked
and yawed as the suspensoray and the crosswind
tried to tear it free of the train.

Margrave got his hands around Forester's throat,
but the heavy material of his flying jacket ham-
pered him. Forester hit him at the left hinge of his

jaw, and he groaned; Forester broke Margrave's hold and hit him again, making something crack. He got to his hands and knees and crawled to the hatch.

On the train roof below, Caladon was scrabbling over to the other side, aiming at another grapple. Forester shouted at her, but she couldn't hear anything. He started to climb down.

Forester barely heard the gunshot, saw the sparks and the reflection of the suspensoray. The ground dropped away at a crazy angle. Forester got a glimpse of Caladon clinging to the top of the train, and then it was too late to jump. He shut what was left of the hatch door.

Margrave was sitting up against the conduit-covered wall of the corridor. "Cong'a'lashons," he said through his dislocated jaw, " 'ou win."

Forester stepped over him, went forward to the airship's bridge. He sat down in a seat that had a stick and pedals, and about two hundred other controls, none of which meant anything to him. A dial marked AIRSPEED read 300 mph; one marked ALTITUDE had pegged at 99,999. He looked out the windows: the ground was barely visible now. He could see the curve of the Earth. The sky was darkening, stars coming out. Frost covered the windows. Forester's head hurt, and he couldn't breathe.

There wasn't anything after that.

There was no road where Forester walked; some-where under the snow there was a trail, so he had a way through the woods and the hills, but it was not easy going. He didn't know how long he had been walking. He had good boots on, and a warm nylon parka, and the cold air was very still; he wasn't uncomfortable. There were some raisins and pieces of chocolate in his pocket; he wasn't hungry. There was a 9mm-short pistol in another pocket; he wasn't worried. But he was tired. It was late afternoon, maybe four o'clock by the low winter sun, when he saw the lodge.

It was at the join of two hills, surrounded by forest; it was built of gray field stone, with a slate roof capped with lead. Smoke rose straight up from four chimneys. There was a curving flagstone path from the buried road to the large front door, and in back Forester could see a stone-paved yard, faced toward the best view of mountains Forester could remember ever seeing. The flagstones were all shoveled off, swept clean. He turned down the path, knocked on the door.

An old man with a round body and a round balding head opened the door. He wore loose twill slacks, worn leather slippers, a ticking shirt, a heavy cardigan sweater. He was smiling.

Forester said, "Dr. Karl Lyman Vogel?"

"Yes, young man. Do come in; you're the first, but the others should be here very soon. Did you walk? It must have been a very long walk. There's a nice fire, and beds if you'd like a nap. Or something hot to drink? Come in, sit down, tell me what you'd like."

Forester took a step. It was quite warm inside, and he felt slightly dizzy. "I want—"

Vogel shut the door behind Forester. "You want

hot cocoa and a soft chair in front of the fire," he said. "And then answers, yes, there will be answers. But not until the others are here." Vogel put his hand on Forester's arm, looked up at him, and his face was terribly, shockingly sad. "And perhaps not the answers you want, and I fear certainly not the ones you are expecting."

Vogel showed Forester to a small room, cluttered with knickknacks. Vogel pointed out the light switches and the tiny bathroom, and demonstrated that the lock on the door was quite secure. "I hope you're not too enamored of television," he said. "There's no television here."

"I can live without it."

"I hope so," Vogel said. "You do take my meaning— there *is no* television here. Rest well."

Forester locked the door, took off his boots, and lay down on the bed; it had a feather mattress, and was quite unreasonably comfortable. He fell asleep without meaning to.

He woke to a sound like an electric arc, and blue actinic light outside the window; he went to look, but by the time he got the blinds open there was nothing to see but a man walking up the path to the front door. The man wore a gray leather jacket and high boots, and a scarf trailed from his neck.

Forester went downstairs. Vogel was welcoming Glenn Margrave, taking his scarf and flying helmet.

"Ah, Forester," Margrave said. "It's been some time. You've been well?"

Forester nodded.

"Pleased to hear it. Who else is here?"

"Just the three of us now, but any moment—"
There was a grinding of tires on gravel from outside the lodge. Forester looked through the window, and saw a black limousine with brass-cased headlights and a long, coffinlike hood braking to a stop before the door. He couldn't see who was driving, but the rear passenger door opened and a man and a woman got out.

Forester turned as the front door opened again, and Jane Caladon came in, wearing a fur-trimmed jacket and an ankle-length skirt; on her arm was the Commander, in a long leather coat with epaulets. Behind them, the road was empty, and there were no tire tracks in the snow. The door closed. Vogel went through his happy-host routine again. Margrave sat down near the fire with coffee and brandy.

Forester watched as Caladon helped the Commander remove his coat. The Commander wore a double-breasted blue suit, brass-buttoned, with miniature medals on the breast; he looked quite frail. Under her jacket Caladon wore a white shirtwaist, with lace and a large onyx brooch at her throat. Forester took a step away from the window, to see her better.

Outside, a horse whinnied, hooves pounded packed snow, and there was the hiss of sled runners. Harness bells jingled, the horse whinnied again, and the hooves and the sleigh stopped. Vogel opened the door.

Irene Kiel wore a white fur jacket over a red silk gown sewn with thousands of crystal drops clear as water, the ruffles of the gown like rose petals wet

with dew. Her hair was in a silk net and her face
was radiant. Forester looked past her with difficulty, but there was nothing beyond but the clean
snow and the trees.

"Please be comfortable, all of you," Vogel said,
bustling about again. "There is warmth, there is
food, there is drink." He swept a hand past the
crystal decanters on the bar; it seemed to Forester
that his fingers passed through the neck of a flask,
but it must have been a trick of the light.

Forester stood in a corner, Vogel leaned against
the fieldstone mantelpiece. The others sat down,
looking warily at one another.

Vogel pressed his hands together, touched his
fingers to his lips, and said, "You have all come
here looking for me, because you believe that I
can help you with some grave societal problem. I
doubt that the road has been easy for any of you.
And I would be a terrible wizard indeed if I were
to send you away. So I will try to answer your
questions . . . but I trust you will not object if I
ask you to pay no attention to the man behind the
curtain."

Forester looked at the windows. Margrave burst
out laughing, an unpleasant sound coming from
him. The others looked blank. Vogel said "A joke,
a figure of speech, I'm sorry. Are you all comfortable? This is rather a complicated story.

"I was interested in the application of the Uncertainty principle to the physics of sensory re-
sponse. You know the principle: to observe a system
adds energy that disturbs the observation. But

what, I thought, if the system being observed is *itself* an observing system? Does it disturb itself?"

"The two-slit experiment," Caladon said.

"Yes, my lady. Yes. Single photons create interference fringes with themselves. There is no such thing as pure data.

"Furthermore, I knew from sensory-isolation experiments that in the complete absence of input, the sensorium would still register inputs. No matter what we did—suspend, anesthetize, cut—"

"You had an extraordinary freedom in those days, didn't you?" Margrave said. His face was intent.

The Commander said, "There was supervision of experiments."

"Oh, in a manner of speaking," said Vogel equably. "There was a man named Lashley, working—oh, decades before me, who was looking for the physical seat of memory. He worked with rats, you see, maze-trained rats, and tried to surgically destroy only those brain cells that would erase the maze training, no others. He cut into the heads of a great many rats."

"And?" Forester said.

"And nothing. He never got his result. Poor Lashley was actually driven to the conclusion that memory was impossible."

"Holography?" Kiel said.

"Holography had not been invented, so he had no analogy. But holography only provides a guess as to the non-locality of memory. It leaves a more important issue unaddressed—which is a bad pun. . . .

"Think of any particularly vivid memory. Think

of all you can recall—sounds, smells, colors, words spoken. How many data points are in that image? And how many such memories do you have? Add the memories that hypnotic regression can pull from you, in massive detail, and we start to run into a serious problem of storage space. You have ten billion brain cells. Ten billion bits isn't nearly enough room for the things you know. In my models, the autonomic responses alone took up thirty percent of that as a minimum."

The Commander said, "Yet I remember, Dr. Vogel."

"Do you? That is, does something inside you, your brain, actually contain the memories? It doesn't, that's the point. There's nothing in there but short-term electrical patterns, and a little bit of RNA firmware. The memories, the truth, *the reality*, is somewhere else. The brain is only the access unit to the great collective of all memories."

Margrave said in an amused tone, "O Jung, art thou sleeping there below?"

"Yes," Vogel said suddenly, "he is."

Kiel said, "But if that were true, we should be able to remember . . . anything."

"Not at all. You're in a library. There are thousands, millions of books on the shelves. How many of them can you read at once? One, of course. Now, you're reading that one book. You find a word you don't know. It's invag to you—"

"What?" Kiel said.

"—so you put down the book and find a dictionary, and it tells you that 'invag' is 'the quality of being baffled by a strange word in an otherwise intelligible sentence'."

"I assume you're now going to discuss self-referentiality and undecidable propositions," Margrave said. "May I have a drink?"

"You may have a drink," said Vogel pleasantly, "and I was only trying to introduce the idea of data that are necessary for the interpretation of other data—of our understanding of the universe's meanings modifying our, well, understanding of the universe's meaning."

Margrave poured dark rum into a shallow glass. "All right, we're self-referential beings, and the quality of mercy is not strained either. But I know where that reference comes from, and it's not some vast collective."

"The problem is not that of access to memories, not at all. That can easily be explained with analogies to language coding, or to cocktail-party effect—the ability to pick out one voice from a roomful. No, the problem is one of origin. Where do all those memories come from?"

"Now you're being absurd," Caladon said, with something less than full confidence. "Experience. The senses."

"Ah. The experience of the senses—and now we are in the knot. For you are not, you are never, experiencing the world directly. You're experiencing what your access unit tells you is out there. Take the rawest of experiences: pain. Suppose we have a group of people being tortured—I'm not shocking you, am I? No, I thought not.

"Now. For the innocent in our torture chamber,

the experience is one of confusion and injustice. For the stoic, it is a mere distraction from his contemplations. The revolutionary finds a means to an end, the sadomasochist pleasure, the spy the price of doing business, the double-agent a sense of getting the job done. The same limbs are twisted in the same ways, but the experiences being fed to the collective are all different. And what is modifying the inputs to the collective but the collective itself, through those extensions of itself resident in the access units? The group mind is reinforcing itself, memory telling mind what to remember." Vogel turned back to Forester. "The reason I cannot answer your question directly and simply is that the whole issue of meaning, of the interpretation of the sensorium, has exploded, and I doubt that we could fit the pieces back together even if we could find them all."

Forester looked around the room. Kiel had a pinched expression, Caladon one of determined disbelief. The Commander did not seem to be paying attention. Margrave chuckled softly to himself.

"It's just cheap solipsism," Caladon said.

"Solipsism is never cheap," Margrave said, "for solipsists have no one at all to love."

"What proof do you have of this?" Kiel said to Vogel. "Your device works, but what does it have to do with this . . . idea?"

"The proof. Ah, there is the bad part."

"It usually is," Caladon said.

"I built a machine," Vogel said, "to tamper with the process of memory access. It worked."

"Yes," said the Commander distantly.

"You remember it, then? But what do you remember it doing? Does your Vogel device destroy access, or enhance it? . . . Mr. Forester."

"I'm listening."

"What lies to the east of the Ural Mountains? East of the United German Republic?"

"The Manchu States."

"I mean just to the east. Between Germany and the Chinas."

"Nothing."

"It's a distance of thousands of miles, Mr. Forester."

"It's all wasteland," Forester said. "Snow and bare rocks. There aren't even trees on it." He was acutely aware of the others watching him, all of them very intent . . . except the Commander, who looked into the fireplace.

Vogel said, "Did you learn that in school? Have you ever actually seen the Great Eastern Waste?"

"Of course I haven't been there. I haven't—" Outside, there was a sound like automatic gunfire. Forester looked out the window. He saw nothing that hadn't been there before.

"Did you hear something?" Vogel asked, very softly.

"I heard—" He stopped. The sound was gone.

"What about the Waste?" Margrave said.

"Ah, the Waste. Does the name Union of Soviet Socialist Republics mean anything to you? To any of you?"

There was no answer. Vogel said, "Not even to you, Commander?"

The Commander said, in a tight voice, "It's all over. It's forgotten."

"Yes," Vogel said sadly. "It certainly is."

Forester heard shots again. Two single shots, and then a muffled thump, like a body falling on snow. He did not turn. None of the others seemed to have noticed at all. He spoke to drown out the echo in his ears. "What was this Union?"

"A bad memory," Vogel said, "as we were a bad memory to them; until the collective rose up together and blocked our access units from them, edited them out. As, surely, we must be erased from their past. . . . I wonder what their world is like, without us."

"This is nonsense," Caladon said. "A nation isn't a closed entity; there are connections, trains and planes, people who cross borders—"

Margrave said, with a glitter in his eyes, "Yes, how does one clean all the bad books out of the library, without also purging good books with bad words in them?"

"I don't believe it was a clean division," Vogel said. "I think it was a fragmentation, a shattering of the glass; not two worlds but many, overlapping. They all run parallel, and sometimes the edges bleed together."

Forester said, "What made the . . . collectives . . . act? What was suddenly so powerful?"

Vogel said, "I can't tell you that."

Irene Kiel said, "You don't remember?"

"I remember, young lady. But Mr. Margrave is right about censorship spreading. I don't have the words any longer, and the dictionary has been burned."

The Commander was looking straight at Forester. "My god," he said, "you must have been there. You couldn't have avoided the draft. And you must surely have been on the front lines. . . ." There was a fascination in the Commander's look, a hungriness too much like Margrave's expression.

"I need some air," Forester said, and walked out of the den, through the lodge to the sunny kitchen. He pulled open the door and breathed in the cold draft.

For several minutes he stood looking out the open door at the fresh snow. There was a whistling noise from somewhere—like wind, but surely too high to be wind—and the specular sunlight on the snow hurt his eyes.

He poured some coffee from the pot on the stove, drank it black and scalding.

You're going to burn your gut right through, partner.

The mug shattered on the floor.

Light, too bright to see by. A whistle that wasn't wind.

Forester stepped through the door, onto the flagstone courtyard.

You want me, call. I'll be there.

Forester reached, trying to pull the fragments together, trying to remember, whoever's memories they were. He walked out of the kitchen, into the cold.

*   *   *

The snow was deep, but packed down, not hard to walk on. The tall firs gave enough cover for two men on the move—but two men on the move a long way from their unit, a long way from the American lines, looking for shelter in a Leningrad winter have no reason to be pleased by hard Russian snow and a few Russian trees.

"So do you figure we're going in the right direction?" Danny Baker said.

"I figure we've got to go somewhere." Forester looked up at the sky: it was completely overcast, no sign of a sun to show direction. He thought it was afternoon, but wasn't sure at all.

There was a wide clear spot ahead, and in the middle of it sat a helicopter. It was American, a UH-90 Gila transport. Its rotors were broken, and it slumped against a snowdrift, but it didn't seem too badly shot up and it hadn't burned. It was shelter, at least. There might be food in it, a radio—but that was blowing smoke. The shelter was enough.

"You cover me from here," Baker said.

"Go up careful."

"Oh, you got *that*, partner."

Forester leaned against a tree, cradling his rifle. Baker loped around behind the copter. They called it "salting the bird's tail" in Ranger school. Baker was good at it. He was just hard to believe, moving in open country; watch him two or three times and you'd swear the guy could have snuck up and goosed a deer.

Baker reached the tail boom, which had a partly obliterated serial number, something-or-other 234

GEA. He slapped it a couple of times, knocking snow loose. "Death or glory, holy shitsky!" he yelled. "Anybody from Kansas in there?"

Nothing.

Baker waved and Forester moved. Both of them kept checking the sky, the horizon, the chopper doors. Still nothing.

"Looks like we got a room for the night," Baker said, knocked ice from the door handle and pulled the door open.

There were two shots and Baker fell down, spread-eagle on the snow.

Forester dove under the Gila. He put two rounds through its belly, heard them bounce inside, heard a yell. A Russian grunt came tumbling out of the bird. "Surrender, surrender," he said thickly, holding an AKD over his head. "No more shoot." He put his thumb on the carbine's trigger, and Forester aimed at his knocking kneecaps. The Russian pulled the trigger. Nothing. No more shoot. He was gabbling; Forester doubted he'd understand even if he knew any Russian.

But in fact he did understand. The guy had two rounds left, maybe for defense, maybe for dinner, maybe for himself. He'd found the bird and thought he was safe for the night. And then the Big Black Amerikanski had come along and scared him. Bang bang.

Forester hit the Russian with his gun butt and knocked him down, kicked the AKD as far as he could, then went to look at Baker, though he knew just what he was going to find. One bullet had punched through Baker's heart, the other his throat, and he was dead. The Russian was a good shot when he was scared.

Forester kicked the Russian. It warmed Forester like a shot of corn whiskey. He kicked the man again. That felt just as good.

Then Forester stopped, because in another couple of kicks he'd be hooked on it, and when he got through he'd go into withdrawal until he could find another Russian.

He grabbed the grunt by the collar and belt and hauled him up. "Get the fuck out of here," he said, in English; he didn't know how to say it in Russian. Not even politely.

The soldier was wheezing. Forester supposed he'd broken a couple of the man's ribs. He didn't care that much. He pointed his gun and said "Go."

The Russian went. He fell once; Forester put a round over his head, and he got up and kept going.

Forester sat in the open door of the copter, looking at Danny Baker dead on the snow. There wasn't anything else to do.

Overhead, there was a whistling sound, not like aircraft, a little like bombs, but bombs from what? Forester looked up at the Russian sky, white as stainless steel, a million miles from anywhere.

He saw the missile, saw three of them, and then he saw the flash. There wasn't anything after that.

Forester looked up, though the precise direction wasn't certain. He seemed to be on his knees, but he wasn't quite sure. The sky was full of light, though there was no discernible sun. There were four moons, or maybe two seen with double vision. Stars were falling all over the place.

"Stop," Forester said, and the word sounded like the crack of doom, but it didn't have much other effect.

"It can't really stop, not now," said Vogel, who seemed to be sitting just in front of Forester, on what might have been a hillside if it would only stay in one place. Maybe it was a big toadstool. There was some smoke in the air, and a gleam that could have been a water pipe. "Did you find what you were looking for out there?" he said.

Forester said, "I don't know. I can't tell what's real any longer."

Vogel said, "We've always defined reality in terms of memory, while forgetting—oops, pardon me, but you see the problem—that memory is subjective. Use anything you want, deep hypnosis, drugs, triplet scanning, torture—memories of childhoods spent on Mars come up in the same level of 'reality' as childhoods in Minneapolis. You want a bottom line of reality—well, there isn't one, not any longer, anyway. There's only the dreadful lot of us who've made this awful mess of things." He sighed, exhaling butterflies. "Here we are as gods, and not only aren't we able to get the hang of it, we've lost what control we ever did have."

"What am I doing here?" Forester said. "I don't have any quick answers."

"Do you mean, one switch to throw, one button to push, one trigger to pull and fix things? Well, of course not, no one does," said Vogel, "but you *recognize* the fact. That's why you're here, I think. That, and one other quality."

"What's that?"

"I can't tell you that," Vogel's voice said, though Vogel was no longer there to supply it. "I can't tell you anything. I was incinerated by the first missiles to hit Cheyenne Mountain."

There wasn't anything after that.

"Vogel's been gone a long time," Irene Kiel said.

"He'll be back," said Jane Caladon. "Though I'm beginning to wonder if we'll get anything useful from him."

Glenn Margrave said, "You're so terribly practical, my dear. I wonder if you and I could—"

The Commander said, "Will you do us all a courtesy, Margrave, and shut up for a while?" and continued filling a water glass with bourbon.

The door swung open with a crash and a shattering of glass. Forester stood in the cracked frame, a bulky black gun in his hand. He fired, one long, long burst. Bullets ripsawed through the tabletop, shattered pictures on the walls, exploded chair cushions.

When the rattle of the gun finally stopped, all of the people in the room were still standing: covered with dust, scratched and bruised by flying splinters, half-deaf, but unhurt. None of them moved at all.

Forester raised the assault rifle over his head and threw it into the fireplace, knocking logs loose, spilling fire on the floor. Then he turned and began walking through the snow, up the hill toward the trees.

The silence and the paralysis went on for some moments. Then Kiel said, "What in God's name was that?"

The Commander went to the hearth and examined the gun. "This is a Kalashnikov AKD," he said. "Russian carbine."

"A *what*?" Margrave said.

"There shouldn't be any of these," the Commander said calmly. He looked through the open door at the distant figure, hard to see now against the snow. They all looked, trying to puzzle out what it was they had just seen happen, the name of the emotion, the name of the act.

But if they had ever known it, they had forgotten.

CHANCE

Nancy Springer

What did it mean to be female in feudal times? Was woman an adored symbol of the Virgin Mary, or did she slave in a cowshed? How separate were the concepts of chattel and chivalry?

Like an early Brotherworld, the Middle Ages tended to suppress or disregard personalities. Marriage was foremost a business transaction. As a system for transferring assets it worked well; one hopes that once in a while, as a coincidence, it also provided some happiness.

The Crusades provided powerful impetus in the slow revolution to courtly love. For centuries clerics had equated women with Eve, the cause of Man's downfall. But in Byzantium men learned the cult of the Virgin, most beloved of all women; and from elsewhere in the East came the experiences of other ways of life, other levels of civilization. Women became the honored subject of hundreds of love poems, songs, and stories carried about Europe by jongleurs and members of the court.

But "Chance" springs from before these times. Here Nancy Springer gives us a young woman whose heart leads her into danger. She has a protector, but of what help is love against a tyrant?

Chance walked softly through Wirral, silent in doeskin boots, more stealthy than seemed possible of a man of his broad-shouldered brawn and middling age. His duty as Lord's Warden was to see what happened in the vast forest named Wirral, whether poaching or spying or, sometimes, murder, a corpse left in the boskage. Sometimes he glimpsed things stranger yet: the small faces that were gone in an eyeblink, vanishing into the hollow of an oak. Denizens. Them he did not report, for Roddarc son of Riol, Lord of Wirralmark, gave no credence to the hidden folk who were even holier than Wirral and never spoken of by name. Chance did not like to believe in them either, for the tales related of them were fearsome. Squirrels, he told himself. Squirrels rustling the branches of the oak.

The beast with two backs was commonplace within the fringes of the forest, especially in the springtime. This activity, also, he did not report, nor did it much trouble him. If squires and servant girls needed a private place to enjoy their sport, he would not begrudge it to them, though another with his secret might have. But he was long-suffering, Chance. He would turn his face away and leave the place as silently as he had come.

Only, this time, he could not help seeing that it was she whose name he never heard without a leap of his heart.

Halimeda. He remembered the day she was born. Her lady mother, dying after the birthing, had chosen the name. Halimeda, "dreaming of the sea." Chance had never seen the sea, but even at the age of ten he had known what it was to dream. It was a lovely name, and the girl had grown to suit it, tall as befit a lord's daughter, her eyes gray-green, her mien quiet, her look often focused somewhere beyond a stormy horizon.

Halimeda on a bed of violets and spring-green moss. She did not moan and squeal like the servant girls, so he had come quite close without knowing. And she was naked, and so lovely, slender as befit a lady of blood, fallow-fawn skin and dark, dark hair. So young, so bold. She lay silent and rapt, her eyes lidded, the dark lashes trembling. Head next to hers—that handsome young buck of a commoner, Blake. "Love," he whispered to her, and her lips moved against his neck.

Chance moved away for a few silent paces, then recklessly abandoned silence. He ran, crashing through the bracken like a stag. When he finished running, he leaned against a birch and retched.

Halimeda would never be his; he had always known that. For more reasons than could be counted. But his feelings were not amenable to such reasons.

That evening Lord Roddarc came to see him in his small lodge that stood outside the forest walls and beyond the tilled ground, under the shadow of Wirral.

Chance heard the rapping, hurried over and flung open the door at once, for he knew that signal well. His lord strode in, but no retainers stood at guard.

"You should not come here alone," Chance scolded. "Have me summoned if you wish to speak with me."

"Bah!" The lord crossed the room in three paces, sat down on a bench by the hearthfire. A tall man, finer of feature than his warden, not as rugged of build but perhaps just as strong. His hair and short beard shone red-gold in the firelight. His high black boots shone even brighter with hours of some servant's polishing.

"Rod, would you think with your mind instead

of your hind end! Out alone in the dusk, fit game for assassins—"

If the lord's retainers had been present, Chance would not have bespoken him so bluntly, nor would he have called him by name. But as they were alone, he let go of ceremony. He and Roddarc had been reared nearly as brothers. As young warriors they had fought the blue-painted barbarians side by side in the front line. Roddarc had been with Chance when he had taken his worst wound—it could as featly have happened to the Lord himself. Roddarc had shielded his comrade while they fought out the rest of the battle, and when Chance had weakened and fallen at last the young lord had borne him away to the tents and cared for him. Ten years and more it had been since that time, but Chance was not likely to forget. And later, when Roddarc came into his holding, he made Chance his warden—Chance, the commoner with the sorrow-child's name, orphan and bastard, unclaimed by any family. Roddarc had made him a man of authority in Wirralmark, and Chance would not forget that either.

Therefore he scolded his lord and friend from the heart.

"All the mutterings of the malcontents, the rumors, and you must come a-visiting when anyone could aim a bolt at you from a shadow!"

The lord of Wirralmark sat grinning broadly, as if he wished for nothing better than to be railed at by his friend. Indeed, Chance could hardly have better rewarded him for coming alone.

"At twilight! Alone, to the edge of Wirral! Of all the jackass—"

"I'll go where I like," the lord interrupted, still smiling, "and alone if I like."

"That's what you said to my lord Riol when you were seven years old, and he thrashed me until I bled."

For Chance, of an age with Roddarc, had been reared at his side as the whipping boy, the one who took punishment so that the noble buttocks need not be scarred. It was an honor, an opportunity for a child of low degree.

Roddarc's smile darkened into a scowl. "The old bully is gone, praise be," he retorted, "and I am not a child any longer."

"You act like one!"

But Chance's ardor merely made Roddarc smile anew. Amused, he was. Chance raised clenched fists in despair and gave it up, slumping onto the other bench. He fed thornwood to the fire. The two men watched the leaping flames companionably.

"Nothing out of the ordinary in Wirral," Roddarc remarked after a while, for Chance would have told him if there were.

"I have seen nothing, no."

Halimeda's dalliance—should he reveal that? He felt a hot flush at the thought, and realized he would not. She was Roddarc's younger sister, ten years younger, and the lord treated her much as a father might. He would be upset, angry with her, perhaps even furious enough to punish her in some way, though he was not a punishing lord. Chance did not care to gift her with wrath. Nor

could Halimeda's affairs have any connection with
his lord's difficulties. Or so he deemed.

"Wirral is vast," he added, "and I am but one
man. What might be moving in the deeps of Wirral
I cannot say."

"I know it." Roddarc studied the flames, their
hearts shadowed with blue and green, and when
he spoke there was unhappiness in his voice that
he would not have revealed to anyone else but
Chance. "If only I knew who was behind this
unrest . . . Old friend, I have not been a bad lord,
have I?"

"Hardly! You are among the best; you know
that." Roddarc was for the most part just, and in
many ways not unkind.

"Then why . . ."

"Because men are fools, that is why!" Chance
spoke with vehemence. "They would prefer a lord
who rules by the sword and torture, it would
seem. For when a gentle lord rules, they can think
of nothing but overthrowing him."

"Well." The lord looked up, his jaw firmed. "If
they should succeed, Chance—"

"Say no such thing! They will not."

"It is devoutly to be hoped you are correct. But
if they should succeed, I want a promise from
you."

"Rod, you know you have it."

"Not so reckless, my friend. It is hard." The
lord was faintly smiling, his look wry. "It is this:
that you should protect my sister. For if I am
killed, this demesne by right goes to Halimeda,
should she ever be able to claim it."

Chance took a deep breath and nodded. Roddarc was right; the task was hard. For likely he would see Halimeda wed to some lord powerful enough to champion her, and he could never make any claim on her except that of a loyal servant, for all of his heart's clamoring.

Chance prowled through Wirral the next day in a panic barely concealed. He had never known Roddarc to speak of his own mortality. And when he had walked his friend back to the fortress, parted from him at the gate, Roddarc had reached out for a moment and clasped his hand, the grip of a comrade facing battle.

Plain battle was a matter ill enough, but this hidden one yet worse. He and Roddarc knew not even the names of their enemies. Who were the conspirators? Where might they be mustering? Six men had been missing from the fortress guard that morning, deserters. . . . If there were rebels gathering in Wirral, they ought to be somewhere in the skirts of it near the Mark. But Chance had stalked all those ways, every moment expecting attack, and found nothing.

A movement—he froze, crouching, bow raised and arrow nocked. But it was nothing. A flicker of brown, a shadowy face peering for a moment from the hollow of a lightning-torn oak, then gone before he could draw breath.

Chance straightened and aimed his arrow at the ground. A daring thought had taken hold of him, and he seized the moment.

"Little one there in the tree," he said softly, "come out, please, and speak with me."

There was a scrabbling sound as of a squirrel inside the trunk, and then the face appeared again, eyes bright. Quite by accident Chance had hit upon a lure well-nigh irresistible to the Denizens of the forest—the lure of words at coupled sport, of rhyme.

Chance stood still, not utterly afraid but very wary. In a moment the small man of a nameless race stepped boldly out of his refuge and stood on a branch at the level of Chance's eyes, entirely revealed.

Chance knew that he had been reckless beyond belief.

The creature was far less human than he had thought. Twig-thin limbs and a torso very narrow, covered with skin like the bark of a young cherry tree, by the looks of him as hard and tough as an ash switch. No clothing. Chance had to force his eyes away from brown genitals that lumped grotesquely large in proportion to the skinny body, scarcely a foot tall. He had heard that the nameless woodfolk were lustful; now he believed it. No wonder Wirral grew so thick. . . . The small man's hands and feet also seemed overlarge, and his nose. Even so, Chance perceived his face as eerily beautiful. A narrow face, fine of jutting bone, subtle of mouth, taut of russet skin, with eyes so large and bright they seemed almost luminous.

"Chance Love-Child," said the oak-dweller in a strong, dark voice, "what do you want?"

Chance could not speak. The Denizen laughed,

a sound like the song of a wren, and strutted on the branch where he stood, his massy cock thrust forward.

"Nearly ten years you have trod this way," he cried, "and never showed lack of sense till today. What ails you, Chance?"

From trees all around came the sound of bubbling laughter. Chance felt his small hairs prickle.

"Is it the maiden who is maiden no more?" the Denizen mocked. "The lady Halimeda who is maiden no more? She lay with Blake in the violet glade, no more a maid, and when Chance saw—"

Anger such as he had not felt in years rushed over him, jarred him out of his frozen fear. He raised his bow. But that scion of Otherness faced him, bright-eyed, fearless and laughing, and he could not take aim. He lowered his bolt again. A saddened ease stole over him, the calm of utter defeat, and he found that he could speak.

"It is for my lord Roddarc's sake that I make bold," he said.

Birdlike chirps of delight rose all around; a subtle rhyme! The brown woodsman strutted again.

"Why?" he demanded. "He has said, the lady is yours, should he die."

Chance nearly lost his voice again. If they had heard Roddarc's bidding, then even in his lodge one of them had been listening. "You go everywhere," he whispered. "You see everything."

"It is our nature so to go, so to see. What do you want to know?"

"Where the rebels muster," Chance said with a

dry mouth. "Who is their leader. When they will strike."

The Denizen stopped his posturing and stood still in what might have been genuine perplexity.

"Surely you know," Chance urged.

"I know full well. But why would I tell?"

Chance stood with his mouth agape. "Why not?" he burst out at last, and the small woodsman warbled with laughter.

"Why not?" The little man turned to the listening forest. "What say ye? Should I tell?"

There arose a piping clamor. A few strong voices shrilled above the others. "Tell! Tell!" cried one. "We love to meddle!" one sang out gaily. "And we meddle full well!" called another.

But before the visible Denizen could speak, another appeared, from where Chance did not see, and stood on the branch beside the first. He was gray, like beech, and mossily bearded, and as massy of cock as his russet comrade, for all that he seemed older.

"Chance," he said in a taut voice, "ten years you have averted your eyes. Now you grow unwise. Think again."

"There will be a price to pay," said the brown one, singsong, "a price to pay, some day, some way."

Their gaze met his as if from out of depths of another time, another order of being, and he knew that he was facing a power he could in no way control, relentless as fate, capricious as the turning of fortune's wheel. Perhaps as cruel as Lord Riol, and not likely to go away, like Riol, and die. The

Denizens would live forever in the forest, and what they might do to him. . . .

Still, he had to know. For Roddarc's sake.

"Tell me," he whispered. "I will pay when I must." *Whipping boy that I am,* he thought.

The forest fell to silence. The brown Denizen sat down on the bough; the gray one remained standing and spoke formally, with no attempt at rhyme.

"The rebels are gathering at Gallowstree Lea. Blake is their leader. Their numbers are small, fifty and a few, but they are clever. They will not need to penetrate the fortress. Roddarc will come to them, for they have with them a hostage."

"Who?" Chance demanded, though already he knew.

"Lady Halimeda."

All the miles to the fortress he ran. The day was more than half spent, but, powers be willing, there might yet be time—if the forest folk had told truth. He had heard tales, and he knew they might be making a jackass of him, burbling their uncanny laughter. Or betraying him, luring him off on a fool's errand, perhaps setting him to lure Roddarc off on a fool's errand while Blake took the fortress. The thought burned in him.

But instinct told him that there was truth in them this one first time. Truth to make him always hope thereafter.

Roddarc was at the gate, on horseback, with a troop of mounted followers, just setting out when

Chance ran up to him, stumbling and streaming sweat and grasping at the steed's mane for support.

"Halimeda is missing," Roddarc told him tersely.

Chance nodded. Gasping for breath, he could not yet speak.

"What is it, man! You have news of her?"

"Gallowstree Lea," Chance panted, finding voice. "Blake, their leader. Fifty men. They will be expecting you."

Halimeda had gone on horseback and left a plain trail. Roddarc rode grimly along it, with Chance on a warhorse beside him but not armed for war. When they neared the lea, they dismounted and left their steeds and men, stalking ahead to scout the enemy's preparations. It was not fitting that the Lord of Wirralmark should do this; Chance should have done it for him. But Roddarc had insisted that they go together.

"I trust no one but you these days," he murmured as they made their way softly forward.

The lea was a meadow in the midst of the Wirral, a place where lightning had seeded fire a few seasons before, now lush with grass and shrubs. Off to one side stood a surviving tree, an elm where outlaws had once hung a renegade. Cocky of Blake, to choose this place; did he not fear the same fate?

Roddarc did not tread as silently as Chance would have liked. But it did not matter. Blake was indeed overweening. He and his followers stood chatting in boyish excitement, and his sentries heard nothing but that babble. Of course, they were not expecting spies, but a troop of men on horseback, blundering along a plain trail.

Halimeda stood tied to the gallows tree.

"How did they lure her here?" Roddarc wondered, whispering, very softly, directly into Chance's ear.

Chance knew well enough how it had been done. A message of love from Blake, an elopement planned, perhaps. Hoping Roddarc need not know, he did not answer. But suppose Halimeda stood bound merely for appearance's sake, actually there of her own will, to watch her brother be killed . . . could infatuation have made her so false? Chance felt sick.

"Go around," Roddarc whispered, "and when you are behind her, signal me with a bolt in the air. Then I will sound the horn, and do you free her and take her to safety."

If Roddarc's troop charged at the blast of the horn, all would be well. But if they tarried, Roddarc would face fifty men alone. Chance shook his head in protest.

"Do as I tell you!" Roddarc commanded, the words soft between clenched teeth.

The bolt, Chance decided, would be in Blake's back rather than into the air. He made his way with all stealth around the lea to the place where Halimeda stood captive.

And when he had stalked to a place where he could see her hands, his heart warmed with relief. She was tied, truly and firmly tied; her wrists ran red with blood from her attempts to free herself.

She stood with her head bowed, her dark hair hanging so that he could only glimpse her face.

He could not shoot Blake. Halimeda and the tree stood in the way. By no maneuvering could he manage it.

At last he gritted his teeth, sent a bolt into the air, and heard the mighty blast of the horn. Halimeda's head came up as if jerked by a hangman's rope.

Then Chance reached her side, cutting her bonds.

And on the far fringe of the lea, Roddarc was striding forward, sword at the ready, roaring for Blake to meet him in combat.

If the rebels had any honor at all, he would not yet be killed. . . . Chance reached for Halimeda's arm, to lead her to safety. But the look on her lovely face, the blaze of hatred, stunned him, and in his astonishment he let her snatch the long knife from his grasp. Dumbfounded, he stood with the hand that had reached for her arm still reaching, in air.

She turned and ran straight toward Blake, the knife raised.

There was small honor in the renegades. They were closing in on Roddarc on all sides; he held them off with mighty arcs of his sword. Running to his aid and her own revenge, Halimeda hurled herself at Blake with a harpy's shriek, clawing at her erstwhile lover's neck, stabbing at his back. The knife hit the shoulderblade, doing little more than startle him. He flung her off, sent her staggering with a blow.

Chance got hold of her around her waist before

she fell. Enemies were everywhere; he flailed about him with his bow, using it like a club. Halimeda raised the knife again, but not, he saw, against him; she was frightened now, and with reason. "Roddarc," she pled.

Her brother was hard beset, taking blows and wounds.

Then the troop thundered in, clearing away the rebels from around him like so much smoke, and Roddarc seized Blake and held him at the point of the sword.

Three days later the execution took place. By hanging, at the courtyard gallows within the fortress walls. It was as well, Roddarc said, that Halimeda had not killed Blake. Treacherous schemer that he was, he deserved strangulation, not the clean death of the blade.

Everyone in Wirralmark was there to witness, for by longtime law all were required to be. Halimeda stood near the wooden stairway leading up to the high keep door, and Chance shifted his place, seemingly at random, until he stood near her, hard put not to look at her too long or too openly. She stood very still, very lovely, in a slim dress of oak-green velvet, the raw rope cuts on her wrists hidden by long sleeves that tapered nearly to her fingers. Threads of real gold bound her dark hair into braids and tendrils that rippled down her back. The bruise on her fair, pale face was already fading.

Not so, Chance thought, *the bruise on her heart.*

Hands bound, Blake walked out of the dungeon

tower between two guards—or barely walked; they more carried him than not. The coward. There was not a mark on him except Halimeda's knife scratch; Chance knew that. Roddarc practiced no torture in his prison, not even on traitors.

The lord came out of the keep and stood by his sister.

"Our father would have ripped out his tongue," she said to him, her voice not quite steady, "and his eyes."

And taken away his cock as well, had he known.

"Do you wish it done to him?" Roddarc asked, gazing at her levelly.

"I—" Her voice failed her, and she was silent.

Perhaps she does wish they had gouged out his eyes that gaze at her so piteously. But no need to take his tongue. He is too craven to speak.

The noose was slipped over Blake's head, hitched to the plowhorse which would draw it tight. Halimeda looked straight at her former lover and proudly lifted her chin.

Roddarc raised his hand and gave the signal.

The horse walked forward, and Blake was lifted into the air. His handsome face turned to a horror. His feet convulsively kicked, and there was a stench as he befouled himself. The watching crowd burst from silence into a vengeful roar.

Roddarc was staring stonily at his dying enemy. But Chance watched Halimeda more than he did Blake, and he saw the pallor of her face increase, a fit of trembling take hold of her. Moving only a few inches, he slipped his strong bowman's hand under her elbow just as she started to sway.

Startled, she looked up at him, but did not take it amiss that he aided her. Chance was her dear and lifelong friend, like an uncle, her brother's all-but-brother. . . . He did not meet her eyes. If he had answered her glance with all the compassion in his own, she would have wept, and it would not be well for folk to see her weeping. Worse yet, she might have perceived the love. . . .

Blake had ceased to writhe. Halimeda took a deep breath. Her brother turned away from the dead renegade, offered his arm to his sister, and Chance eased away from her without, he hoped, anyone's noticing. The lady walked up the long flight of stairs to the great hall at Roddarc's side, her head held high, and Chance went back to the Wirral.

He had an inkling what tumult was in Halimeda. He thought of her as he walked in the shadow of the forest. And on toward dusk he made his way to the place where Wirral groped nearest the fortress, where he had a clear view of the postern gate, and there he waited.

And there, when day had nearly turned to dark, she slipped out and came running as if hounds of hell were after her.

He met her as she plunged into the forest, tears already shining on her face, and he blocked her way. "Lady—"

"Oh, Chance, let me be!" she wailed, trying to make her way around him. He knew what she was thinking. She had spent a long day withstanding the gaze of all the world, denied even the wretched release of tears. And now this big, bumbling fool of a warden was keeping her from entering her only refuge, the wild place where she had thought no one would see her weep.

"Lady, no, you cannot! There is danger. Listen to me, Halimeda!" He took her by the shoulders, met her eyes; she could not see much in him now, not in the dying light. "There is no need to hide your grief from me. I know you loved Blake."

She stood still, gazing up at him. "You—you *know*?" Her voice rose on the final word; she sounded glad.

"I know much of what happens in Wirral," he said, then winced and tried to soften it. "Couples walking—clasped hands—"

She did not care what he had seen. She was weeping freely, and for all that caution cried out to the contrary he gathered her into his arms so that her head rested against his shoulder. Words joined her torrent of tears.

"The—more—fool I—"

"You couldn't know he was a liar," Chance said.

"Handsome—liar. He—made a laughingstock—of me."

"No one is laughing."

"They—will be." She raised her head, tears clinging to her face. "Chance, you don't—know all."

His heart froze.

"He—I—I am with child."

A spasm afflicted his arms so that he pulled her yet closer to him, rocked her against his chest. "Could you be mistaken?" he begged when he could speak.

"No. I am—sure."

She grew still with a despair too deep for weeping, turned away from him and spoke numbly.

"He sent for me, and I went riding out to meet him like a—like a—"

"Brave and loving lass that you are," Chance told her.

"Happy," she said with a bitter wonder. "I was so happy, all the way, I had such news for him. When I reached the lea, I ran to him, he kissed me. And I told him I was bearing his baby—I could scarcely speak for happiness. Then he was laughing at me, and there were men all around."

Anger was boiling up in Chance. "I did not see him laugh when you came at him with the knife," he said.

She turned her face to him with a grim smile. "I wish I had struck more true! I wish I had done it sooner. But I could not believe what I was seeing, hearing. They were leering, and telling me that I was going to help them kill my brother and take his lands."

"The scum," Chance raged. "The piss-proud dregs! And they needs must tie you to that foul tree, like a felon—"

"Not then, not yet! It was worse. Blake—Blake seemed to think that I would stay with him willingly, that I was so much besotted—"

Choking on the words, she wept again.

"So much his toy, that you would betray your own brother," Chance said huskily. "Well, the more fool Blake, for thinking so." *And I, for thinking it even for a moment*. He put his arms around her, and she wept wearily against his shoulder.

"Roddarc was—so magnificent—"

Chance nodded. Roddarc had indeed been splendid. His feat capture of Blake and his outlawing of the remaining rebels had made him shine in the eyes of his troops and his people. Trouble was behind him, for the time.

"How am I—ever to—tell him."

His despair matching hers, Chance had no answer for her.

The Denizens danced in the mushroom ring.

A place of great antiquity, this, where the revels had been held time out of mind. All the woodsfolk came, swarming in their hundreds, as thickly as tadpoles in a rainpool. Not all were like the first ones Chance had met, with their sapling bodies and twiggy limbs, their smoothbark skin and the gall-like swellings between their legs. Many were like them, and there were females like them, too, with tough brown protuberant breasts that reminded him of oak apples. But some of the females were miniatures of the most lovely of human maidens, so slender, so dainty, that they seemed nearly transparent. Looking at them, Chance thought achingly of Halimeda.

He sat off to one side in the starlight and firefly glimmer of dusk, watching the swirling and strutting of the dance with a quiet half-smile, listening to the wild skirling of reed pipes and squirrelgut strings. If the small folk had taken a fancy to invite him to their vernal revels, it was hardly his place to refuse, but he would not be drawn into that ring of yellow mushrooms. Knowing the Wirral

Denizens better day by day, nevertheless he knew
only that they were changeable, as likely to mock
him as greet him. Or as likely to harm him as
help, he deemed. If Blake had bespoken them
fair, perhaps he would be alive and Roddarc dead.
Perhaps they would have aided him instead of
Chance. None of this would Roddarc have believed had Chance told him, so Chance told him
nothing of it, though he disliked having even so
small a secret from his lifelong friend.

Halimeda's secret was the heavier one. . . . She
was pale and silent whenever he saw her, and
there were whispers among the people; what ailed
her? But her secret would not keep much longer.
It was blossoming in her, as spring blossomed into
summer.

When the dancers in the starlight ring began to
pair off into couples and slip away amongst the
ferns, Chance rose and took his leave. He smiled
wryly, walking back to his lodge. No lover awaited
him there, but Wirral would grow lush this year.

Roddarc sat waiting in the lodge when Chance
came in.

"Are you a werewolf," he asked sharply, "that
you have taken to roving under the moon?"

"Have I bitten you?" Chance retorted. He lighted
a lantern and looked at Roddarc, then sat down
with him by the cold hearth.

"What is it?" he asked.

"What is what?" Roddarc snapped.

It was the chilling anger in him that Chance

meant, anger such as he had never seen in his friend. But he did not say so. "What you came to tell me," he said instead.

"Halimeda." Roddarc hurled the name out as if it were a curse. "She is with child."

Chance stared. Perhaps Roddarc took the stare for shock. It was shock indeed, but at the lord's rage, not at the tidings.

"I looked at her today," Roddarc went on with a terrible fury, terrible because so cold and controlled, "and I saw the swelling of her belly. It is just beginning, but I knew. So I made her tell me the truth of it, and name a name, and I did not take tears for an answer."

So there had been shouting, ugliness. And Halimeda was disgraced. Chance felt ill at the thought.

"You must have guessed some of it before now," he said stupidly.

"Of course I guessed. What sort of fool does she take me for? She goes about all ribbons and smiles before Gallowstree Lea, and then she turns into a wraith afterwards; how am I not to guess? I knew she was lured there. And who would her lover be but that calf-faced, honey-tongued Blake."

"Whom she tried to kill for your sake."

"She tried to kill him because he had betrayed her," Roddarc said coldly, "using her as bait to bring me to him. If he had confided in her, belike she would as readily have killed me."

"Rod! You cannot believe that!" Chance spoke with a force that gave Roddarc a moment's pause.

"What am I to believe?"

"All good. She is ardent, innocent, betrayed. She has suffered. She came to your aid, and stood by you bravely while you exacted a lord's vengeance on a traitor."

"If she is so brave," said the lord in cutting tones, "then why did she not brave my ears and my presence with some words of truth?"

"She was afraid of hurting you. I'll warrant she thought to spare you pain as long as she could."

"Spare me pain?" Roddarc laughed harshly. "As if it were no pain to wonder! I guessed from the first, and my heart went out to her, and I wanted nothing more than that she should confide in me. More than once I asked her in all gentleness what was wrong, and she would make no reply, only look at me and weep. After a while I grew annoyed with weeping."

Chance said nothing. He knew Roddarc, or so he thought. Heartfelt gentleness was painful for the lord to sustain; annoyance, far easier. But perhaps, after he had vented his spleen, gentleness would return.

"If only she had spoken with me," Roddarc railed, "trusted me, I could have forgiven her. Even though her foolishness means the disgrace of us both. But she was afraid to tell me. Afraid! I, who do not practice torture even on felons and traitors, what was I likely to do to her? I, who do not use the lash even on my horses and dogs?"

"Lady Halimeda is no coward," Chance protested, but Roddarc seemed not to hear him.

"Child and youth, when I had done wrong I had to stand before my father and endure his wrath—"

"Which was visited on my body!"

So that the lord need feel no constraint. It was a wonder, Chance thought, that he had not been killed entirely. A hard edge of anger nudged somewhere inside him, edge which had never been there before, or not for more years than he could number on the fingers of both hands. And without clearly knowing why, he began to remember things he had not thought of since he had been a man.

Starting with the day Roddarc had scanted his courtesy before his lordly father's seat of honor.

Not so great an offense, merely a stripling's newfound arrogance. The two lads, Rod and Chance, had just turned thirteen. But it was not in Riol to humor anyone's arrogance but his own. Not even that of a stripling, not even his noble son. His face flushed bloody red with rage, and he darted out a long hand and snatched Chance by the arm as he made his own proper obeisance, jerking him forward and landing a blow on his head that sent him sprawling, all within the moment.

"Again!" he thundered at Roddarc.

Roddarc was very thin at that age. His limbs looked as if they might be broken by two fingers of his warrior father's heavy hand. But there was a look on his fine-boned face as of something that refused to be broken. He made a sweeping parody of a courtly bow.

"Strip!" Riol roared at Chance, tapping at the tops of his high leathern boots with the whip that was always in his hand.

Strip, before all those present in the great hall.

But it was not so uncommon an occurrence, and Chance stolidly did as he was told. To do otherwise was unthinkable. Powers of hell only knew what his punishment would have been if he, himself, had ever scanted a bow. But looking back, with a flare of fury and anguish he wondered if little Halimeda had been there to see his humiliation. Belike not. Belike she was yet too young to eat in the great hall, or a nurse had taken her away so that she would not be frightened. Though he seemed to remember a child's crying. . . .

Riol had lifted the whip, a sort of rod covered with knotted leather, meant for the disciplining of hounds. With it he had commenced to scourge Chance's legs and buttocks.

This, also, was an occurrence all too common. Riol was easily angered, no matter how Roddarc tried to please him. Eyes narrowed with pain, Chance stole a glance at his foster brother's face, expecting the more inward, bittersweet pain that sustained him through these times. Roddarc would be starting to weep. In a moment, he would begin to plead with his father for Chance's sake. It would take much pleading to satisfy Riol, much begging before the flogging would be ended. But for days thereafter Roddarc would do whatever his father wished. . . .

The young lord's face was hard and dry.

"Bow," Riol commanded his son.

Roddarc stood without moving, jaw set, chin raised at a stubborn angle.

"Bow!" Riol roared, and he beat Chance with such fury that blood burst from the boy's mouth

and nose; he would have fallen if it were not that
the lord's hard hand held him up. His eyes, blinded
by pain and tears, could no longer seek Roddarc's.

"Lash all you like," he heard the young lord
coldly say. "Chance is a commoner and a bastard.
He deserves whipping."

"Aaaa!" Chance panted suddenly aloud in a new
experience of pain. He could not have said which
hurt him more, Riol's rage with the whip or
Roddarc's betrayal. Though of course Rod could
not mean it—

"Is that so?" the lord queried in a soft voice, far
too soft for comfort. "Chance deserves punishment?"

"Certainly. He is a commoner, and we of the
blood do with commoners what we like. Do we
not?"

"Truly? You flog him, then." Riol stilled his
whip long enough to offer it to Rod. Not an offer,
but a command. . . . Knuckling his eyes so that he
could see, Chance looked at his friend. With an
angry, arrogant smile, Rod was shaking his head.

"But I choose not to. And what will you do to
me, my father? Turn the lash on me?"

With a wordless roar of fury Riol struck Chance
across the face. Only the boy's raised hands saved
his eyes from the rod.

"Go ahead. Kill him," said Roddarc. "And who
will you beat then?"

Riol spun the whipping boy around and struck
him with the rod featly across his cock, bending
him double with agony. His head swaying above
the floor, Chance felt that his world had spun
upside down. Rod, condemning him?

"Cut it off," Roddarc said. "I don't care."

Riol straightened Chance with a blow of his heavy fist, then struck again with the rod.

"You are a filthy tyrant," said Roddarc with something of heat, more of disgust, and nothing, nothing at all, of heart.

Even in his agony Chance felt the lord's shock, the sudden silence, the rod hovering, stilled. "What did you say?" Riol inquired through clenched teeth.

"You heard me," said Roddarc with a weird calm. "A filthy, bloody tyrant. All goodly folk hate you."

Riol flung Chance to the floor and started to laugh, yell after yell of comfortless laughter. "Very truth, very truth!" he shouted amidst his laughter. "And someday you will be another."

It was over. No thanks to Roddarc, and not because the lord was merciful, either. Merely because he was amused. Lying half drowning in his own blood, slipping away into a swoon, Chance heard the yells of laughter, the lord's tipsy shouts. "Tyrant, is it? And someday you will be one, just like me."

Servants carried him away after the lord's back was turned, tended to him hastily and heaved him into his bed. He knew nothing until he awoke groaning in the dark of night.

"Stop your whimpering." Roddarc's voice sounded irritably across the chamber they shared. "Let me sleep."

"You swine," Chance breathed. "Every part of me is on fire. Do you not care—"

"Hold your tongue," Roddarc commanded more coldly, "or I will thrash you myself."

From mere pride Chance kept silence. He would not have Roddarc hear him weeping.

Later he understood, in a dim way, how Roddarc had needed to free himself from the trap formed by his own noble birth and the happenstance of his loving Chance. But at the time, the pain of the flogging had seemed as nothing compared to his heartache.

He lay in his bed for days, past the time when he could have been up and about, for all parts of him were healing cleanly. No one troubled him. Let the lad sulk; there were events afoot. Lord Riol was going off to war.

The war from which he never returned, all good powers be praised. And after he was gone, Chance and Roddarc had drifted gradually back into their former, brotherly ways. No lasting harm had come to Chance from the flogging, except a quietly continuing pain of spirit. For there had been no apology from Roddarc, nothing said between them of trust betrayed. No need for words, Chance had told himself. Forgive and forget. Better truth was that he was too needful to risk a quarrel with Roddarc. The young lord's regard was all he had. The young tyrant. . . .

"I still bear the scars," he said angrily. The old, buried dagger-blade of anger, all but forgotten, edging up in him, after all the years; why? Roddarc's ice-pale face before his eyes.

"You think it is the easier lot," the lord said, "to stand by and let a—a brother be beaten? You will scoff, Chance, but it may have been almost—harder for me."

Long habit is not easily broken. Chance did not quarrel.

"Yes," he said, "there are punishments worse than blows." How well he knew it. "And my lady knows it as well as you and I. If she fears, it is not for her body."

"She knows full well I will never lay a finger on her to hurt her," Roddarc said stiffly. "I did not touch her even today to wrest the story from her." He stood up, his face stony. "But by all the powers, it will be many a long day before she sees my smile."

Chance stood up as well, trying to pierce that locked gaze with his own. "You're no gentle lord, then," he said. "Blows would be kinder."

But Roddarc only gave him a black look and strode out.

He will be over it in a few days, Chance thought, or hoped, for he had no basis for thinking so. And at the back of his mind he seemed to hear still the yelling of dead Riol's laughter.

As summer warmed into high summer he learned what Halimeda had somehow feared but he, Chance, had never admitted: that Roddarc was capable of an icy and relentless wrath day in, day out, sustaining it and feeding it as he had never been able to nurture tenderness. And even though his demands were the same as they had ever been and his rulings in the court of law not unjust, all his people felt his mood and began to mutter under it.

Every ten of days Chance went to see Halimeda. At first he found it hard to find excuses. Business had never brought him much within the fortress. Later, he simply went, not caring for sly looks or whispered comments, taking blackberries, a delicate flower found beneath the Wirral shade, a drinking noggin carved and polished out of oaken whorl.

Halimeda needed none of these things, for she was a lady and had all she could want of baubles and good food, clothing and the gardens for roaming. But as her belly swelled with child, Chance sensed she needed his visits for nurture food could not give her. Though, truly, she was strong: all through the summer and early autumn, strong in body and steady in spirit, "bearing up well," as the gossips would have it. With awesome strength, for one so slender, so young, so defenseless, Chance thought.

"Does my brother come to see you still?" she asked him when summer was hot and golden before autumn.

"From time to time, yes." *Fleeing his own wrath*, Chance thought.

"Maybe there is still hope, then, if there is that much heart in him. I—sometimes I think he will never be a brother to me again."

"He provides for you," Chance said awkwardly, meaning, *love underlies the silence*. But Halimeda only pulled a face.

"Yes, he checks on me as he might on a well-bred bitch in whelp, cursing me with his concern. He speaks to the servants, not to me." She shrugged, dismissing the matter as out of her control.

"He speaks of you from time to time," Chance added after a moment.

"None too kindly, I am sure," said Halimeda with bitter amusement, and Chance could only keep silence.

He sometimes took issue with Roddarc for Halimeda's sake, but not too strongly, hoping to do more good if Roddarc continued to think of him as a friend. Moreover, he was afraid to speak ardently of Halimeda. Afraid of what Roddarc might see in his eyes.

By harvest time, the lady had grown as round as the fruits of the vines, a very emblem of the full lofts. Those golden days were darkened for Chance. A fear was growing in him as the babe grew in the lady, and one evening when the smell of frost hung in the air he spoke plainly to Roddarc.

"It is time for you to give over this wrath," he said.

"Give over?" The lord glanced up, his look chill even in the warm light of the hearthfire.

"Yes. I know well enough that you love your sister, Rod. You cannot keep on this flinty shell forever. Suppose she dies in the birthing of the child?"

Chance felt his voice falter, speaking of that fear. But Roddarc's hard stare did not change. Chance plunged on.

"She is very young, very slender, it is not unlikely. How will you feel if she dies and you have not made your peace with her?"

"As I feel now," Roddarc stated. "That it would be her own foolish fault, for dallying."

"You cannot mean that!" Chance whispered, shocked and vehement. No use, any longer, trying to hide his vehemence.

"I do mean it," the lord said, all too evenly. "No one made her conceive a child. It is not as if she were wed."

"Roddarc of Wirralmark," Chance shouted at him, "for whatever goes wrong, the blame will be on your head if you send her to childbed grieving!"

"Is it not fitting," the lord said with icy calm, "that a sorrow child should be born amid tears?"

"Does it mean nothing to you that she is your beloved sister?" Chance was on his feet now, raging. "Lord Roddarc, you are blind, locked like a felon in a dungeon of your own digging, as bad as your father Riol at his very worst, for all that you give yourself airs of kindness!"

That stung. "Speak not to me of Riol," Roddarc snapped, and the lash of the words brought him to his feet in his turn.

"I will speak what you need to hear! My lady Halimeda was wise not to confide in you. She knew that you can be as cruel as any tyrant who ever wielded—"

"Speak no more to me of that wench!" Roddarc thundered. "What, are you besotted with her?"

"You pledged me once to protect her!" Chance shouted back just as fiercely. "With my life I was to shield her! What, am I to desert her now for the

sake of your ill humor? Is she worth less than she
was before?"

"She is worth nothing!"

"She is worthy of all love," Chance whispered.
But the lord did not hear him, ranting on.

"What man of rank would have her? There is no
noble in the land who will take such a sullied
bride, be her dower far richer than I can afford.
Once I had thought there would be perhaps a
prince for her, but now—"

"I would take her in an instant," Chance said
softly, and this time Roddarc heard him.

For the space of three breaths there was utter
silence. Eyes met in a complicated communication; memory was part of it, memory of a time ten
years and more before, of a battlefield. Pain for
Roddarc in that memory, and pain angered him.

Lord Roddarc spoke.

"How very fitting, how suitable for her. You, a
commoner, a bastard, and a castrate."

Chance stood as if frozen, unable even to breathe.
When he drew breath and moved, it was to stride
across his small home and fling open the door.

"Get out," he said.

"I will go when I please."

"It is not fitting that a lord should come so
familiarly to the home of a commoner. Out!"

Roddarc shrugged and ambled out with apparent indifference.

The next time he went to see Halimeda, Chance
found that he was no longer to be admitted to her
presence. Nor did Roddarc come any more to his
warden's lodge.

*   *   *

Autumn waned toward winter. Chill winds and rains tore the leaves from the trees until only a few remained, hanging in dark tatters, like rags.

The Denizens seemed not to mind the cold any more than the bare trees of Wirral did. They wore no more clothing than they had in the heat of summer, nothing more than their barklike skins.

Making his rounds of the forest one day, Chance went back to the same lightning-hollowed oak where he had first spoken with a small brown man. There he paused, feeling diffident, for he had been mocked and snubbed by the small folk often enough. He stood gathering courage until he heard a birdlike giggle within the blackened hollow.

"Little one there in the tree," he whispered, "come out, please, and speak with me."

A face popped into view. But as the body followed it, Chance saw that it was a female he had summoned this time. Her jutting breasts and pudenda were no less daunting than the cock of her male counterpart had been. More so, to Chance.

She saw as much, and grinned at him. Her narrow, bony face yet had a broad and sensual mouth. Chance forced himself to look not at that mouth, nor at the handspan height of the rest of her, but at her eyes, both merry and haunted, as he spoke.

"Have you any tidings—I mean—know you anything of the Lady Halimeda?"

The Denizen grinned more broadly but answered

him directly enough. "We have seen her walking in Gallowstree Lea."

"Lately?"

"Yestereen."

"Alone?" Chance exclaimed. With her time so near, Halimeda ought to have been sequestered in her chambers. It was not right or usual that she should have been wandering so far into Wirral.

"Lone, lone, all alone, under the bloated moon."

Chance frowned uneasily. "No tidings more?"

"We stay in Wirral, we. Nothing more."

Chance slept restlessly that night, half waking. The wind was high and whined even through the stone walls of his lodge. Moonlight shone in through his single window, and tossing trees seen against that white luminous mushroom made him moan, dreaming first of flailing rods, then of the revels of the Denizens. Clouds torn into dark tatters by the wind passed across the face of the bloated moon, casting shadows that crawled eerily in his floor. A skein of wild geese flew somewhere in the dark, their cries like the yelping of the hounds of hell.

Other cries, singsong cries, on the wind with the piping of the geese.

"Lady, Lady Halimeda,
Lone, alone, under the moon,
Lady, Lady Halimeda,
Lone, alone, under the moon,
Left the fortress, left her home,
Lady Dreaming-Of-The-Sea,
Bound for Gallowstree Lea—"

Chance sat bolt upright. The voices were real.

"Bound for Gallowstree Lea!"

Chance sprang up, pulling on trousers and boots in a panic, not pausing for further clothing. At a dead run he sped through the windy, shadowy Wirral.

Gallowstree Lea was swept with stormwind, cloud gloom and shifting moonglades. In the trickster light Chance could not at first comprehend the dark, billowing shape by the lone tree that groaned aloud in the night. Then he saw. It was Halimeda, round with child, all robed in black, with the black cloth whipping about her, Halimeda standing on a waist-high boulder under the boughs of the gallows tree—

For a heart-sickening moment Chance thought that already the loop clung around her neck, that she had only to jump and she would be swinging, strangling. Then he saw that she was still tying the rope. She was having difficulty in securing it. The storm had delayed her.

He was heartsick still, that she stood there so desperate.

Possessed by her own desperation, she did not see him until he stood panting before her. Then she screamed with fury.

"Chance, no! Let me be! I—"

He lifted her down and led her away, an arm around her shoulders. She went with him unresisting, though she was still crying aloud.

"I cannot stand it any longer! He hates me! He glares at me with a curse in his eyes."

Her shoulders sagged, and she started to weep.

Blinded by her own tears she walked, and Chance led her to his lodge, as it was the closest dwelling.

He sat her by his hearth, put fragrant apple wood on the fire, drew water and set it to boil for hot herb tea to soothe her. She looked up at him. Her face was white, drawn down by grief, ravaged by tears, her hair hanging down her forehead in strings.

"There is nothing for me any more," she told him with deathly calm, "for my babe, nothing. No hope."

"Hali, please." He had not called her by the pet name since she was a tiny girl, but that night it burst from him. "Do not say that!"

"How am I not to say what is but simple truth? What is there for me but to be a whore, and my baby a whore's brat? Unless I die—"

"Hali, no!" He knelt before her, his shoulders broad and bare in the firelight, reached up to touch her face, as if his touch could somehow heal her of tears. It did not.

"Far better that I should die. I am a blot, all goodly folk scorn me. My own brother hates me—"

"I love you," Chance whispered, his face upraised and his eyes meeting her eyes.

Her face grew very still, and she looked back at him as if she were seeing him for the first time.

"That was not spoken as my brother's warden," she said slowly after a moment, in a hushed voice.

"No." Chance swallowed, and shame tugged at his face, but still he met her eyes. "And it should not have been spoken, for it is unseemly, except that—it is truth, Lady, and something you needed to hear, tonight."

"You—love—me?"

The tremor in her voice smote him to the heart.

"How not?" he said. "Hali, you are of all maidens most beautiful, most brave, most—most dreaming. What man can see you and not love you? And you are wrong, Lady." His voice grew stronger and yet warmer. "There will be a worthy lover for you someday, after these dark days are behind you. A noble lover, I feel sure of it."

"You call yourself unworthy?" Halimeda's voice also grew stronger, and with her own hands she reached up and brushed away her tears.

"I, a commoner and a bastard?" He laughed briefly, harshly. "Yes, manifestly unworthy. I am a fool to speak."

"No fool. I know better." Halimeda was looking at him thoughtfully, desperation turning into a bold thought, and Chance saw. In a few moments, he knew, his heart would break—for still he must speak truth.

"Hali, I have—nothing to give you."

"No name, you mean, for the babe? No family? But already I am bereft of those. I came here with nothing, and you have offered me a commoner's love. It is that much more." She spoke not warmly, but in a settled, collected way. "Perhaps, in time, I could learn to return it."

Looking up at her, hope dawning in her gaze, he faced at last the agony that for years he had held at arm's length. He sobbed, bent as if by a blow, hiding his face behind his hands.

"Chance, what is it?" Halimeda drew him toward her, letting his head and shoulders lie in her lap, against the warm curve of her pregnant belly, as he choked on pain. "My life's friend, what is wrong?"

He stopped struggling and found the calm in the vortex of the pain, looked up at her.

"I have—nothing to give you, Hali."

Scarcely comprehending, unwilling to comprehend, yet she began to understand, and her face grew very still. She did not speak. He got up, found a shirt and put it on, made the tea, gave her some and himself some as well. Sitting near her by the hearth, he told her the tale.

"It happened the day of our victory in the long war. Roddarc and I fought side by side always, and he in the fore, as befits a lord's son. And he is a splendid warrior, I was proud and joyous to stand by him. And many a time had he taken a spear on his shield. But this one time of those many times, he erred somehow, and instead of deflecting the spear harmlessly he let it slip down and to the side, and it struck me featly in the groin."

He had never spoken of that day, not to anyone, and it was as though he felt again the blow; he shuddered and winced. But the lady's steady eyes were on him, and he went on.

"We fought on, both of us. We had to, or be killed. Luckily the battle was nearly over before I weakened. . . . Roddarc carried me to safety, and laid me down and tore open the clothing to bandage the wound. And when he saw what had been done to me, he wept. When I awoke, the next day, he was still weeping."

"How—how horrible," Halimeda whispered.

"He never told you?"

"No!"

"I think—he does not speak of it, any more than I do. I think— my lady, he has never said this to me, but it may be why he has never wed. So that he would not enjoy what I could not. He is—he is all bound up in honor and loyalty; he would think in that way. And he was a merry enough wencher before it happened. We both were."

Halimeda grimaced at him. "Did you make yourselves babes in the wenches?"

"We may have. I know Roddarc did." *And his punishment, as usual, was visited on me.* The thought, new to him, took his breath away, until he saw the look the lady was giving him. "No, it is not right," he told her.

"Or fair," she said hotly. "Men share the pleasure and escape the blame."

"It was a long time ago. We were young fools. And—Halimeda, do you think it may be part of Roddarc's spleen now, that you have enjoyed lovemaking. . . ."

She flushed and glanced down at her hands. Impulsively Chance reached over and touched her hair, straightening the straggling locks.

"I don't know when I began dreaming of you," he said softly. "Years ago. It happened stealthily. . . . And, you see, it did not matter to me that you were unattainable."

"I must think," she muttered, still staring at her hands.

"Take note, my lady, you are not so willing to hurl yourself away after all."

She looked up at him with a small, shamed smile, and he nodded.

"Truly, there will be someone better for you. Your case is not so desperate that you must settle for a bastard commoner with no manhead. Life's course is full of strange quirks and turns. You are so lovely, there must yet be a worthy lover for you. I cannot believe otherwise."

"Chance," she said slowly, "I am all in confusion. You have made me see outside myself, and it is a comfort, but strange."

"Then go home, bear your child, wait. It will come clear. Only, Hali. . . ." One last time he permitted himself that love-name, and he looked at her in plea. "Think no longer of Gallowstree Lea."

She gave him her hand for a moment. That was her pledge.

On a day when bone-chilling drizzle fell from a gray sky, Chance paused along a deer trail in the Wirral to relieve himself against an oak—a thing he had done often enough before, forsooth. But this time he had no more than undone the lacing of his trousers and parted the fabric when a trilling laugh sounded, to be echoed from several directions.

"No nuts, and only half a stem!" a fey voice sang. "Chance, don't you miss them?"

Chance scowled and started to cover himself, then considered that it would be worse to be pursued elsewhere. He emptied his bladder, and as he did so the Denizen who had accosted him strutted into view. It was one of the tough-breasted females, to his chagrin, and he flushed deeply. The woodswoman laughed again.

"Chance, it is a wonder they call you man!"

He closed his trousers, fumbling with the laces in his haste, and burbling laughter sounded from all around. Then a small brown form shot through the air and landed like a squirrel beside the other. It was the Denizen Chance had first bespoken, the handsome russet-colored young prince of them all.

"Pay no mind, Chance," he said. "Fate is unkind."

"And you, I suppose, are kinder," Chance retorted sourly.

"Indeed so! Listen, and you shall know." The young Denizen paused for effect, and crouched down on his bough in a manner as of a conspirator. "In the midst of Wirral," he said in a lowered voice, "in the very fundament of it, stands a tree which bears nuts such as those you lack."

Chance snorted aloud. "You must take me for an ass," he said.

"You doubt it? When Wirral grows thick as grass?"

Chance scowled; they were rhyming with him, now. "What of it," he said curtly, "if there is such a tree?" For he did not know all that lay in the penetralia of Wirral; no one did. Stranger things than what the Denizen named might be there.

"What of it? Chance!" The Denizen prince seemed aghast. Still standing beside him, the female took up the tale.

"Just do as we say—"

Other voices joined in.

"Pluck the nuts from that bole,"

"And you will be whole,"

"And join the dance within the day!"

"Bah!" Chance exploded, but he did not turn away. If the small folk were bejaping him, they had judged nicely as to their bait. He could not turn away, not while there was even the fool's chance that they were speaking truth. In no mindly sense did he believe them, but he had heard tales of these folk, their many powers. He had to risk. . . .

"Danger?" he demanded.

The Denizen prince stood up, stiffly erect, cock jutting. "Some small peril," he admitted. "Do you care for that?" Glint of his amber eyes gave the dare to Chance.

"Bah!" Chance sputtered again. "Which way?"

Instead of replying, the copper-colored Denizen turned to the surrounding forest. "What say ye?" he cried. "Shall we guide him thither?"

Blast the cock-proud rascal, Chance fumed, *he'll have me begging next for my chance to be gulled*.

The cry went up from all around.

"Away, say we!"

"To the cullion-nut tree!"

"Whither, thence! Hither, hence!" the Denizen prince shouted crazily, and he vanished as handily as a squirrel, within an eyeblink. A birdlike laugh sounded somewhere, and then there was silence. Chance lurched forward.

"Where are you?" he shouted, trying to keep the fury out of his voice. Be cursed the lot of them, truly they would have him begging! For what folly? A ball tree!

"Here!" came a teasing voice from somewhere far ahead.

"This way!" another cried gaily from a somewhat different direction. "With a dildo hey! Away, we say!"

Panting with anger even before he began, Chance ran toward the voices.

"Full merrily away say we!"

And indeed they led him a merry chase through the drizzling rain. Tearing through bracken and stumbling through stones, up scarp and down dingle, into thorn thickets that pierced him even through his leathern clothing, that would have liked to have taken his eyes. The Denizens, he decided, must have some plan for him after all, for they slowed their pace to wait for him. But as soon as he stumbled out of his difficulties they were off again as wildly as ever, and he must needs trail after, with no breath left even to curse.

"Chance Lord's man, he ran and ran . . ."

Already they were making a song of it. They would be amusing themselves with the tale, Chance deemed, for the winter's span, perhaps longer. No matter, for he had to know the end of the story. He ran through the waning day until the gray sky darkened into dusk. No matter, again. There was no loved one waiting by his cold hearth.

He splashed into fen. No matter, still; already he was wet to the skin. Though never before, even in Wirral, had he met with such a bog. Thick mud oozed up to his thighs, almost up to his crotch, slowing him to snail's pace.

"How much farther?" he called into the dusk.

A babble of laughter sounded instead of an answer, and Chance stiffened: something large was
bestirring the fen, rising luminous into the dusk.

The laughter of the denizens rippled and warbled from the forest all around. There must have
been hundreds of them watching, as dense as a
flock of starlings.

And Chance shouted with terror, falling back
into the muck.

Looming over him, a sort of a snake of single
eye, a dragon—but no, the thing was too stubby to
be called a snake, too formless and squalid for a
dragon. More like a huge worm or a maggot,
fungus-colored, with the glistening soft skin of a
catfish. Slimy fen water dripped down from it, and
the single eye deepset in the center of its head
peered toward him.

Chance floundered back from it, thrashing for
balance and footing, and the Denizens shook the
small tree limbs with their laughter. Gleeful voices
shouted.

"Don't hurt it, Chance!"

"It only wants to dance!"

"Wirralworm, we call it!"

Above them all the voice of the young prince
carried.

"Chance, there is no cullion tree. But see, we've
found a phallus for ye!"

If I had a sword, he thought grimly, *if I had a
nobleman's weapon.* . . . But what would be the
use, indeed, of doing battle with the nodding monster? It had not moved from its place amidst the
muck, and even as he crawled at last onto solid

ground and stood, streaming bogwater and greenish slime, to face it, the thing went limp and
collapsed beneath the surface. There was a faint
glow as of something rotten, and it was gone.

"But it's always there," said a voice close by his
ear, "hidden deep yet not asleep. Just like the
manhood in you, Chance."

He turned, sluggish with disgust, to face the
copper-brown prince of the Denizens, barely visible in the nightfall darkness.

"Very well," said Chance, "you've had your play.
Now which way to my home?"

The handspan youth chuckled in delight at the
happenstance rhyme. "The sun will show you the
way, come day," he sang. "Sleep well!" Within the
moment he and all the others were gone. Their
laughing farewells echoed away into the Wirral.

Chance did not wait for day. He blundered off,
on the move to keep his chilled blood from pool-
ing in his veins, and roamed all night though he
could see nothing beneath cloud gloom that shut
out the moon and stars. He did not mind the
darkness; it matched his wakeful rage.

Halimeda's babe was born as the first snow fell
thick and cold on turrets and trees. It was a girl. A
hard labor, but the lady would be well enough
after a ten of days, if she did not weaken with
fever. This much Chance learned from the talk of
the alehouse—he went often to the alehouse, those
days, and made friend with those who muttered
there in the evenings after a day of wearisome toil
in the lord's service. He inquired of Halimeda also

from Roddarc's steward, to whom he made his reports. The lord himself he had not seen since the night he had ordered Roddarc out of his lodge. Nor was Chance admitted to see Halimeda.

The talk had it, after several days, that she was on the mend and the infant thriving. But the tenth day came and passed, and there was no courtly gathering, no ceremony of welcome for the little one, no bestowal of a name.

Near Chance's cottage lay a broad, hollow log of apple, the most auspicious of woods. When that day had passed he worked the evening by lantern light and cut a section of it, took it in by his hearth. There in days that followed he cleaned and shaped it, polished it with wax, fitted ends to it, and rockers.

Snow after snow fell. The Wirral stood shrouded, white and cold.

"Any tidings?" Chance asked of a tree one day.

A small, cross face looked out at him. "We have said we will tell you, Chance Lord's Man."

He believed them in this, for he considered that they might be inclined toward kindness since the affair of the fen. For a time.

"But someday—" the Denizen grumbled.

"I will pay," Chance finished impatiently. The small woodsman scowled at him.

"Think not, fool, that you can pull from one of us a thorn. We take care of our own."

"Just tell me quickly when she comes."

As it chanced, he saw her himself and needed no telling. Barefoot in the deep snow she came, in the pale winter's daylight, slowly walking, gowned in black, carrying the baby in her arms. So as not to be seen from the fortress, he let her come well within the shelter of the trees before he met her.

"Chance!" she gasped, then burst out at once with her trouble. "He has said I must leave the little one here in the Wirral!"

"I know. So it would have been done to me if your kind lady mother had not taken me to the keep." Easily, as if he had done nothing in his life but handle children, he reached out and took the babe. "Now the little lady of Wirralmark comes to me."

"But Chance—oh, I am filled with hope, but how will you care for her? How will you feed her?"

"I will find a woman to nurse her. I will cherish her, my lady."

Halimeda's eyes filled, and she touched one of his weathered hands.

"How is Roddarc?" he asked her gruffly.

"Much the same." She sounded more weary than bitter, but then her eyes widened with fright. "He will learn that you have sheltered the babe, he will punish you for it!"

"He will learn," Chance agreed, "but I think he will not trouble me. There has to be shame in him, or he would have killed the child outright."

The infant in his arms stirred and began to wail.

"Go back quickly, Lady, before you freeze," Chance urged. "Only tell me, what is this pretty one's name."

"I have called her Sorrow."

"She is worthy of better than that, Halimeda!"

The lady hesitated only for a moment. "Call her Iantha," she said softly, and she touched the babe's petalsoft cheek, kissed her on the forehead, glanced once at Chance and turned away, running.

Iantha. The name meant "Violet."

Chance hurried her to his lodge, and the babe howled loud with hunger.

He satisfied her with a sugar-teat and the rocking of the cradle until after dark. Then he carried her to the village huts that huddled beneath the fortress wall. But he had misjudged, thinking his fellow commoners would be as brave as he. Not a woman of them would take the infant to nurse, or a man permit it, for fear of the lord's wrath.

By the end of the next day Chance knew that Iantha was starving. She could not hold down the milk of cows or goats, or even that of mares. Her wailing grew weaker, mewling and piteous.

Frantic, Chance bundled the baby warmly and began to stride through Wirral toward the distant demesne of a neighboring lord. He would be a renegade to Roddarc thenceforth. He had thought it would be a while yet before that happened; Iantha was upsetting his half-formed plans. But he could not let Halimeda's daughter die. . . .

"We will feed her, Chance Love-Child!" a voice piped from the beech tree at his elbow.

Chance stopped short, but he looked doubtfully at the twiggy female Denizen who had spoken. Great-breasted she might be for her size, but the whole of her was no more than half the length of the infant, and maybe a quarter the mass.

"How?" he demanded, and the woodswoman

gave him a dark smile. She was greenish gray as
well as brown, with hair that hung in airy tendrils
like liana, and Chance realized suddenly that her
tough, narrow face was both grotesque and beautiful.

"Simply, as the sap rises in the tree. Take me
up in your hand."

He did so, conscious of his own daring—he had
never touched a Denizen, and he found this one
dry, cool and pleasantly hard, almost like a lizard.
He held her beside the baby's head, and she gave
the breast. Her entire dug fit into the infant's mouth.

For a moment Iantha did not respond. Then she
began to suck greedily, and she sucked at length.

"Is she being nourished?" Chance asked doubtfully.

"Does earth nourish yonder beech?" the small
woman retorted. "Open her mouth; I must change
breasts."

Chance pried apart the infant's lips with a fingertip, and Iantha bellowed angrily, a strong sound
that was good to hear. Sucking on the second
breast, she fell warmly asleep. Chance took the
Denizen and set her back in the tree.

"Many thanks," he said, hoping thanks were
warranted, for he felt a stirring of misgiving even
as he spoke. The woodswoman did not speak to
the thanks. She seemed exhausted.

"Take the babe back to your dwelling," she said,
"and we will tend her." She turned, slipped away,
and Chance did as she had said.

When Iantha woke and cried, some hours later,
another great-breasted Denizen slipped down

through a gap in the eaves, between rafter and thatch, climbed nimbly down the stones of the wall and gave the breast to the babe in the applewood cradle.

So it went for the space of many snows. A different woodswoman came each time; Chance never saw the same one twice, to his knowledge. Nor were his nursemaid visitors ever the lovely dancers he had seen, the ones shaped like the most lissome of human damsels, but always the bark-brown, twiggy-limbed females. The others would be too delicate, Chance decided, their breasts too small and fine. But he would not have minded seeing one of them again. They were in their way nearly as beautiful as Halimeda.

Of the lady, he heard nothing. She kept to the fortress. Presumably, she yet lived.

Sometimes he carried little Iantha with him as he made the rounds of the Wirral or went to speak with certain folk he met within the forest for secrecy's sake. Sometimes he left her sleeping in his lodge, and the Denizens cared for her. Often he shirked his duties, but he always turned in a semblance of a report. In the evenings, and often during the day as well, he would hold baby Iantha in his arms and lull her and hum to her in his husky voice. No one from the fortress troubled him; if it was known that he harbored the babe, nothing was said of it.

By the time the snowmelt came, Iantha was drinking cow's milk and eating mush, and the Denizens no longer came to her.

* * *

Spring warmed. In Wirral glades the violets were blooming.

One day of soft rain, as Chance stirred porridge and rocked the little one in her cradle, his door opened and Roddarc strode in. By his side walked Halimeda, more lovely than the violets, robed in a dress of amethyst velvet, her hair looped up in braids plaited with thread of gold.

If Roddarc had come alone, Chance would have challenged him. But as it was, he simply stood and stared at Halimeda, porridge dripping from the spoon in his hand. The lady seemed well, her bearing grave but quiet, as if she had settled something within herself. She stood gazing at her daughter, and her smile shifted Chance's glance there also. Roddarc knelt on one knee by the cradle, putting his finger into the infant's tiny fist.

When his eyes came up to meet Chance's stare, his look was full of shame. "Ten thousand thanks," he said in a low voice.

Halimeda came with a rustle of velvet, as if she could not longer restrain herself, gathered baby Iantha up and cuddled her, conversing with her in the private way of mothers. Roddarc stood up, and Chance scowled at him, more than a little uncomfortable.

"Do you want me to go away?" Roddarc asked him.

Chance kept silence, undecided what to do. The lord's diffident manner both touched and annoyed him.

"I have hurt you," Roddarc said, speaking awkwardly, "and I have hurt Halimeda more. So much, both of you, that I doubt if I can ever make amends. But I want you to know—I am sorry."

Chance flung the spoon into the porridge pot. "Gaaah! Sit down," he growled, not wanting to hear any more. "What woke you out of it when all my shouting could not?"

"My own misery." Roddarc sat. "But it is a hard thing to face. . . . Chance, I am more like my father than I knew. My methods differ, but the venom is the same."

"It served him well," Chance said curtly. *Powers, can we make this limp worm into a man again?*

"In the long war, you mean? Then I am worse than Riol. He turned his poison against his enemies, but I vented all of mine on my sister and my own true friend."

"Gaaah!" Chance exploded again. "Be done!"

"There are things that need to be said. I know I still have your loyalty, Chance, but I know I cannot expect—"

I should say not. Though you do.

Roddarc swallowed. "I cannot expect your friendship. I cannot blame you if you hold it against me, what I have said, what I have done."

Chance looked over toward Halimeda, where she whispered to her baby, swirling about the room and rocking the little one to the imagined melody of a carrole. "Does your lady sister hold it against you?"

"Halimeda is more noble than I can comprehend."

Chance wondered, but he could not disagree.

With a grunt he sat down across from Roddarc at the hearth.

"If you can forgive me," the lord said to him, "it will be blessing far more than I deserve."

"Would you *stop* that!" Chance roared at him.

Halimeda looked over at them with a smile, came over and crouched by them, still holding tiny Iantha.

"She does not know me," the lady said wistfully.

Iantha gazed solemnly up the three of them. Though she was but a fourmonth old, already her features were delicate, her pale fawn skin very fine and scarcely touched with pink, her eyes of a startling green. The wisps of hair on her head were reddish gold, very bright and true. When Halimeda caressed her cheek, she did not answer the caress, not even with her glance. She looked skyward with a mien at once innocent, knowing and very old.

"She is the same with me," Chance told Halimeda, meaning to comfort her. But the lady clutched her daughter in alarm.

"Changeling," she whispered, and Chance sat stunned at her boldness, that she should have spoken so nearly of the Denizens who were never named. Even Roddarc, startled, gestured her to be silent. But she stammered on, unheeding. "They—folk say babes left in Wirral will be taken—"

"Lady, please!" Chance exclaimed, nearly knocking her over as he blundered to his feet. She caught at his hand, and he pulled her up.

"The babe is very young," Roddarc soothed, rising also. "She is not yet aware of us."

Sighing, yet smiling, Halimeda placed the baby back in her cradle, and without much more speech she and Roddarc went out. Chance did not need to wonder why they had not taken Iantha back to the fortress with them. He deemed he already knew.

Whisperings had grown louder. Rumor was turning into certainty.

Some few weeks later Chance went to Roddarc— for he was no stranger to the fortress any longer, but went there often, with Iantha or without her. He found Roddarc in his chambers and spoke to him in privacy. "Louts wink at each other again. It is said that you will be overthrown before the year is done."

The lord answered with a smile. "You had not heard ere this? The little one must be keeping you out of the alehouse."

"You *knew*?"

"There have been mutterings since before Iantha was born. When I was in my dudgeon, I bruised many a nose, it seems."

And a few hearts, Chance thought. "Why did you not tell me?" he asked coldly.

"Could you keep watch better than you already do?" Then, seeing the stony look on his warden's face, the lord reached out to him. "Old friend, if I had told you, perhaps you would have thought I spoke you fair only for this, that you should aid me. And it would not have been true." He sat back, his manner quite settled and calm, almost happy. "Truth is, I do not care what happens."

"You—what?"

"You think I left little Iantha with you out of the hardness of my heart? When Halimeda longs every day to hold her? Chance, I entrusted the babe to your care because she will be safest with you. Pay no heed to the scheming of renegades. Tend the child, and let them do to me what they will."

"You cannot be serious!"

Roddarc laughed. "Oh, I will put up a fight, never fear! But I want you far from it, Chance."

Chance murmured in wonder, "You really do not care."

"Why should I care, with Riol's ghost leering over my shoulder and the smell of blood everywhere? Let some other lout take this cruel seat and rule by the sword. Why should I be lord when my folk scorn and spurn me, rule I foul or rule I fair?"

Chance could only stare at him. Taking the stare for shock or protest, the lord stood and grasped him by the shoulders, very seriously meeting his eyes. "Chance, please hear me, please trust me. I have seen the way to my redemption."

"It is true, folk scorn Roddarc," Halimeda said, eyes lowered. "And that is my fault."

Chance stirred broth and snorted. "As it is the cricket's fault that frost comes?"

"Things just happen, you mean?"

"Yes," he said, "they do."

His glance strayed to the baby sitting on her

lap. Halimeda came often to see little Iantha, talking to her and trying to teach her pattycake and singing to her in a pure, sweet voice. The little one did not respond, not any more than she responded to Chance. Unsmiling, she looked past her mother with vivid green eyes, gazing off into the distance at the treetops of Wirral, as if she heard somewhere a yet sweeter music.

"But it was when I went about huge with child, and unkempt," Halimeda insisted, "that folk began to mutter again."

Chance snorted. "Say it is my fault, then, if old Riol rules anew in his son."

The lady looked at him in perplexity. "What have you done but show me kindness and care for my babe?"

"I could scarcely have let her starve!" His voice roughened, for it troubled him to remember how the babe had been fed. "And what have you done," he challenged the lady, "but give love?"

The word resonated in her. She met his eyes; silent echoes flew about the room. Slowly she sat Iantha down, turned to look at him across the width of the stone lodge.

"There is love," she said in a low voice, "and sometimes there is lasting love."

"Lady, you know you have it."

She gaze at him and nodded, but pain flickered in her eyes. "I have been thinking," she said very softly, "that manly prowess is not the most important thing about a man."

Powers, she could not mean it! He would not let hope rise. "Lady," he told her, dry-mouthed, "do not let my devotion make a vestal of you. Love where you will."

She looked at him with an odd, saddened smile. "If only I could," she said, and she came over to him and laid a hand on his massive chest. "But, Chance, I think it will not be a matter of loving for me, after all. I deem my brother will not long be lord of Wirralmark. I have had a dream of a dragon, and Roddarc lying bloody under its claws."

And which is the greatest tyrant, the dragon or Riol's son or love itself, I scarcely know.

"A woman taken as booty of war . . . there will be few enough choices for me, Chance."

"Then stand farther from me, Lady," he said huskily, "for this closeness brings but pain to both of us."

She nodded, kissed her daughter and went away.

Thereafter, when she came to see Iantha, there would be a doomed dignity about her, an acceptance, that made her seem older than her less-than-twenty years. She had grown, Halimeda. There was something in her as sturdy as oak, as tough as a Denizen's skin. Not for her, any longer, a noose at Gallowstree Lea.

Often Chance would leave Iantha with her and spend hours in Wirral, searching for the haunts of the rebels, or so he let her think. He lacked courage to tell her otherwise. . . . Summer had reached its height. The days were long, and Chance often stayed until after dark in the forest while Halimeda tended the child.

Iantha was growing rapidly, more so than seemed

natural. She had long since outgrown the applewood cradle, and slept by Chance's cot in a great wicker pannier. Already she walked, and no longer needed diapering. Though tiny, she possessed nothing of baby plumpness; she was small and graceful, with the proportions of a slender four-year-old. She did not talk or even babble, and she never smiled, not even when her mother braided her red-gold hair and whispered into the flower petal of her ear. Iantha seldom cried, but she played listlessly with the toys that were provided for her, and often for hours on end she simply sat and rocked herself or stared.

Roddarc came to see her in the evenings sometimes.

"She is so very beautiful," he said to Chance with a touch of awe. "So delicate. Almost as if—what Halimeda said—have you ever seen such folk, Chance, in the forest?"

"Many times," he answered promptly, facing his lord across a cup of ale. What made him divulge such truth after all the years, he could not have said, except that Roddarc truly no longer cared. And in an odd way Chance felt closer to his foster brother than ever before. Before too long, he would be meeting him as an equal, to do him the final favor.

For the time, he told him how he had first made speaking acquaintance with the Denizens. "But there is no dependable aid to be had from them. They are full of caprice, as happenstance as a puff of wind."

"A lucky chance, eh? Well, so were you, my friend, that ever you were born."

He said it so easily that Chance did not need to growl. The two of them sipped their ale, and in her basket the love-child slumbered.

"Have you yet arranged a marriage for Halimeda?" Chance asked after a while, just as easily.

"Powers know I have tried. I have sent missives as far as the Marches. But no noble scion has yet proved willing to take her."

"The more fools, they," said Chance with feeling, and Roddarc looked at him intently.

"You told me once, you would take her in a moment. . . ."

"Rod, all powers know I have loved her these many years."

There. At long last it was said. Pain flooded into Roddarc's gaze.

"By my mother's bones, how I wish I had never been born," he whispered. "Better that ill-fated spear had taken me instead of your manhood. It was meant for me." Roddarc sprang up, hands to his head. "Chance, every step I take, it seems I am a curse on you."

"Had you not heard?" Chance spoke lightly. "Old Riol cursed us both, on his deathbed."

The tyrant had died on a distant battlefield, and no one had heard his last words. But Roddarc stared intently at Chance, as if for a moment he believed him. "By blood, I would not put it beyond him," he muttered, sitting down again, limply, leaning against the table.

"Bah! If it had gone otherwise, Rod, I would have been wed to a wench. Long since."

"Think you so? Chance, all has come to naught now, but how it would have comforted me if . . ."

"If?"

"Folly." Roddarc roused himself with an effort. "I am an ass, as you have often said. Does Halimeda know of this?"

"Yes. She was so in despair, last autumn, that I told her. It cheered her."

"More than cheered her, I think." Roddarc looked at Chance steadily. "And a dolt I may be. But I like to think that somehow—had a spear struck differently, Chance, I would have found a way to give you your heart's desire."

Chance woke with a start in the mid of night to see little Iantha out of her basket and pattering toward the door.

"No!" In a few steps he had overtaken her and gathered her up. The tiny child did not cry, for she rarely cried, but he felt the stiff protest of her body as he carried her back to her bed. He knew she would not go back to sleep at once.

For his own part, he pretended to.

There had been a dream of voices, he remembered, before he awoke. Voices like those once heard in an autumn storm.

This time there was no wailing of wind. Instead, the small urgings, when they came, chanted and whispered amidst the insect chatter of a late summer's night.

"Come away, little one,
    Come away, Violet!"
Dance in the ring
    And all mortals forget."

Once again, dreamily, intent, the child got out
of her bed and started toward the door, and once
again Chance sprang up and grasped her.

"No!" he shouted at the night. "You shall not
have her!"

All that night until sunrise he sat holding the
child, with his arms locked tightly around her.
When the day had begun and folk were about, he
went to the village and spoke with an old woman.
Then, carrying Iantha and a length of vivid red
cotton, he went to the fortress keep.

"My lady," he hailed Halimeda, and she left her
morning meal to greet him and the child.

"I need a drop of your blood," he told her in a
low voice.

She looked somber, but asked no questions—
the less such uncanny matters were spoken of, the
better. She took the dagger he offered and stabbed
her fingertip with it. Chance blotted up the blood
with the wadded end of the blood-red cotton cloth.

"Some of yours," Halimeda told him, "on the
other end. You are like a father to her." For she
knew the blood was for Iantha.

Chance looked at the lady a moment, then did
as she had said. When his blood had moistened
the cloth, he folded it into a sash and tied it around
Iantha's waist, knotting it firmly in the back.

"There," he muttered to the child, "you're blood

bound to this mortal world." The child stared up
at him, great-eyed and soundless.

"Leave her here with me for today," Halimeda
said, and he did so, but went to get her again
before nightfall.

He made Iantha wear the sash at all times, even
in her bed. And when, a turning of the moon
later, the voices sounded again in the night, he
did not get up, but lay watching.

"Come away, little one,
    Come away, Violet!"

Iantha also lay still for a while. Then she struggled up, but her baby steps were slow. Staggering, she made toward the door. But before she
reached it she slowed to a stop and, standing as if
abandoned in the middle of the floor, she began a
terrible weeping.

Chance hurried to her and put his arms around
her, picked her up and rocked her against his
broad chest, whispered to her, calling her by all
the names of love. But all his comforting failed to
soothe her.

"Let her go, Chance!" commanded a stern voice
close at hand. The Denizen came in through the
eaves, stepped out on the chimney ledge to con-
front him. Their young prince, he of the massy
cock and the wide, fey smile, but he was not
smiling on that night.

"You shall not have her!" Chance shouted wildly
at him.

"But she is already ours! One of us! Let her go!
You are hurting her."

It was true; his heart smote him, knowing it was

true. "And you," he railed, "gentle one, have never done hurt."

"Not to my own kind!"

"Go away!" Chance roared. But the Denizen came closer, his look grave.

"Chance, the child belongs to us. She has suckled on our sap. Many of us gave up their lives for her sake, drained dry. Noble was their willing sacrifice, for we need not die."

The words only made Chance clutch the child more fiercely. "And why do you want her?" he challenged.

"For the wellbeing of our race! We do not die, but—listen to me! We become rootbound, voiceless, with age. We become immobile, like trees. If we did not quicken our blood from time to time—"

"So you want her for breeding." Harsh anger in the words. The Denizen creased his brow at the sound of them.

"She will not be unwilling, believe me! Chance, if it will comfort you, I will give you a promise to cherish her as my own. She will be my bride."

Iantha stretched out her arms toward the woodland prince and gave a gulping wail. Chance swore, suddenly blind with anger.

"You cockproud buck!" He snatched up a butchering knife from the table and hurled it. Startled, the Denizen dodged, and the knife clattered against the stone.

"Out!" Chance raged. A cooler fury answered his own in eyes the color of woodland shade.

"Many have been the favors you have asked

from us. You were told that you would pay someday."

"Take your payment some other way!"

"We have already taken it. Iantha will come to us. Her hands will grow clever enough to tear off that rag you have tied around her—"

"Out!" Chance roared, and he drew his dagger. But luminous eyes met his, and he found he could not lift it. After a long moment, the Denizen prince turned and at his leisure took his leave.

Iantha did not cease to weep until morning. Chance held her close to his heart, and his heart wept with her.

When summer was waning toward autumn, the leaves not yet yellowing but the nights growing chill, the rebels formed their line of siege around the fortress. Their numbers were large, for nearly every man of the demesne stood among them, as well as outlaw rebels venturing from their refuges in the penetralia of the Wirral. And few were the servants or warriors who remained at Roddarc's side.

After dark of that night, a starlit night of the dark of the moon, Halimeda slipped out through the postern gate and walked toward the rebel lines. Once again she went robed in black, but this time she wore it proudly, and the long flow of her dark hair was starred like the night with small gems. A larger brooch of silver and ivory pinned her mantle, shining like the missing moon.

At the points of polite spears, the rebel sentries took her to be seen by their leader.

Halimeda was very calm. Her child was safe
with Chance. She had come to offer herself to the
rebel leader for wedding, so that he would not be
obliged to kill her on the morrow, and she expected him, whoever he was, to accept her offer.
She could only hope that the man would not be
utterly a lout. . . . A bleak prospect for one who
had dreamed of love, but Halimeda faced it with
wintery calm.

Her calm deserted her when she and the sentries reached the campfire where men drew lines
in the dirt. The leader of the renegades was a
broad-shouldered, blunt-featured man in tall boots
and leathers. The heavy hobnailed boots of a war
leader, but instead of a sword he wore a bow,
and he held a child by his side. Dagger in his
hand, stabbing the earth; he laid it down when he
saw her.

"You!" she exclaimed.

Chance came and put Iantha into her arms.

"Lady," he said, "take the little one to the lodge
and wait there. When all is over, you will be ruler
here, if you wish. You will wed me or not, as you
wish. I hope you will not hate me." His voice
faltered for an instant, then grew firm and hard,
the lines of his mouth very straight. "As for the
lord your brother, I have a lifelong score to settle
with him. The whipping boy has spurned the rod."

"You—he—I do not understand," Halimeda stammered. "After all, you hate him?"

Chance shook his head. "I hated him for a while,"
he said, "when he had you so in despair, when I

remembered my own despair. But it is you who
should hate him now, my lady."

Her eyes widened hugely, shadowed in the firelight, as she stared at him. Chance's voice sharpened.

"Lady, your brother is no fitting lord. He craves
to be killed. Do you think I should let the neighboring lord oblige him, then hunt you like a deer
through Wirral? Or some lout hack him down,
carry his head on a spear and take you to wife?
You are the Lady of the Mark, Halimeda! If Roddarc
is too cowardly to care for his own honor, he
should yet care for what is rightfully yours."

Misfortune had made Halimeda tame, but his
tone moved her. Listening to him, she felt her
chin rise, her shoulders straighten.

Chance said, "For the sake of my own hatred it
would have been sufficient to look him in the face
and kill him. But for your sake, my lady . . . these
many months I have planned and labored and
brought folk together, since before the little one
was born. The outlaws of the Wirral. I knew the
ways to their lairs, though it was a subtle matter
to speak to them without being killed. But after
we had struck bargain all was easier, for they have
no desire to skulk in the woods, and there are
those in the village who want their comrades and
brothers back. I made promises, and received the
one I wanted in return: that you should not be
harmed."

"I would rather you fought my brother for your
own sake," Halimeda said.

Chance's straight mouth quirked into a smile;
there was yet some pride left in her! "Indeed, it is

also for my own sake," he said. "When I have made an end of him, I will deem myself a man again."

"Have you ever been less?"

His face grew still and haunted. "Can you doubt it? I have always been lessened by Roddarc, and still am. Halimeda—have you not felt it, too? How he speaks you fair, and yet old Riol peeps around the corners of his deeds?"

"I have come to an enemy encampment in the night," she said, her voice hard, "offering my body to save my life. Yes, I feel it, how once more my brother has had no thought for me. This indifference is what he calls forgiveness."

"There is food in the lodge," Chance told her, for though Roddarc had taken no thought for her, Chance had. "Enough for you and the child for some days. Go there, bar the door and wait."

There were not enough men within the fortress, Chance deemed, to hold the shell, the circular outer wall of the stronghold. Though all the next day they did so, for Chance preferred to spare his followers and take Wirralmark by degrees. Not for him, the piling of bodies in the ditch outside the wall. He and his outlaw archers picked off defenders one by one until nightfall stopped them. During the night four more of Roddarc's followers deserted to join the ranks of the challengers, and at daybreak Chance found the shell deserted. Roddarc's force had fallen back to the keep, the square tower where the lord made his home, and they had knocked away the wooden steps that gave entry. The only door, heavily barred, stood well above the level of a man's head.

Chance and his rebels spent that day battering at the thick stone of the corner buttresses, hoping to knock a hole, stretching ox-hides over the laborers to fend off the many deadly things hurled from the parapets above. Chance took his turn with the maul and wedge, but for the most part he watched from the shelter of the dungeon tower, waiting. Once his men had succeeded in loosening a stone, it was only a matter of time. In any event, Roddarc's overthrow was only a matter of time.

They made their entry, and widened and defended it during the night, and on the third day they stormed the keep. Roddarc met them at the top of the first spiral of stone steps.

"Chance," he breathed. "They told me, but I did not believe them."

"Who else? Would you wish an enemy to have the slaying of you?"

"Mischance, I will have to call you now."

Roddarc raised his sword, and Chance struck with his cudgel, the commoner's weapon of choice. All around them men fought hand to hand, with staffs and daggers, the renegades forcing the defenders back, opening the high, barred entry so that those outside could put up the scaling ladders to it; more rebels poured in by the moment. And Chance had not yet succeeded in touching Roddarc, nor had the lord harmed Chance, but with swift strokes of his sword he killed rebel after rebel as he and his few remaining men gave way. He was splendid, magnificent, as magnificent as he had been at Gallowstree Lea. Flung back at every charge, Chance could not come near him. Only sheer press of numbers forced Roddarc back.

One more stone stairway led to the upper chambers, the lord's last refuge. Roddarc leaped to a vantage on the stairs, planted his feet in the fighter's stance and waited there with bloodied sword at the ready, and for a moment no rebel came near him.

"Why!" the lord panted at Chance. "That is all I want to know; just tell me why!"

Chance's anger rose up in him like the one-eyed monster in its fen at the center of Wirral.

"Tyrant!" he roared. "You yourself are the rod that has always scarred me the worst, son of Riol! You with your sniveling and your so-called friendship—be an honest tyrant, would you, or no tyrant at all!"

Rage flushed Roddarc's face to the hairline, twisted his mouth, blazed in his eyes, and those who watched stepped back as if they had seen a revenant; for a moment it seemed as if Riol stood there.

"Where are your balls, whipping boy?" the lord taunted, and Chance lunged.

Up that spiral stairway they fought, and this time Chance took cuts, and the lord took blows. Roddarc fought on alone; the last of his followers had been captured or slain. He slashed Chance on the head and nearly toppled him, but others stood ready to steady their leader, to drive back the lord; Chance and the others drove him back to the head of the stairs, then quickly halfway to the wall. But at the center of his lordly chamber Roddarc let his sword fall with a clash to the floor, kicked it toward Chance.

"I'll not be taken in a corner, like a brawler," he said, standing lance straight. "Take that and use it, whipping boy." The sword spun on the stone floor, then came to rest with a clatter against Chance's feet. Chance stood as still as Roddarc, and a ring of rebels formed, watching.

"Take it, bastard, and my dying curse on you! I'll not be slain with a commoner's weapon."

Chance picked up the sword, hefting it, accustoming his woodsman's hand to the feel of this unfamiliar weapon. "And what is the curse?" he asked mildly.

Roddarc smiled, a hard, dark smile. "Riol have you," he said.

Chance killed him with a single blow of the sword.

Chance came to Halimeda in twilight, with a bloody wrapping on his head. The lady came out of the lodge and stood beneath an oak tree to meet him, the child in her arms, a question in her gaze. He met her eyes and nodded.

"Roddarc is dead," he said, "and he died well. The women are preparing his body for a lord's burial."

"I thought it more likely, the men would have put his head on a pike," she said.

"That, too."

Laughter like the shouting of birds fluttered out of the foliage of the oak. A rustling like that of squirrels, and small woodland folk by the dozen stood on the spreading limbs, broad smiles stretching the tough skin of their faces. Halimeda gasped and clutched at her child, but Chance merely rubbed his nose in annoyance.

"What do you want?" he demanded of the Denizens.

Despite himself his glance shifted to the child. Having not seen her for a few days, he saw Iantha anew. The beauty of her—but how pale and thin she had become, the little girl so quiet in her mother's arms.

The Denizens trilled with laughter and did not answer his demand. Instead, they chanted at him. "Well, indeed, Chance! And you've become like us, as hard as trees, as fickle as mothflight; was it happenstance? Or mischance, Chance?"

"What do you *want*?" he asked them fiercely.

"Why, to honor you, Chance." It was the russet-brown prince who spoke. "The lady and thee. Come to the dance. A revel for your bridal."

He gave a single snort of laughter. "A quaint revel you'll have from me!"

The prince of the Denizens beckoned. "Come."

There had been no time to talk with Halimeda concerning bridals. Nor was there now much choice. "It is best to do as they say," Chance told her in a low voice, and she nodded, only her widened eyes showing her fear. He took the child from her, shielding the small head against his shoulder.

Leaping and scampering atop the branches, the Denizens led them through the darkening forest. A new moon, rising, gave not quite enough light.

Chance and the lady stumbled over logs, felt their way through thickets, fending off twigs that seemed to search for their eyes. Iantha slept in Chance's arms. By the time they reached the meadow and the mushroom ring, Chance and Halimeda felt weary enough to sleep as well. They sank to seats on the tussocky grass. Chance laid Iantha down, wrapped his mantle around her.

All that happened that night seemed like a dream. The music, humming and buzzing and piping amidst insect music and birdsong in the moonlit darkness. And the whirling and circling of hundreds of tiny dancers within the luminous ring, the mushrooms that glowed like small yellow moons amidst the grass. And wine served in acorn cups. And a heat in the blood. . . . Chance dreamed that he took Halimeda by the hand, led her within the moonglow circle, danced with her there, and she came with him willingly, and he danced with a nobleman's skill. Later, he dreamed that he was lying with her there, her warm, womanly body close to his. And the passion, the sensations he had thought long gone, long dead and turned to dirt and worm on a distant battlefield, his once more. Dreaming . . . but such a blessed, vivid dream. Hands moving, and Halimeda's mouth meeting his, and soft importunity of her breasts, and the welcoming, sweet, warm haven under her skirt. He entered it. Reverent, nearly weeping with joy, home coming, he entered it.

With sunrise he awoke, blinked, gazed. Her face lay close to his, her hair in disarray, and her tender smile matched his own. His mantle covered both of them. Around them grew a ring of yellow mushrooms.

"Chance," she whispered, "darling Chance, you rascal, will you never stop surprising me? There's nothing amiss with your manhood."

"But—Hali, I've not deceived you—" Hope growing in him like passion itself, but still he hardly dared to believe. . . .

"I know." She kissed him. "I felt it happen. The healing. Wirral magic."

Healed. He was whole, entire, a man again, as he had not been for many years. He hugged her wildly, shouted aloud in joy. From somewhere close at hand, someone laughed.

Chance started to jump up, but something jerked him back. Looped from his wrist to Halimeda's, and knotted around each, lay a bright red sash. He untied it and fastened his clothing in haste, all the while glaring around him, but even as he did so he knew that it had been no human laugh, no human trick played on him, no human joke. He had nothing worse than Denizens to face.

Denizens. . . .

"Iantha's gone!" Halimeda exclaimed.

Chance got up, numbly winding the blood-red sash around his hand. Halimeda scrambled up as well.

"Come, hurry," she pled, "we must find her!"

"No," Chance murmured, "perhaps it is for the best." As she turned on him to protest, he pointed. "Look."

A birdlike laugh sounded. At the outer edge of the mushroom ring a delicate beauty faced them, a

fawn-gold maiden less than a foot tall. Shining
red-gold hair curled down below her waist, and
her large eyes sparkled vivid green, full of leaf-
shifting woodland light. She was smiling, the sun-
niest of wayward smiles. Before they could do
more than gape, she waved at them merrily and
scampered away.

"She's gone," Halimeda whispered, "to—"

Gently Chance hushed her. "Say no more."

"She—she looks happy."

"Is a butterfly happy, on the wing?"

They gathered up their things and walked away.
Halimeda wept softly until they came to the lodge.
There she washed her face, brushed dirt from her
clothing.

"We must go to the fortress to live," she said.

"Yes."

"We will—have our own child, Chance. . . ."

"I hope, more than one." He kissed her.

"Our children will—rule after us."

"We will have to be canny," Chance said, "to
rule so long. We will have to be hard as the trees,
merciless as winter."

*Though few are the trees I will leave standing. I
will make prisoners of those who disobey me, have
them hew at the Wirral until it is leveled. There
will be no refuge for outlaws or rebels near my
realm. Or Denizens.*

"A pair of tyrants, we will be, you mean,"
Halimeda said.

"Yes. Old Riol did not toughen my hide for
naught."

He looked at her with a fey, changeling's smile

tugging at the corners of his straight mouth, and in a moment she lifted her chin and gave him back the same wry, elfin grin. Her eyes lit with caprice, the willfulness that would save her heart from breaking ever again. For she also had suffered.

From some hidden place in the eaves came a warbling laugh.

"Rule by the sword, Chance my lord," the unseen Denizen sang.

WE PARTICULARLY RECOMMEND . . .

ALDISS, BRIAN W.

Starswarm

Man has spread throughout the galaxy, but the timeless struggle for conquest continues. The first complete U.S. edition of this classic, written by an acknowledged master of the field.　**55999-0 $2.95**

ANDERSON, POUL

Fire Time

Once every thousand years the Deathstar orbits close enough to burn the surface of the planet Ishtar. This is known as the Fire Time, and it is then that the barbarians flee the scorched lands, bringing havoc to the civilized South.　**55900-1 $2.95**

The Game of Empire

A *new* novel in Anderson's Polesotechnic League/Terran Empire series! Diana Crowfeather, daughter of Dominic Flandry, proves she is well capable of following in his adventurous footsteps.　**55959-1 $3.50**

BAEN, JIM & POURNELLE, JERRY (Editors)

Far Frontiers – Volume V

Aerospace expert G. Harry Stine writing on government regulations regarding private space launches; Charles Sheffield on beanstalks and other space transportation devices; a new "Retief" novella by Keith Laumer; and other fiction by David Drake, John Dalmas, Edward A. Byers, more.　**65572-8 $2.95**

CAIDIN, MARTIN
Killer Station

Earth's first space station *Pleiades* is a scientific boon—until one brief moment of sabotage changes it into a terrible Sword of Damocles. The station is de-orbiting, and falling relentlessly to Earth, where it will strike New York City with the force of a hydrogen bomb. The author of *Cyborg* and *Marooned*, Caidin tells a story that is right out of tomorrow's headlines, with the hard reality and human drama that are his trademarks. 55996-6 $3.50

The Messiah Stone

What "Raiders of the Lost Ark" should have been! Doug Stavers is an old pro at the mercenary game. Retired now, he is surprised to find representatives of a powerful syndicate coming after him with death in their hands. He deals it right back, fast and easy, and then discovers that it was all a test to see if he is tough enough to go after the Messiah Stone—the most valuable object in existence. The last man to own it was Hitler. The next will rule the world . . .
65562-0 $3.95

CHALKER, JACK
The Identity Matrix

While backpacking in Alaska, a 35-year-old college professor finds himself transferred into the body of a 13-year-old Indian girl. From there, he undergoes change after change, eventually learning that this is all a part of a battle for Earth by two highly advanced alien races. And that's just the beginning of this mind-bending novel by the author of the world-famous *Well of Souls* series. 65547-7 $2.95

DICKSON, GORDON R.

Hour of the Horde

The Silver Horde threatens—and the galaxy's only hope is its elite army, composed of one warrior from each planet. Earth's warrior turns out to possess skills and courage that he never suspected . . .

55905-2 $2.95

Wolfling

The first human expedition to Centauri III discovers that humanity is about to become just another race ruled by the alien "High Born". But super-genius James Keil has a few things to teach the aliens about this new breed of "Wolfling." **55962-1 $2.95**

DRAKE, DAVID

At Any Price

Hammer's Slammers are back—and Baen Books has them! Now the 23rd-century armored division faces its deadliest enemies ever: aliens who *teleport* into combat. **55978-8 $3.50**

Ranks of Bronze

Disguised alien traders bought captured Roman soldiers on the slave market because they needed troops who could win battles without high-tech weaponry. The legionaires provided victories, smashing barbarian armies with the swords, javelins, and discipline that had won a world. But the worlds on which they now fought were strange ones, and the spoils of victory did not include freedom. If the legionaires went home, it would be through the use of the beam weapons and force screens of their ruthless alien owners. It's been 2000 years—and now they want to go home.

65568-X $3.50

FORWARD, ROBERT L.
The Flight of the Dragonfly

Set against the rich background of the double planet Rocheworld, this is the story of Mankind's first contact with alien beings, and the friendship the aliens offer.   55937-0 $3.50

KOTANI, ERIC, & JOHN MADDOX ROBERTS
Act of God

In 1889 a mysterious explosion in Siberia destroyed all life for a hundred miles in every direction. A century later the Soviets figure out what had happened —and how to duplicate the deadly effect. Their target: the United States.   55979-6 $2.95

LAUMER, KEITH
Dinosaur Beach

"Keith Laumer is one of science fiction's most adept creators of time travel stories ... A war against robots, trick double identities, and suspenseful action makes this story a first-rate thriller."—*Savannah News-Press*. "Proves again that Laumer is a master."—*Seattle Times*. By the author of the popular "Retief" series.
                                    65581-7 $2.95

The Return of Retief

Laumer's two-fisted intergalactic diplomat is back— and better than ever. In this latest of the Retief series, the CDT diplomat must face not only a deadly alien threat, but also the greatest menace of all—the foolish machinations of his human comrades. More Retief coming soon from Baen!   55902-8 $2.95

CHERRYH, C.J. AND MORRIS, JANET
The Gates of Hell

The first full-length spinoff novel set in the Heroes in Hell® shared universe! Alexander the Great teams up with Julius Caesar and Achilles to refight the Trojan War using 20th-century armaments. Machiavelli is their intelligence officer and Cleopatra is in charge of R&R ... co-created by two of the finest, most imaginative talents writing today. *Hardcover.*

65561-2 $14.95

MORRIS, JANET & MARTIN CAIDIN, C.J. CHERRYH, DAVID DRAKE, ROBERT SILVERBERG
Rebels in Hell

Robert Silverberg's Gilgamesh the King joins Alexander the Great, Julius Caesar, Attila the Hun, and the Devil himself in the newest installment of the "Heroes in Hell" meganovel. Other demonic contributors include Martin Caidin, C.J. Cherryh, David Drake, and Janet Morris.

65577-9 $3.50

SABERHAGEN, FRED
The Frankenstein Papers

At last—the truth about the sinister Dr. Frankenstein and his monster with a heart of gold, based on a history written by the monster himself! Find out what really happened when the mad Doctor brought his creation to life, and why the monster has no scars. "In the tour-de-force ending, rationality triumphs by means of a neat science-fiction twist."—*Publishers Weekly*

65550-7 $3.50

VINGE, VERNOR
The Peace War

Paul Hoehler has discovered the "Bobble Effect"—a scientific phenomenon that has been used to destroy every military installation on Earth. Concerned scientists steal Hoehler's invention—and implement a dictatorship which drives Earth toward primitivism. It is up to Hoehler to stop the tyrants.

55965-6 $3.50

WINSLOW, PAULINE GLEN
I, Martha Adams

From the dozens of enthusiastic notices for this most widely and favorably reviewed of all Baen Books: "There are firing squads in New England meadows, and at the end of the broadcasting day the Internationale rings out over the airwaves. If Jeane Kirkpatrick were to write a Harlequin, this might be it."—*The Washington Post.* What would happen if America gave into the environmentalists and others who oppose maintaining our military might as a defense against a Russian pre-emptive strike? This book tells it all, while presenting an intense drama of those few Americans who are willing to fight, rather than cooperate with the New Order. "A high-voltage thriller ... an immensely readable, fast-paced novel that satisfies." —*Publishers Weekly*   65569-8 $3.95

ZAHN, TIMOTHY
Cobra

Jonny Moreau becomes a Cobra—a crack commando whose weapons are surgically implanted. When the war is over, Jonny and the rest of the Cobras are no longer a solution, but a problem, and politicians decide that something must be done with them.
65560-4 $3.50

Cobra Strike

The sequel to the *Locus* bestseller, *Cobra*. In *Cobra Strike*, the elite fighting force is back, faced with the decision of whether or not to hire out as mercenaries—under the command of their former foes, the alien Troft. Justin Moreau, son of the hero of *Cobra*, finds that it take more than a name to make a real Cobra.
65551-5 $3.50

Rogue Bolo

A new chronicle from the annals of the Dinochrome Brigade. Learn what happens when sentient fighting machines, capable of destroying continents, decide to follow their programming to the letter, and do what's "best" for their human masters.   65545-0 $2.95

BEYOND *THIEVES' WORLD*

MORRIS, JANET

Beyond Sanctuary

This three-novel series stars Tempus, the most popular character in all the "Thieves' World" fantasy universe. Warrior-servant of the god of storm and war, he is a hero cursed ... for anyone he loves must loathe him, and anyone who loves him soon dies of it. In this opening adventure, Tempus leads his Sacred Band of mercenaries north to war against the evil Mygdonian Alliance. *Hardcover.*

55957-5 $15.95

Beyond the Veil

Book II in the first full-length novel series ever written about "Thieves' World," the meanest, toughest fantasy universe ever created. The war against the Mygdonians continues—and not even the immortal Tempus can guarantee victory against Cime the Mage Killer, Askelon, Lord of Dreams, and the Nisibisi witch Roxane. *Hardcover*.   55984-2 $15.95

Beyond Wizardwall

The gripping conclusion to the trilogy. Tempus's best friend Niko resigns from the Stepsons and flees for his life. Roxane, the witch who is Tempus's sworn enemy, and Askelon, Lord of Dreams, are both after Niko's soul. Niko has been offered one chance for safety ... but it's a suicide mission, and only Tempus can save Niko now. *Hardcover.*

65544-2 $15.95

MORRIS, JANET & CHRIS
The 40-Minute War

Washington, D.C. is vaporized by a nuclear surface blast, perpetrated by Islamic Jihad terrorists, and the President initiates a nuclear exchange with Russia. In the aftermath, American foreign service agent Marc Beck finds himself flying anticancer serum from Israel to the Houston White House, a secret mission that is filled with treachery and terror. This is just the beginning of a suspense-filled tale of desperation and heroism—a tale that is at once stunning and chilling in its realism. **55986-9 $3.50**

MEDUSA

From the Sea of Japan a single missile rises, and the future of America's entire space-based defense program hangs in the balance. . . . A hotline communique from Moscow insists that the Russians are doing everything they can to abort the "test" flight. If the U.S. chooses to intercept and destroy the missile, the attempt must not end in failure . . . its collision course is with America's manned space lab. Only one U.S. anti-satellite weapon can foil what *might* be the opening gambit of a Soviet first strike—and only Amy Brecker and her "hot stick" pilot have enough of the Right Stuff to use MEDUSA. **65573-6 $3.50**

HEROES IN HELL™—THE GREATEST
BRAIDED MEGANOVEL OF ALL TIME!
MORRIS, JANET, & GREGORY BENFORD, C.J. CHERRYH, DAVID DRAKE
Heroes in Hell™

Volume I in the greatest shared universe of All Times! The greatest heroes of history meet the greatest names of science fiction—and each other!—in the most original milieu since a Connecticut Yankee visited King Arthur's Court. Alexander of Macedon, Caesar and Cleopatra, Che Guevara, Yuri Andropov, and the Devil Himself face off . . . and only the collaborators of HEROES IN HELL know where it will end. **65555-8 $3.50**

Here is an excerpt from PYRAMIDS, Fred Saberhagen's newest novel, coming from Baen Books in January 1987

YOU ARE HERE TO ROB THE PYRAMIDS? COME THEN: THE MONSTROUS GODS OF ANCIENT EGYPT AWAIT YOU . . .

Whether or not that monstrous, incredible mass of stone up on the hill was the original Great Pyramid of Giza, it was still there when Scheffler went back again to take a look at it through heat and sunlight. Still there, in the broad daylight of what was either mid-morning or mid-afternoon, though it had been dusk in Illinois when he pulled the tapestry-curtain back into place and closed himself into the elevator once more.

Standing in the savage sun-glare on the lip of the rocky fissure, he pulled the cheap mass compass out of his shirt pocket and established to his own satisfaction that here it was mid-afternoon and not mid-morning. For this purpose he was going to be daring and assume that, whatever else might happen to the world, the sun still came up in the east.

So the river was east of him, and the pyramid about the same distance to his west and a little south. Last night Scheffler had done a little reading on the geography of Giza, the district of the Pyramids just east of modern Giza, and he had to admit that the situation he was looking at here seemed to correspond exactly. Everything he could see indicated to him that he was standing on the west bank of the Nile.

The hardest part of that to deal with was that if Khufu, or Cheops as the Greeks came to call him, was still building his great tomb, the year ought to be somewhere near three thousand B.C.

Whatever, and wherever, *here* was.

A Fascinating New Twist on the Time-Travel Novel, by the Author of The Book of Swords, Berserker, *and* The Frankenstein Papers.

JANUARY 1987 • 65609-0 • 320 pp. • $3.50

To order any Baen Book by mail, send the cover price plus 75 cents for first-class postage and handling to: Baen Books, Dept. B, 260 Fifth Avenue, New York, N.Y. 10001.